Armour Piercing

Peter Aengenheister

Clink Street

London | New York

Published by Clink Street Publishing 2018

Copyright © 2018

First edition.

The author asserts the moral right under the Copyright, Designs and Patents Act 1988 to be identified as the author of this work.

All rights reserved. No part of this publication may be reproduced, stored in a retrieval system or transmitted, in any form or by any means without the prior consent of the author, nor be otherwise circulated in any form of binding or cover other than that with which it is published and without a similar condition being imposed on the subsequent purchaser.

*ISBNs:
978-1-912850-02-0 paperback
978-1-912850-03-7 ebook*

*To Mum, for her patience, love and understanding
and in appreciation of all that she has done for me.
Her capacity for giving, in the face of adversity,
is her legacy because it continues to inspire.*

Chapter One

DATELINE – 1978

He was tired, aching, and deep down he wondered if this was really, truthfully going to be all that he hoped for. Would all his yearnings be satisfied and would the torment, the nightmares that haunted so many of his nights, come to an end, here in England? Or was he about to die, either at the hands of the British when they knew what they wanted to know, or by his own countrymen after being hunted like a wild dog?

It had been a long and arduous journey and he was very ready for sleep. He, right at that moment, didn't much care what happened to him.

He thought of his two-roomed apartment and his small circle of friends in the tight-knit scientific community at Bikanor.

He knew exactly what they would be doing at that moment. He knew what they would be doing the next day and the day after that, following their 12 to 14 hour shifts at the research centre.

And now, finally, he was back in England. He wished his old friend had been there to meet him.

They arrived late at night in an unmarked van. It was

pitch dark. The vehicle swung round on a coarse gravel drive and backed up to the side door of a large black creosoted barn.

Vasilli had been bustled, not roughly but firmly into a room while the door was slammed shut, and only then did bright lights flood the room, brutally piercing his optic nerves. It was musty and smelled of hay.

They had been travelling for 26 hours non-stop, and, despite the fact that he had been in the dark most of that time, there had been not the slightest chance of sleep.

The safe house was a large old farmhouse on the outskirts of the small Warwickshire village of Flecknoe. It was old, but looked comfortable. It stood in a commanding position on a slight hill, one road in and the same road out – easily defended.

After the shortest of meetings in Lubeck, on the Baltic where East Germany met West, Vasilli was looking forward to seeing again, the man who had been the last man in the world he had expected to see – it would be very strange to have his old friend, his only friend in this country, Pete Armour, of all people, debriefing him.

Why? Because he spent two exhilarating weeks with Pete Armour during a cultural exchange during his university days, many years before, and yet, in the years they had been writing to each other since, he had become perhaps his best friend. They had fleetingly crossed the East–West divide together when the divide had been at its widest, but they built an inexplicable bond… maybe it was the times, perhaps partly an empathy that students everywhere share.

Even though they had written to each other regularly – at no time had there been even the slightest hint that they worked in the same industry… well, they didn't, but they were now inescapably entwined in it.

After their arrival he had been told he would have a day to rest and that Pete would be there the next day, so he settled in, took in the atmosphere of the house and particularly the books in the library, which passed the time very quickly.

The farmhouse itself was very old he guessed but then updated several times over the years. There were very definite Elizabethan features, the shape of the tall leaded windows, exposed wood and huge fireplace he had spotted earlier in the main entrance hall, flamboyantly-dressed Tudor noble with slightly pinched features and long curly flowing locks, and across an expanse of flagstone flooring and expensive rugs, grew a pair of broad reach, carved and curving staircases, which went left and right and met at an exposed landing.

Tapestries and hatchments and two suits of armour from even earlier times adorned the walls of this magnificent great hall.

The property had been lovingly looked after, and the decor fitted several periods but was beautifully balanced. The place oozed history and charm, elegance and style. By comparison to the great entrance hall, all the other rooms, possibly apart from the sitting room and library were very small.

Vasilli would have happily stayed here for as long as they liked. He dreamed of having a home like this.

He wondered if space guidance system experts in the West could afford such a place.

He mused at the vast chasm between his two bedroom flat in Russia, with its own dining-cum-sitting room, and this vast edifice.

His flat, amongst the privileged scientific community in which he dwelt, was considered to be extravagant – for a man on his own.

Here in England though, he knew things were different. He had experienced a taste of life among the spires of Oxford, and knew there was another way of life.

Vasilli knew also that his work in Russia was no longer anything to do with all for man's exploration of space, finding new worlds and furthering the glory of his mother country. It was a far more sinister thing. In his mind his guidance systems work would help propel space probes, and, later, manned ships throughout the solar system. He hoped, one day, to be allowed to go on one of those space missions or even spend time aboard one of their space stations.

Star Wars projects for some time were just a rumour and when he learned eventually, that this was the main thrust of what he had been working towards, Vasilli lost interest.

Nuclear proliferation had been bad enough, but the thought of having a hand in this type of death and destruction, gave him nightmares, and eventually had led him to consider the drastic measures he had taken over the past few weeks. His defection would be a severe body blow to his country and that too sickened him, he had not wanted that either.

He eyed the wall of books in the library. There were thick dusty volumes, from massive encyclopaedia, to mighty geographic and scientific tomes. All of Shakespeare's works, including the sonnets he could see, and most of the Greek classics. There were all the other great British poets, Keats, Byron, Shelley, Coleridge and many others and then the more contemporary, quite a few of which he did not recognise. He spotted the works of many great authors. He picked out a favourite, *Hamlet*, and then another book caught his eye.

He hooked his finger over the spine of a black covered hardback and pulled it back on its base to reveal cream-coloured writing that offered to reveal *The Mind of Adolf Hitler* by Walter Langer.

He was interested in history and wandered how the West's perspective of the Second World War might differ from the version told to Soviet students. With both books in his hand he crossed the room, lolled in the huge swing, swivel, rock, captain's chair, and easily swung his left leg over the arm.

Occasionally, to consider a point, he would raise his eyes and gaze through the tall windows. He could see down over trimmed lawns and carefully tended flower beds, and then further over rolling hills and a deep wide valley. In the distance he could see a tractor and trailer moving across a field.

His attentions were neither totally on the book he was reading or the scene set out before his window.

And as time passed there were serious moments of nagging worry, he could not help but think about the action he had taken, the culmination of which had resulted in his flight from Russia in the last few days.

He knew one way or another he would suffer for his 'betrayal', but also, looking out that window, absorbing the peace and tranquillity of the pastoral beauty below him, he knew he was right to turn his back on his country, rather than betray himself and his own soul.

Vasilli had often thought deeply about what and how the British, and Americans(he knew when you talk about one you include the other) might use any information they could get from him.

He believed his technical research and knowledge to date, was probably in advance of the West. Western space projects had developed very quickly, often using new and untested designs and technology. The hardware looked very sexy, but the result was a horrific lack of consistency, and very poor results.

The Soviets on the other hand kept the good parts of their technology and design. Much was tried and tested and they simply, and inexpensively, added to it. The result was that they were using a lot of older hardware, but had far better reliability and success in space.

It was the Americans who started the race for Star Wars, but even so, it was less likely to be used by them against the East. The fact was that the East was a lumbering giant with a terminal disease, and probably could not last much longer anyway.

Vasilli, albeit privileged and knowledgeable, was a civilian and he recognised this, so it was certain that the intelligence agencies of the West knew it and a lot of the detail of just how critical the situation was. They would not have to shoot their Star Wars rockets at anyone. They just had to wait for the USSR to roll over and die. And when that happened all the old factions of the Soviet Union would be at each other's throats and half of them would be welcoming the advances of the West with open arms. Even he, Vasilli Vasilovski could see that!

There was far more chance that Vasilli's specialist knowledge would see the early hopes of his imagination fulfilled in the West. His was a quest for space!

Vasilli had enjoyed a light, but more than adequate lunch of ham salad, so fresh and crisp, the colours so bright… tomatoes and radishes redder than he had seen for years and the lettuce, cucumber and cress a million miles from the limp and pallid version he and his comrades were used to. The soft granary bread that had come with it had been slightly warmed and the aroma made his head swim.

He could not understand why he felt so guilty every now and then. He tried to dismiss these thoughts and concentrated instead on looking forward to his coming talks with Pete Armour, there was a lot to talk about.

He had been in the Warwickshire safe-house since 11.30 pm the previous night. He had slept until 11.30 that morning. He was not allowed to leave, or walk in the grounds.

There were armed men in the house itself and more outside.

He had expected it, and most of the Military Intelligence and secret service people he had met so far had been friendly, but business-like. But there was more security than he had anticipated.

Vasilli had enjoyed a very relaxing day, and as he looked outside for a second he could see the night closing in. A security man crossed the reddened sky between him and the dying sun. They seemed to be everywhere. He was surprised at the level of protection, he had not realised that he was that important.

He turned another page, enjoying a gin and tonic – he promised he would own a library like this one day. His English was pretty good and he was able to appreciate most of the books there. As he rocked slightly with that thought, the door quietly opened and a man in a grubby wax jacket and cords walked in…

He was tall, and lean. His blond hair was long and although he was calm, his steely eyes darted around the room.

Instantly, Vasilli knew something was wrong. He had not seen this man before and he did not look like the others.

He had been promised protection. He had been told he would be given a new life after he had unburdened his secrets to military intelligence… to Pete Armour, but now he knew he was facing his killer.

He could not believe that the KGB could have caught up with him already. At any time during the journey, perhaps, but not now. There had been so much changing of transport, lying low, switching this way and that, moving quickly, diving on to trains, jumping off buses, fast cars, boats, brief moments in farmhouses and hotels…

The man's eyes were everywhere. In the second that he had entered he had scrutinised the room, positively identified Vasilli, and in the next second seemed satisfied.

As Vasilli rose from his chair, the farmworker's hand went

inside his jacket. Vasilli had seen enough over the past few days and instinctively knew what would emerge from it. He threw the book he had been reading, and at the same time dived for the panic button on the desk. Without glancing back at the hitman in a completion of his first movement his hand continued to sweep up a vase, hurling it through the window.

All this had taken place in a split second, and as he continued to sail through the air, he half smiled at his amazing presence of mind and incredible agility and… a bullet thumped into his shoulder. It changed the direction he was travelling in, and he crashed into the drinks trolley.

As glass shattered showering him in booze and splinters, the assassin moved round the room with incredible speed, and he must had known that the agents around the farm would be upon him in a matter of seconds.

Almost in the same breath two secret service agents who Vasilli had earlier seen outside, crashed in through the window, and another smashed through the door, two died, their heads exploding, the walls behind them hideously splattered red and strangely it matched the curtains as the dying sun flashed on them.

Vasilli took another bullet before the hitman went down – one of the guys from the window, and another entering from the door finished him… but the firing was still going on outside.

Just as they had come in, the agent crashed out again – no one stopping to check on him or his health.

Vasilli was lying on lush, thick pile carpet, his head two foot from the gaping eyes of the farmworker.

His shoulder and ribs started at first to sear, cold, like he had been stabbed with a stalactite, then turned inside out and burning as if a blowtorch was being played on his skin. His head throbbed and spun. He had never felt pain like it, but he knew he had been lucky… to feel any pain.

He knew that the first bullet had gone right through his body from low to high, between his collarbone and his shoulder blade. It was a small calibre bullet from specialist-made weapon. The entry and fortunately, although a little surprisingly, the exit, were neat fine holes. The exit wound wept blood. The second bullet, as he had been turning in the air, had glanced his ribcage, near his heart, but had not entered him.

As the firing continued, he knew he was not out of danger – the hitman, whom he had presumed to be a Russian, would not been alone. Somehow Vasilli decided he would have to get out, and probably on his own. With the adrenalin surging through his body, and keeping near to the ground he moved to the door, and opened it. The corridor outside and the cellar stairwell to his right was clear, and the gunfire was coming from behind him. Turning to the left he moved quickly, and as he did so he passed an open door.

Inside in a panelled room, was a large oak table with paperwork strewn around on it, and ten seats around, had been abandoned, obviously when the firing started.

As he surveyed the room he heard footsteps in the stairwell, and voices from somewhere outside. Orders were being barked. He dived into the room closing the door except for a small crack. He heard the stomping feet of two or three men crashing into the library and out through the window. He stayed for a few seconds more, but just as he turned to leave the draw of the set of documents closest to him was magnetic.

He looked down at the paperwork, picked up a set of five A4 sheets, stared for a minute, his eyes narrowing as he recognised a name. Quickly, he stuffed them down the front of his trousers and left.

Finding a large stable-style door, he was soon in the gravel courtyard into which they had driven the night before, and moving as silently as he could, he kept close to the barn wall, to fences and hedges.

The darkness was falling quickly, and all the shooting was on the other side of the house, on the lawns leading down to those peaceful rolling hills.

Vasilli headed quickly along the quiet farm track towards the village where he could see lights glowing and flickering. Near to the houses Vasilli found a small copse. He entered and kept to the shadows.

He was in a strange country and with only one chance – to get in contact with Pete Armour. After what he had seen he needed to do that – it was imperative for him… and for Pete. He knew the documents he had retrieved from the room next to the library, were vitally important. A powder keg. The relevance was not lost on him. He had to get the documents to Pete. Pete was the only one he could possibly trust now, but what had Pete said in Lubeck?

It was 1960. Pete had been studying East European history and culture, and was part of an Oxford group chosen to be invited to Russia. Armour was selected to be hosted Vasilli Vassilovski, only son of a good party member, who was a cleric in local government in Minsk. Vasilli was talented and because of his good family name was to some extent privileged, and because of an intelligent analytical mind won his way through university.

He recognised his privilege and special option and took advantage of them, but never took on that sanctimonious air that some of his similarly 'exulted' party elite peers did.

In fact they irritated him considerably, and often he found himself on his own, or mixing with those involved in sport or entertainment, not that he was particularly artistic, but he did love story-telling and amateur dramatics, poetry and reading.

Although it took a little time, he and Armour soon became firm friends. They had similar interests, albeit that Armour did not have the same scientific bent that Vasilli had, he did share the same clear analytical mind of Vasilli. Both enjoying sport, they soon became very close.

Vasilli could never quite understand how Pete could be so relaxed. They both knew that they were being watched, but Pete had an air of confidence that was almost annoying. It eluded Vasilli for some time, but then he recognised what it was. Pete was not scared. Nothing fazed the Oxford undergraduate, who at the same time showed considerable reverence for his hosts and their country, and a surprising knowledge of the culture. Russian people could not help liking him, despite western decadence, and their visitors' irritating proclivity for always being cheerful, whatever happened. How lucky he was, Vasilli often thought, and he tried to reflect Armour's good humour. He did for much of the time, but he noticed Armour often fended off questions about England and tended to underplay things. He was slightly embarrassed that his visitor did so, but understood why he did.

For his part Armour was stunned by the generosity he encountered. He knew these were not wealthy people, and they were not only 'giving' with their hospitality but their hearts.

He guessed that food and wine supplied by the party boosted normal provisions so there would be no loss of face.

There were theatre trips, concerts, museum visits and cultural receptions – all strictly controlled and monitored. The host families had 'get-togethers', which despite the language barriers proved entertaining. The three week visit passed very quickly.

It was with great astonishment then that the following year, an amazed Vasilli Vasilovski had been allowed, with an exchange group, to travel outside the country. He had been allowed to come to Oxford for a month. The authorities had taken a chance.

But he was a science student and not considered a radical free thinker, or very political.

He was a student of great social conscience, but certainly not considered by his seniors as one who would question Soviet authority or be a risk-taker.

And at that time they had been correct in their assumption. Despite the provocation of youth, and the temptations of the West, there had never been any doubt that Vasilli would take full advantage of his trip to the UK, and return a model Russian citizen.

Later the authorities, his bosses, his colleagues and friends would never have imagined his total about-face and his need to escape Russia, despite growing rumours that the Soviet Union was breaking up and the Iron Curtain was coming down.

From the moment the plane left Russian airspace back in 1960, Vasilli felt as if he might as well be going to the moon. He had read about the outside world, heard from people who had travelled before, from Armour, but now he was going to experience it first hand.

He wondered if it would be as decadent as he had been led to believe… Would he be led astray, corrupted?

Those days, Oxford had been a total amazement to Vasilli. Oh, he had seen the travelogues, heard about the colleges, the spires and imagined punting along the river Cherwell, but nothing could have really prepared him for what he would encounter…

What a truly amazing, beautiful, bountiful city… so full of freedom, of thought and of action. And what a night life! Always busy and always bright. In the first few days of his stay Vasilli tended to shuffle in his walk… from turning to see if anyone was following.

But soon he didn't care too much – this place was bliss to the repressed Russian – and one spot in particular.

During that short stay, Pete had shown him as much as he could. He knew that time was precious for Vasilli. Vasilli had taken in as much as possible.

While others stayed out late and slept in late, Vasilli burned the candle at both ends.

He stayed out late and got up early. But everything he saw was absorbed. Everything was somehow vital.

Even if their time had been idly spent punting, Vasilli appreciated it to the full. Once he suddenly stood up in the boat, spread his arms and filled his chest with air. From the bottom of his soul he cried out, a long, deep yell that seemed to quieten the birds in the trees for a second or two. It sent a shiver up Pete's back and made the skin on his neck and lower jaw tighten, almost in embarrassment that he had missed a great significance.

But he always seemed to understand the differences between him and Vasilli with quiet respect. Vasilli then lay in the bottom of the punt with his copy of a Shakespeare play… *Hamlet*. Not looking at the pages Vasilli would rustily, but confidently, quote.

"Oh that this too, too sullied flesh would melt, thaw and resolve itself into a dew…"

Somehow he managed to say it in a more melancholic manner than any Prince of Denmark performer Armour had ever seen – his voice drifting over the lapping water to be absorbed by the cascading willows. Vasilli certainly did not mind who else might have heard him.

Four short weeks and Vasilli had returned to his mother country disturbed slightly, but at the same time happy to be back, or was it a sort of relief in a way. It might have seemed strange to a Westerner, he had absorbed so much, but he was not sure he was ready to handle so much freedom. And certainly he knew that he had to go back. Staying was not an option. He had to face the reality.

He graduated and the Party found him 'interesting' work at Baikonur.

Although not a lot was happening, Vasilli became involved in the space programme, and guidance systems particularly. He knew the investigation of deep space would require probes and they would need guidance. He enjoyed the work. It was challenging and he dreamed of space and where it might lead humans in the future. He hoped that one day he might make it into space.

Not a lot happening? That was, until someone found another purpose crucial to the programme. He was soon reassigned. Although not happy with the reason for the programme, Vasilli carried on. He did not have much choice, but he hated the idea of working on weaponry of any kind, for any reason.

Vasilli's work was secret of course, but he lived and socialised with many other scientists. He still wrote to Armour, a long letter, every six months or so, and Armour would reply.

Vasilovski talked about literature, international news (to show he was allowed such information), and sport, but never anything about his work, and for some reason, maybe obvious reasons, Armour never asked about it.

Armour responded with similar material, but would often talk about his 'normal' work. Neither Vasilli, nor the Russian censors had the slightest idea of Armour's 'unusual' side line.

It had been in a cosy quiet bar, shortly after they had met in the cold and wind-swept medieval centre of the Baltic resort of Lubeck, Armour in low tones, and well out of ear shot of unwanted listeners, told Vasilovski: "If you are in real trouble contact Mart Burricks at the evening paper in Northampton and tell him your name and to pass on to me, the message:

Peter Aengenheister

'That special bottle of Scotch you requested is now available', then go to the old Grand Hotel in the town and book in under the name of Dieter Schmitt. I will find you."

When they had first met in Lubeck, Vasilli could not quite believe the face in front of him.

It had been some years since they had seen photos of each other, and Vasilli tilted his head from one side and then the other and squinted.

Armour had hoped for this. It gave him just enough time to lead the Russian quickly to one side. The element of shock shown by Vasilli's expression would be misconstrued by the British agents guarding Vasilli, as a response to Armour's somewhat abrupt treatment. Armour was the debriefer and they would not question his techniques as far as preparing a defector.

Strangely picking up the serious face of his old friend, he hushed his tone, but said: "Pete, Pete Armour, is that really you? What are you doing here?"

It was a stupid question really. Pete drew Vasilli a few paces further away from the agents who were escorting him, and kept his voice low.

Vasilli appreciated the seriousness of what he was saying, fascinated by the change in Pete Armour. He had always known him to be gentle and laid back about everything, and he had not perceived any change in recent letters.

But then, if Armour was now some kind of agent, that should not be a surprise.

Fortunately, Vasilli had studied maps of Great Britain, and particularly the Midlands, because it held special memories for him. Despite the dark, he soon picked up of the main road signs and although he had never heard of Flecknoe before, he quickly sussed how to get to Northampton.

Armour Piercing

A little earlier he had found another farm on the outskirts of Flecknoe, had stolen a bicycle, and decided to stick with it all the way to Northampton. The bike would be slower but he decided not to take the obvious route along the A45, but kept to the back road from Daventry to Duston on the edge of the town – only the locals used it, although it was nearly as quick at the main road, which is partly dual carriageway.

Amazingly the bleeding from his wounds has stopped. As soon as he was on the eastern side of Daventry he had passed a golf club. He crept into the club car park for a moment to bandaged himself with the remains of his shirt that were almost clean.

Over the hill he saw the lights of a small village and as he got closer and in among the houses he spotted a rotary washing line. He stole two shirts from a washing line to wear – he felt guilty, but he was getting cold. He decided he would later need the second one to re-dress his wounds.

What haunted Vasilli now about his course of action, was another comment made by Armour in Lubeck: –

"Only contact Burricks as a last resort. He is totally safe, but he is not one of us."

What is 'one of us'…?

He would probably be able help, but not to any professional level. Well, he now needed all and any help he could get. But by not being part of the organisation Armour had thought he would be safer.

From the documents he had seen, he knew Armour was right about that, and he now assumed that both MI5 and the KGB were after him, and he was not too sure which intended him good or harm. He had to avoid both until he had contacted Armour.

Armour, he knew, somehow, would sort out the mess.

It was almost midnight. He needed some sleep.

Chapter Two

Pete Armour, and far as the non-spook world was aware, was a freelance journalist, working with several newspapers in the Midlands. He often did shifts with the *Coventry Evening Telegraph*, and the *Chronicle & Echo*, Northampton. Occasionally he helped out on the weeklies in Leamington, Banbury and Daventry, but only because he knew the editors well and enjoyed the change.

He would work equally well reporting as sub-editing, but sub-editing was the skill most papers wanted him for. He was good at it, and quick at page design, and the standard of accuracy was extremely high. He was known to be very reliable, but not particularly cheap, which was why he did less for the weeklies – they wanted him but couldn't readily afford him.

Over the years Amour had become well known for his remarkably agile mind. Armour had made numerous contacts during his university days at Oxford, and as a result of one of these, six years after graduating, he was recruited by British Intelligence as a de-briefer.

He had always regarded the job as a short-term thing, and at the very most he had always insisted that it should be a side-line. He had never quite fancied the idea of being permanently or completely 'on the government payroll'.

Although obviously having to sign the Official Secrets Act and all that, it went a little further. Some defence mechanism, if it could be called that, made sure that he never totally relied on any single organisation, especially British Intelligence, for his living.

But British Intelligence wanted him, and he had to admit to being fascinated by the role. They made an exception, allowed him his side-line position, safeguarded his retirement, and, as it happened, tended to reserve some of the more interesting and sensitive cases for him to handle. Over the years they had found that it had paid off.

But for Armour, he found it very difficult to actually like anyone in the service, not that he had actually tried too deeply. They were strange – even the most apparently 'relaxed' did not know the meaning of the word.

He knew one agent, a former SAS man, who while on leave, had been to a disco one night. During the evening he had fallen asleep and 'friends' had watched as the cigarette he had been holding, burned itself away through his fingers. He never stirred.

And yet, three days later the very same man had very nearly killed his own 12-year-old daughter. He had been asleep on the sofa, when she had skipped in from the kitchen, after playing in the back garden, and tapped him on the shoulder. His reaction had been instantaneous, blindingly fast… and almost deadly.

In less than a moment he had moved from his reclining position to one above her. He had her neck savagely twisted to her left by his left hand, with the elbow of his right arm ready to crash down on her exposed head or neck – either would have led to her final breath as the vertebrae popped and her spinal cord snapped like a twig.

The blood had drained from his body as he had realised

what he had so nearly done, and he spent six months on a 'company farm' getting his head together.

All this complicated Armour's life too much, so he did not seek it out. This was not a career, simply an interesting and unusual diversion. His only regular contact was with his immediate boss, Sir Michael Staveley-Smythe – a 'hooray', but not too bad, and in his own way he empathised with Armour.

'Mick', as Armour liked to called him to his face, because he knew it slightly irritated him, had been his third 'control'. Who knows what his title, or official role was, or any of the previous ones who had done the job. He had chosen never to ask, but Mick seemed to be in fairly constant contact with Personal Private Secretaries and junior Ministers, and occasional dragged in with the big boys when the shit really hit the fan.

And it had been hitting the fan recently. Not with any of the subjects Armour had been debriefing, but with two or three others. People had died mysteriously, including the service's own agents, and on one occasion the subject and debriefer fell rather ignominiously from the rooftop of a very dodgy hotel in a red light area of Seattle.

Of course there had been internal investigations – the probes had gone deep and wide, but had revealed very little – two guys fiddling their expenses, and one chap fiddling with his partner's wife – sad, but trivial. Things had gone quiet just recently… It was Mick who had contacted Armour to tell him that a very special operative was 'coming over' – the information on him was incomplete. He could not have been aware that Vasilli and Armour knew each other. Armour had just done a stint at the *Daventry Express*, one of his favourites, when he switched mode for Mick.

He did not say much at the time except that his subject's name was Vasilli Vasilovski and that he was a 'Star Wars' expert – Armour of course, was to debrief him…

Being on the other end of the phone, Mick could not see Armour's reaction. He sat down suddenly, as if dealt a swift, sharp, body blow. He had recovered quickly, and none but the most observant, would have recognised the slight hesitation, possibly a waver, in Armour's voice, because it was just as quickly gone.

He was given the address of the safe house, and a time to be there. He had used this house once before and like it. It was comfortable, Vasilli would be impressed, and it was convenient. In fact, it couldn't be better.

Some of Armour's debriefs had involved travelling abroad. That had been OK, but he actually preferred to do it somewhere close to home – his mind was far more in tune. If it was abroad, he much preferred to get it out of the way and then go and explore – it was his weakness. In fact, this had been recognised by Mick, who cut his cloth accordingly, and trips were only on if the subject was insistent, or Armour was simply the best man for the job.

Because Armour was freelance, none of the papers he worked for queried his availability, and even when he had to let someone down at very short notice, he would make amends in the future by doing a shift for free, depending on how much he had messed them up – there were those editors who didn't mind if he did. They got someone cheaper to do the job and then Armour would come in on another occasion for nothing… but it didn't happen very often.

Armour's life was not too complicated at the moment. A partner had finished a year-long relationship they were in about five months earlier, which had left him a little 'jangled' for a few of weeks – he had not been expecting it, but got over it. In the 'post mortem' it became obvious she had been seeing someone else in recently months. He had had no idea.

Armour had never married. He had obviously had a few

relationships, some of them fairly important, but none had galvanised him enough to think seriously about getting married… well it was probably the right thing, he often thought – he was a loner.

But now, Armour was worried. He was on edge. He could not get it out of his mind that Vasilli was coming to Britain. That he would be seeing him for the first time since that university exchange – he was 40 now, they had been 22 then…

Bearing in mind some of the things that had been going wrong, he had every reason to worry for Vasilli's safety – he was already at more risk than was necessary, but how was he going to avoid it? Why had it been so crucial to bring him out now? Couldn't it have waited a few months until they had sorted out their internal problems… because that is what it had to be.

It was unusual, but he persuaded Mick to let him meet with Vasilli in Lubeck, on the way to Britain. It was unusual, but he said he was particularly concerned because of the cock-ups… that was true. Armour had something up his sleeve in case things did not go according to plan. It was unorthodox and unauthorised, but it might just work. It might just save Vasilli if he got into a squeeze.

"Bloody hell!" hissed Staveley-Smythe brushing dust and dirt from his now crumpled trousers, as he picked himself up from the patio outside the library window.

"What the fuck is going on?"

His main operator, Blake, had just given the all-clear, but there were six bodies scattered around the Flecknoe farmhouse. Two were unidentified and the others were his men. The search was already on for Vasilovski.

Blake reported this fact, said he was convinced there were no other hostiles in the vicinity, that this was a two-man operation. He flicked open his Motorola mobile phone and arranged a clean-up, and a cover-up.

Men were running into outlying fields and checking hedges, walls and outbuildings in the area, radios cackled and then more men were drafted in. The noise that had been created was bound to cause a stir among local people, who were often slightly bemused by the comings and goings at strange hours, and occasionally the big black cars and strange number plates – but never had there been a major gun fight.

Hushed rumours and guarded whispers about the place were not rare but a pretty good whitewash story was needed very quickly to cover this one. But that was OK, probably the least of their problems, he was confident of that part of what they had to do now, but there was still a major worry – some supposedly precision timing had gone very wrong. The hush hush meeting that had been conducted should not have been interrupted under any circumstances – there would be repercussions.

By the time Blake snapped the cover of the Motorola shut, Staveley-Smythe had regained his composure, but there was still a slight tremble of anger and indignation as he swore again and said: "I need to get to the bottom of this. This is the last operation that goes wrong. I want to know everything about anyone who had anything to do with it, from start to finish."

He turned on his heel and headed back into the house, and to the room beside the library where they had been conducting a meeting.

He hoped above all that no one from that room had been hurt, it could cause considerable embarrassment if they were.

Staveley-Smythe, a tall lean, well-educated man in his late forties, was met at the door by General Sir Bryan

Calder-Maynes, who was a good ten years his senior. The general was strong, stockily built, but with very little fat. He had dark, deep sunk eyes which flashed incredibly when he was excited. Not quite so well-educated, he had served with the army all his life, was flamboyantly decorated with an extremely impressive array of medals, and had seen action in most theatres of war – whether Britain was actively, and/or officially involved or not.

"Ah Bryan, are you alright? What about everyone else."

"They're OK In the circumstances I told them to go. We will have to reconvene later.

But this attack," and he whispered out the side of his mouth, "Or the timing of it, is very unfortunate Michael. It could have been very embarrassing. Have you got any leads on who these mechanics are and under who's orders?"

"No idea yet, but we will. Bryan, you go too. I'll call you this evening… shame, the meeting was going so well. I'd better tidy up in here. Do you want to keep copies of the documentation?"

"No, shred it all," said Calder-Maynes and he walked off down the corridor without another word.

Staveley-Smythe walked into the room and started gathering the papers. He stopped, counted… counted again and then gathered them again. He crossed the hall, to a small room opposite which housed a copier, fax, small personal computer and printer, and the shredder, and he fed the documents in.

It could have been that one of the people in the meeting had mistakenly taken their agenda and brief. They had been told not to. He would have to ring round on their mobiles or when they were all back in their offices, to check. He could not help being slightly uneasy, but did not intend to tell Calder-Maynes for the moment, although he knew he was taking a huge risk. The general would, of course, be furious and Staveley-Smythe would, no doubt, get it in the neck. But frankly he was getting a little fed up with getting all the flack, which the 'old git' as he had coming to mentally label him, sat around lording it over him.

General Sir Bryan Calder-Maynes' steps across the gravel were a brisk march, and the sound of the stones under his heel were amplified round the yard.

He climbed into his maroon Jaguar saloon and gunned up the V12 engine and letting the tyres spin slightly, smacking pebbles into a barn wall. The tyres then gripped and he pulled away from the farmyard.

He too was seething. Another cock-up. A vital meeting curtailed, and the integrity of the Group seriously threatened. He had power and influence, but he hated this nagging feeling that recently things were more than slightly out of control. These meetings were vital to the future, his future, and if he was able to orchestrate the situation well, things would be far more efficient, less people would be killed, missions were accomplished and 'everyone' would be happy... and rich!

He would make sure that things were not left totally in the hands of Staveley-Smythe, someone he knew was, although not military, quite professional, and the two of them had had long discussions about the purpose of the meeting. Both were key to its success. The trouble was Staveley-Smythe was just a prat. He couldn't help it, that's the way he was.

That was not a reason, in itself, to distrust him, but he didn't have a great deal of time for him. Now there were things going on that were worrying. In his own mind he knew that some of the problems MI5 were confronting were of his doing, but that was calculated, if a little dangerous. But the risk was measured and in his control.

It was the bits he could not calculate that were beginning to worry him.

This latest farce at Flecknoe had been the closest to wrecking his own operations and plans.

The general decided he would bring in his own professionals, people he knew. They would start with the missing Russian.

Staveley-Smythe was relieved that Calder-Maynes had gone. He of all the people he knew in agency circles was the most influential, and the most dangerous. He had an air of confidence and affluence which was based on personal achievement and skill, not inherited… as with Staveley-Smythe.

It was petty he knew, as he watched a plume of dust from the disappearing Jag in the distance, but he wondered how Calder-Maynes had acquired his double-barrelled name.

Staveley-Smythe too was concerned at the speedily halted meeting. He had not wanted that. He believed there was real benefit for him and fellow colleagues in what had been discussed. He wanted to see things progressed, and he was very concerned at the continuing problems they had been experiencing. In fact it did not help with the negotiations. It was becoming increasingly clear there was a leak… strange… because that was almost what they had been talking about.

And now, there was a missing set of documents from that day's meeting.

"Shit," he said through his teeth as he put the phone down from talking to the people who had been there. Clearly, there were three possible scenarios.

Either someone in his own staff had grabbed a copy of the papers; there had been a third person in the attack who had gone straight for the documents, the attempt on Vasilovski being a half blind, and then thirdly, that Vasilovski had taken a copy of the documents in his scurry from the farmhouse. He favoured the third option.

Was Vasilovski what he purported to be? They assumed

he was the rocket guidance scientist his records said he was, but his biographical details, although very patchy early on, had been clear and corroborated over the past 20 years or so.

One of his first questions when they brought him back would be why he had run from the safe house?

Secondly, although using agents from MI5, there were a few who he knew he could rely on for extra work and with total discretion. Certainly he needed more help if he was going get an edge, and an edge was what he needed. The first priority was to get the Russian back – it shouldn't be too much of a job, where could he go? He already had Blake with a team on it. He thought he might set a second team on as well.

He would have to ring Armour and let him know the debrief was likely to be delayed.

Armour… he had been a bit strange over this debriefing, demanding to meet with Vasilovski before his arrival in England.

It was the first time that had happened, but at the same time Staveley-Smythe had a sneaky admiration for Armour. He wasn't too clear why, but he had seen him debriefing a few times and was impressed by his line of questioning in certain circumstances, and then his incredible intuition.

It would have Armour following an understandable line and then suddenly change tack, and Staveley-Smythe would watch enthralled, as the two lines of inquiry magically became entwined, and then produced an answer. It sometimes appeared as if Armour had orchestrated it himself.

That was why Staveley-Smythe allowed this peculiar unprecedented 'part-timer', 'on the fringe' status to continue. But he also respected Armour for his independence, and never for a moment doubted his loyalty to queen and country. And he liked him, although they had never mixed socially.

Armour had explained that he wanted to meet Vasilovski prior to his arrival, partly because he was to reassure himself that things were running smoothly in the light of the troubles they had been having, and get some handle on the man. He also fancied a trip to Hamburg.

This had seemed pretty weak to Staveley-Smythe, and he thought there might be another reason. He now wondered if Armour had given Vasilovski instructions about what he might do if anything went wrong. Staveley-Smythe couldn't see why he should want to go to such great lengths in this instance, but he didn't think it would do any harm. The trouble now was that if that was the case, he had to figure out what this enthusiastic amateur would do. What possible arrangements could he make for Vasilovski? What would Armour do if he did?

If Vasilovski had taken the papers, it would sort of suggest that he immediately understood their importance… or had been after them in the first place!

If that was the case he would probably be outside the country within a few hours, along a pre-arranged route with a pretty well-planned exit from the country.

Staveley-Smythe was in his office off the back of Shepherds Bush Green, which he tried to use as little as possible, and you could tell. It was plain, simple and only embellished with official-type pictures – military equipment, aircraft, ships, beachhead landings. The room had a dull view over towards Olympia.

There was a high-back black chair in which he lolled behind a large wooden, leather inlaid desk.

Despite his lolling, the telephone was red hot.

"Good God Michael, Why didn't you bloody tell me earlier. This is suddenly a very much more serious matter. Have you any idea what is at stake? Michael… Michael, what have you got to say…?"

"Alright, keep your hair on old boy, I do understand the situation, and I have got every available man on it. I can't help it if people are careless and leave their papers lying around. I am doing my best. It was you who sent everyone away so quickly…"

"Well listen to me sonny boy," said Calder-Maynes with his steely eyes narrowed and his teeth gritted. "You hosted that meeting, it is down to you, that's the way I see it, so your best may not be good enough. If this situation is not sorted and bloody pronto, I'll personally make you eat your balls. I'm setting some of my own people on this too, shit, Christ, what a fucking shambles."

Staveley-Smythe actually did not doubt that Calder-Maynes meant his highly personal threat, but there was something else nagging at Staveley-Smythe. It was something that Blake had said to him about Armour's meeting with Vasilovski in Lubeck.

There was nothing concrete, but Blake said he had noticed something in Vasilovski's expression when he first saw Armour. It had been strange… it seemed to be a mixture of shock and surprise. But then, Armour had marched straight up to him and bustled him physically away, which was a bit odd as well. Armour had not made any explanation about why he had done this, but then it was not Blake's job to question debriefers… they were usually more senior to him in the service, but he was observant and he had worked closely with Staveley-Smythe on many occasions. Staveley-Smythe had not particularly made much of this at the time Blake had told him, but now it could be relevant. He was checking anything that occurred to him.

He had decided to review closely anything in Armour's past that might shed light on it. Could he have known Vasilovski? There was certainly nothing in the files to suggest that they knew each other. Their information, although patchy concerning the Russian as an adolescent, was quite comprehensive.

Armour's background had been politically uneventful. After university, incidentally, where he had met Staveley-Smythe, he had trained as a journalist and travelled extensively.

Staveley-Smythe tried to cast his memory back to his Oxford days, trying to recollect when he had first met Armour – they were not good friends, but fairly good nodding acquaintances. They may have had a drink together once or twice, and probably in the company of others.

He was sure they first met at a varsity rugby match, although that was more Armour's bag than his. Staveley-Smythe had been in the debating society, more of the cultural side of things and also in at least one of the secret societies which riddle the colleges.

It had been five years after graduating that during a reunion they met once again.

Though Armour did not know it, Staveley-Smythe knew Armour's previous two controllers, and how Armour had been recruited. But he was fascinated for some time how Armour had managed to be allowed to build up his unique position, half in and half out of the service.

But the one thing no one could argue with, was that he had been extremely successful and had an exemplary track record.

It was generally accepted that had other people been involved with some of Armour's most difficult debriefs, the subjects would not have been so co-operative and their information not as full, detailed and relevant.

Again, incredibly, everyone who had contact with him, even some of the toughest, meanest foot-soldiers, who were rarely required to give an opinion, liked the guy.

With people clearing up around him, Staveley-Smythe made his way to the kitchen. He was peckish, and swung open the door of the fridge…

Chapter Three

The road had been quiet. Vasilli had passed the occasional cottage and through the small village of Nobottle. He skidded to a halt close to the gated entrance to a wooded area. It was now very dark – he was about three miles from Northampton. He went in through the gate and leaned the bike against a tree.

He walked a few yards and saw an obviously deserted old cottage. He was not to know that he was on the Althorp estate, home of the Spencer family.

In the gloom his eyes were becoming accustomed, and it looked as if the cottage was being refurbished. Around the back there was scaffolding, planks and a concrete mixer.

The windows were all boarded up, but he found the plywood board on one window a little loose, and so, using a spade that had been leaning up against the wall, he was able to force a couple of nails out and squeeze through the gap.

He managed to work his way from room to room. He could smell that a plasterer had been at work and the rooms were musty, but dry. All the windows were boarded and when he noticed a bulb in the socket in the main downstairs room, he tried the light switch.

Luck was on his side. The light flooded the room. He went outside again to see whether the light could be seen, but was pleased it could not. He found a couple of workers' donkey jackets, and a wooden cabinet which had tea, coffee, some bread, still quite fresh. He noted that the sink had running water. He rooted around in a cupboard beneath he found some plasters and disinfectant. There was an old two-bar electric fire which he plugged into the wall – it lay on its back and he assumed the workers used it like a grill to make toast, and like a burner to heat the beans… anyway that's how he used it. He ate using his fingers and washed.

Using the second shirt that he had stolen, he tore the cotton into strips. With some difficulty he managed to re-dress his wounds, which were in pretty good shape. He was happier now that he had been able to wash and disinfect the red raw hole in his flesh – one he could see clearly, bending his chin to his chest, the other only just visible by cricking his neck round and then pulling his shoulder forward, which caused quite a lot of pain. When he had completed this task he spread the donkey jackets as a bedroll.

Before trying to sleep, he pulled out the documents he had grabbed from the safe house room next to his, re-scanned them, and then started again, reading each sentence thoroughly – this was pretty important stuff, clearly top secret, but something a bit more than that. Someone was up to something very dangerous, and the initials of all the people concerned, were on this paper. He did not know any of them, except perhaps one, and that only gave him a hint of who they might have represented.

He thought over what he would do the next day. He would contact Mart Burricks, but then thought he might not be being very careful. He simply could not afford for anything else to go wrong. Apart from his life being on the line, if these documents were to be believed, so were most of the secret service agents in most of western Europe.

Mart Burricks was a last resort, which meant that meeting with him should not be the first course of action – desperate though things seemed.

Another plan was needed – another safeguard. He racked his brain… and it wandered back to his time in Oxford. This could be the key. His exact plan would hopefully formulate on the way. He only hoped that Pete Armour would be on the same wavelength… God forbid that he should have to be.

He drifted into a fitful sleep.

The birds woke him early and after more beans, he was washed and away by 6 am.

Heading back towards Daventry and the rocket guidance expert guided himself to Flore. He would cross the A45, cut through to the A5, by the Narrowboat pub, where he would hide the bike behind a hedge and risk a hitch – the first lift would be the most dangerous.

Arriving there, he saw three guys in jeans and sweatshirts leaving the Narrowboat, and one of them, seeing Vasilli was about to stand and hitch at the side of the road, and obviously going south, called to him.

"Want a lift mate? We're going that way, come on, jump in!

The other two seemed quite OK with that, and one echoed

"Yeah, come on, we'll give you a lift.

As they set off, driving a Ford Mondeo, they asked where he was going. He lied that he was going to Southampton, and they told him they would have to drop him off in Brackley.

They seemed very personable, told him they were building site labourers.

Most European people would not be able to tell the difference, so he said he was Polish and that he was on a cultural exchange, and had been in the country for three months, staying with student friends in Southampton. His English was passable and he felt his story sounded plausible. In fact they did not even ask him what sort of cultural visit it was and were more interested in club football in Poland.

Vasilli didn't know, and confessed as much. He apologised. But they then changed the subject and talked about shortages in the shops and Vasilli, relating it to how things were in his own old home town of Minsk, was able to talk freely about this and other social and economic problems.

They seemed genuinely interested, the time flew and very soon they were dropping him off the Juniper side of Brackley, so he was in a good place to get a lift into Oxford.

A plan had come into his mind as he got that second lift. He was not a spy and unused to cloak and dagger stuff, but he was fighting for his life. Very simple though it was, he was pleased with the plan he had come up with and what he had done in the short time he had spent in Oxford. He was sure that he had not been seen and had not aroused suspicion. He would definitely try and get back there when he had sorted out his new life.

The return trip to the Narrowboat was uneventful and he picked up his stolen push bike at about 3 pm and following the back roads through Nether Heyford, Bugbrooke and Rothersthorpe and into the town…

It was very busy. He had to ask a couple of times, but he soon found the *Chronicle & Echo* building – a large block building with narrow vertical windows and a large glass fronted reception, at The Mounts. It was only two to three hundred or so yards from one of the shopping centres, and the town centre pubs and hotels.

Inside the unusually heavy swing doors, the foyer was light and airy. There were several people around, and he looked along the signs above the counter, 'accounts', 'advertising', and 'enquiries'. He went to the 'enquiries' desk, had to wait while someone in front was dealt with and then asked to speak with Mart Burricks. The receptionist, who had a name tag saying 'Margaret', rang the newsroom.

Mart Burricks was a tall chap, about 6ft2 tall. He was well proportioned, had a lean, clean-cut face with hair back-combed and lightly waxed. He was single, well-dressed, generally thought by the female staff to be good-looking and stylish.

Career-wise he had moved around a bit. He had started on the *Bucks Herald* in Aylesbury, spent the three years on the *South Wales Argus* in Newport and two as a crime reporter at *The News* in Portsmouth, before becoming news editor at the *Chronicle* in Northampton, a year ago.

He was highly regarded and had been identified by the editor and managing director as someone they would want to fast-track into management and greater seniority.

But with all that, Mart was a genuine sort of chap, easy-going and popular, but also a good hard news journalist.

He knew Pete Armour pretty well, or so he thought, and when Pete did work for the *Chron.*, it was usually Mart he went for a drink with at lunchtime. They had also met a few times socially in the evenings, and had been to the Sheffield dry-ski slope together a few times to brush up.

Mart had always found Armour intriguing. He was older, more experienced and yet had a glint in his eye. There was always something mysterious about him. No one knew a great deal about him, even though he never played the part of a solitary character. He was always pleasant, convivial, knowledgeable. Perhaps Mart hoped that when he was 40, he would be a bit like Armour.

Mart did not know what to expect when Margaret told him there was someone with an East European accent, insisting on seeing him, and only him, in the reception. He had initially said the man would have to wait, and Margaret duly told Vasilli this and he took a seat. He thumbed through various leaflets on a coffee table, which included an advertising rate card, information about staff with a 'who's who' in editorial, a town guide with a map, which Vasilli decided to keep, and information about the other newspaper titles in the group.

Mart suddenly thought better of making his mysterious guest hang around, and anyway he was intrigued.

He was slightly taken aback when he entered the reception and saw the man sitting on one of the big easy chairs.

He looked between 40 and 45, dishevelled, and his hair was all over the place – he looked rough. Mart knew he had never met this man before and so, a little gingerly, he held out his hand and introduced himself.

The return grip was firm and held on just long enough for Mart to feel the genuine warmth it exuded.

Vasilli's eyes, deep and blue, said: 'Its OK, you can trust me,' as Mart hesitated… but he believed them.

Vasilli asked if there was somewhere more private where they could talk, and Mart checked and chose to use one of the aluminium framed training rooms behind the reception area.

"Thank you for meeting me", said Vasilli, "My name is Vasilli Vasilovski. You are going to find this a little strange."

"Oh, why?"

"You know Pete Armour?"

"Yes, he is a freelance journalist. He works here from time to time."

"Yes, well, he is very old friend of mine, and he said I could trust you. For your own good I should tell you as little as possible. I will tell you that I am Russian scientist who Pete is helping to defect – something has gone wrong, there was a lot of shooting at a place near Daventry, and I need to get a message to him, and it is impossible for me to do it directly."

Mart had heard about the shooting at Flecknoe, there had been a piece on the police media-line early that morning. They had sent photographers and reporters out there but they had been kept well away. The police had said it was a siege situation – some gun-toting farmer had flipped and started shooting at a milkman, and neighbours, and then killed some visitors to the village, firing also at a couple of police officers with a 9 mm machine pistol.

Mart, believed Vasilli, and asked what he could do – he also felt he might be on the biggest story of his life. He was, but he wouldn't be writing it…

"Pete said to get you to pass to him this message – ' That special bottle of Scotch, Excelsior Reserve, you requested, is now available.' Have you got that?"

Mart said that he did, and repeated the message.

"As you may have guessed, I had to leave the farm in a rush last night and I need money, but Pete will know where to find me. I could do with a new bandage on this."

He showed Mart his wound.

First things first, Mart got Vasilli some coffee and went in search of a first aid kit. He returned with the necessary bandages and ointments, and re-dressed Vasilli's wound. He pointed out that really Vasilli could do with proper medical attention for his shoulder.

"Do you want to let me know where you will be?" asked Mart. He was rather loathed to let Vasilli, or the story, out of his sight.

"Better you do not know," said Vasilli conclusively, "Do you have money? I will make sure you get it back I promise."

Mart readily handed over about £50 he had on him – he could always go to the cashpoint on his way home.

"I can let you have this now and more later if you need it."

"No, this should be plenty," said Vasilli, and thanked him.

"Will you try and get that message to Pete, now, or tonight… the sooner he gets it the better," said Vasilli.

From the extension in the training room, Mart tried Pete's number, and got his answer machine.

Vasilli, who was listening at the earpiece, signalled, using a cutting sign across his throat, not to leave the message on the machine.

Mart promised that he would keep trying until he got him.

Vasilli got up, thanked him again and headed for the door.

"Hey, hang on," said Mart, "tell me a little more. If you are from Russia, how do you know Armour. How can he be 'an old friend'? How did you get here? Perhaps you should tell me where you are going to stay. Will it be safe? You could stay at my place."

Mart was desperate not to leave it there. He wasn't worried about the money, but he had a gut instinct that to simply let this chap back out on the streets was not a good idea.

But Vasilli was adamant.

"My friend, I thank you, but this is a very dangerous situation, and people are getting killed. Pete said to come to you, but only so you could pass on my message. Neither he nor I want anyone else to get hurt, and involving you more could prove very, very dangerous. You have already done more than enough, but please keep trying Pete's number. Pete will know what to do."

With some reluctance, Mart showed him to the exit.

He was sorely tempted to follow him. He stepped back into the reception, and then decided to go for it. He stepped out among others on the pavement, in the dying light, and headed after Vasilli as he moved off towards the ABC Cinema.

Street lights had been on for about half an hour already. Vasilli turned right into Abington Street, the main shopping street in the town. It was still bustling with people. He stopped and spoke to someone, apparently asking directions, and then carried on into Gold Street. He crossed over on to the south side of the street and entered the foyer of the Grand Hotel, which was anything but. Mart saw him go in, but hung back. He stopped in the narrow road next to the hotel, to think.

He returned to the *Chron* building via the cashpoint and tried Pete, but still got the answer machine. Pete was a bit of a dark horse. He had not the slightest idea that Pete carried on a 'secret life', but actually, he had not been totally surprised. He obviously knew about Vasilli's imminent defection, but why had he chosen Mart Burricks to help?

Why had he not said something? He could have been better prepared.

By now most of the reporters had left the building with just one doing late duty – he would be there until seven-thirty, and another waiting to go out on a night job, a public meeting of some kind Mart recalled seeing the item on the diary earlier.

Finding it incredibly difficult, Mart finished the story he had been working on before Vasilli showed his face, and then rang Pete again – still the machine. He keyed Armour's number into his mobile phone memory, and then slinging his jacket over his shoulders he made for the town centre again and strolled nonchalantly along Gold Street and approached the Grand.

It all happened so fast. He really didn't have a chance. As he passed the little lane at the side of the building, arms reached out to grab him.

Before he had the instinct to yell, there was a thud to his solar plexus which kept him silent and fighting for breath that just would not come.

Before he could force oxygen back into his lungs, he was bustled 30 yards towards the back of the building and a thin blade entered between his ribs and punctured his heart.

Before another second had passed there was not enough life in him to see the great lid of an industrial-sized wheeled rubbish bin at the back of the hotel come down on him.

Also in that time he had been relieved of his wallet, cheque book, money, mobile phone, and anything else that would quickly identify him, and of course it would just look like a particularly brutal mugging.

Staveley-Smythe had reluctantly agreed to receive Calder-Maynes' call. He told the switchboard to put it through. He had 30 men locally, hunting for the Russian. It had been ten hours since he skipped the safe house and there had not been a sign of him apart from a stolen shirt from a clothes line in Flecknoe. This was made even stranger because they knew that the mechanic had hit his target with at least one shot… there had been blood in the library that did not match up with anyone else. This did not lend any weight to the theory that he had been working for the opposition, as an agent.

They didn't know which direction he had gone. All local roads in all directions had been covered, several times, all ports and airports had been alerted.

"Yes Bryan."

With no hesitation he said: "Well, what's happening? Where are those documents? Is he out of the country?"

"We have everything covered. I think it is more likely that he is laying low somewhere locally. He stole a shirt from a washing line in Flecknoe. He wouldn't need to do that if he had outside help. He is obviously scared and running, we'll get him."

"You had better. If you don't, and soon, I will. And if that is the case, it could be quite messy. Your see, I don't care about debriefs and what suits MI5. What hinges on that Group meeting and others, is far more important to me, and should be to you."

"Look Bryan, I'll keep you posted. I am just as concerned as you about what is happening. As you say, it affects me as much as you… so bloody keep your hair on."

He hung up. He was fed up with Sir Bryan coming over all high and mighty. He had done his best and would continue in a similar vein… bugger him!

It was four hours later, the Russian had been spotted!

On the outskirts of Northampton, heading for the town centre, Vasilovski had been seen on a bicycle in an area called 'Jimmy's End'.

The report came from a member of his staff, working from a photo, a chance spotting, but called as a ninety-five per cent positive ID. That would be good enough to concentrate all their efforts in Northampton. All units had been moved there.

It did not take too long before he was spotted again walking into Abington Street, the town's main shopping street, in amongst the crowds, heading towards Gold Street.

Calder-Maynes' man, Carter, a thin, wiry man in his late twenties, with short hair, wearing a heavy wax jacket that made him look a lot bulkier than he was, had also seen him, but he had also seen the man trailing him… Blake had not!

While another man kept an eye, Carter used a pay phone.

"I don't know who the guy is, I have never seen him before, and I would guess he is not a professional. He followed the Russian out of the newspaper building, and he is definitely, and pretty obviously tailing him."

That's all they needed, thought Calder-Maynes, some nosy reporter poking his nose in.

Why had the Russian gone virtually straightway to a frigging newspaper, it hardly made sense, unless the guy was trying to set up some kind of insurance policy or bargaining chip.

"Where is the Russian now?"

"He has just gone into a hotel."

"And where is the other chap?"

"He is in the street outside, he looks as if he might go in…"

"Get rid of him," said Calder-Maynes hanging up.

Carter signalled to a man across the street.

They did not know or care who he was… Burricks was dispatched quickly and quietly.

Calder-Maynes did not bother to tell Staveley-Smythe, the work his men had done that night. Fact was, he would find out quite soon.

"Sir, Blake here."

"Blake, what's happening for Christ sake?" demanded Staveley-Smythe.

"Everything's under control, I think, sir, The Russian booked into the Grand Hotel under the name of Dieter Schmitt. Twenty minutes later he came out and grabbed a takeaway from McDonald's and then returned to the hotel. He had one drink at the bar and went to his room. I've organised a stake out."

"Strange thing is sir, there seems to be someone else showing an interest."

"What?"

"Yes sir, a two-man surveillance team with back-up. Someone brought them food and drink a little while ago, then disappeared when we tried to trail him… he had to be good.

"I'm pretty positive that it isn't anything like the local Plod, they are too sharp, almost military. I don't know, but there's something about them that isn't Ruskie either. I don't know who they are. Do you want me to find out?"

Staveley-Smythe really liked the way Blake dealt with things and reported back. He was always crisp and concise. He always used his own initiative in running things and was good at it, and his reports added his own intuitive commentary.

"No, leave them alone. I think I know who they are. You've got enough men down there, just keep an eye on them. Report back first thing."

"Goodnight, sir," said Blake and crossed over to the large Bedford van that they were using. There was a single bunk in the van. He would use that to get some sleep, while two men would keep watch from the vehicle. There was also a man on each of the roads leading into the street. One was the wino sitting on the steps of All Saints Church, and the others were hidden in the shadows. All would be relieved twice during the night.

Chapter Four

Claire Willans, known to her friends as 'Mac', because that was the way she liked her whiskey, did not feel or see anything, when the middle-aged man in the reception of the *Chronicle*, slipped the piece of paper into her open bag. She had briefly talked to someone and then turned to the door-way.

She slid her swipe key card through the slot and went through to the stairs that led up to the editorial department, she lightly skipped the first three steps and walked the remainder.

Slender, dark-haired and attractive, it was not too difficult to see why Mac had caught Vasilli's eye. She was stunning.

She was wearing a dark business suit, a silk blouse in bronze and blue, lightly tanned tights and black court-style shoes.

But it was not just that, there was something else about her that made Vasilli choose her.

She was about 26, but had freshness – a frank, open, face and a bright glisten in her eye.

Without causing any attention and in the time she had crossed the reception to the inner door, she had met eyes, winked and smiled at Margaret and one of the cashiers.

Margaret held up her hand and Mac stopped.

"Oh Mac, can you drop in and have a word with Lucy, the editor's secretary on your way through?"

"Yeah sure," she replied, said a couple of words to the cashier and carried on again.

He added something hastily scribbled to the note he had already written, and slipped it into her bag. Mart was not there, which surprised him, but now he knew that his options were very quickly running out.

As they passed each other, Vasilli's nose caught a gentle waft of elegant French perfume that had been lightly dabbed behind her ears, neck and between her breasts.

Earlier, Margaret at the enquiries desk, who had recognised Vasilli from the previous day, told him that Mart Burricks had not reported for work that morning although the newsdesk told her they had been expecting him.

Sitting for a moment in one of the foyer's deep comfortable settees and again leafing through literature on a coffee table, his brain working ten to the dozen.

Vasilli could not believe Burricks would not be there, he had been so interested, so willing to help, let alone keen to pass on his message to Armour. Horrendous though it seemed, Vasilli could only come to the asumption that something must had happened to him. And if it had, it meant that they had him spotted, knew his movements and knew perhaps that he had tried to establish contact.

Vasilli realised that perhaps two countries' agents were closing in on him, but had not imagined that Burricks would be dead but then he would never know…

He did assume, however, that Burricks had not been able to get his message to Pete… it was a very reasonable assumption – Burricks was missing and Armour had not made contact with him at the hotel. But now, time was running out and Vasilli felt he had to act.

Vasilli decided there was little point in trying to talk to

anyone, even though he knew what he was intending to do, so had written the note, before she had come into the building, But something clicked when he saw Mac. It had been in the information leaflet on the coffee table.

He saw the confident way she approached the entrance, and then the inner door with the card key entry system, and knew who she was, and knew that he had to move fast. He scribbled…

He did not even have to bump into her, her bag was gaping carelessly and she did not feel a thing. He guessed that when she read the message, which he was now beginning to hope would be very soon, she would ring Armour quickly.

Had he received a note like that, he would have, but they were different here. He decided to return to his room at the Grand because if Armour did try and make contact, it had to be there.

It was mid-morning, as Mac rooted in her bag for a cigarette, that she found it. It would have been earlier if she had not been trying to give up the weed, but there it was. She pulled it from her large floppy bag as if it was some mysterious archaeological artefact, turning it over from one side then the other…

It was only folded twice, but she opened it very slowly… like it was booby-trapped. She did not know where it had come from, but just knew that it shouldn't have been there.

As her eyes read the words and digested the meaning, her hands and quickly folded the note into her lap, as if prying eyes were looking over her shoulder.

They weren't, and she lifted her hands and brought herself to look at the message again.

It was hard to believe…

"I am dead. This is no joke, ring Pete Armour… or I

am dead. Tell him 'That special bottle of Scotch, Thane's Excelsior Reserve, you requested, is now available.' Don't talk to anyone please, just do it!"

Could she really treat this seriously? Some of the guys in the newsroom were capable of pulling a stunt like this. It could have been put in her bag at any time…

Small beads of sweat appeared on her brow, she felt a rumble in the pit of her stomach, and she considered the options.

She could throw the note away, ignore it and get on with her life, at least that would safeguard against a possible prank.

She could talk and get others involved and see what they thought… and everyone would have a good laugh at her expense.

She could talk to the editor… no… she did not think so.

Where was Mart Burricks? – He had taken her under his wing a bit, she could have talked to him in confidence, she could trust him, and he would have known what to do, he would have understood, and he would have helped?

Mac knew the most simple and probably most effective course of action was to do what the note suggested… to ring Armour. She knew him, although not well – she had only been at the paper two months – something inside her told her this was not a joke. It was too simple to clarify… to sort out. There was a slight twinge as she thought about this option, and that was because she did not want to appear a complete idiot to Armour.

Then again, there wasn't that much to lose and even the big Pete Armour would understand why she had acted in this way. And she could not rule out that if this was a genuine note, someone obviously needed help, and fast.

"Yes."

Pete never acknowledged that a caller had rung the right number by announcing it, he obviously took it that they knew the number they were ringing and should not need it clarified.

"Pete," she recognised his voice," This is Mac… Claire… from the *Chron*. Something strange has happened, and somehow it involves you."

Armour had been expecting it, but not from Claire Willans, where was Mart Burricks?

"Pete," she continued, "I found this very strange message in my bag a little while ago…"

Thank God, he was still alive.

"Mac hi, how are you?" he tried to keep his voice normal, but showing mild curiosity.

'I'm fine Pete, look, can I read it to you, I think it might be important…

'No! No don't, not now,' he said firmly, startling her slightly – she hadn't expected his reaction to be so assertive.

The way things were going, he thought it fairly likely his phone might be tapped.

She heard his voice again.

"Look, I'm coming over to Northampton soon, I'll come into reception – can you get away for an hour, about lunchtime?"

"Yes, I have got the afternoon off anyway, so yes, I'll see you soon."

"OK don't worry. Could you keep that message to yourself until we have talked about it… Oh Mac?"

"Yes?"

"Have you seen Mart Burricks today, I need to speak to him?"

" Err… no… people were expecting him, the funny thing is he has not rung in to say he is ill or anything."

"OK, not to worry, I'll see you later," and he hung up.

She felt he had been a bit curt, but she knew she had done the right thing.

But there was every need to worry. Vasilli was totally exposed and not being very subtle about it – but at least up until a very short while ago, he was alive and well, and passing the note to Mac…

Since his meeting with Vasilli in Lubeck, Pete had been locked away in London with the case study on him, and getting further backgrounders on Vasilli from Mick. It was the normal pattern leading up to a defection debrief. There were things that Military Intelligence needed to know before they got down to the details of Vasilli's work – if it had not been for that, he would have been able to give Vasilli his own number or address… highly against the rules though it was. He had thought about ringing the Grand Hotel, but he could not get there any quicker and could not actually suggest anything to Vasilli but to wait until he did.

Where was Burricks… he was the one Pete had been expecting to hear from after the farce at Flecknoe. He had known almost straight away that Vasilli had got away from the farmhouse… and would eventually be seeking refuge in Northampton and he would soon be able to contact him at the Grand.

Everyone at Military Intelligence was after Vasilovski, and running around like headless chickens and without a clue where to look. Mick had told him the news and told him he might as well go home. Armour decided against telling him anything.

The police forces of five counties, Northamptonshire, Oxfordshire, Warwickshire, Buckinghamshire and Leicestershire, had been alerted, but were hardly given enough to go on, and where and what were the opposition up to, only a vague description of Vasilli – it was a major mess.

The Flecknoe farce amazingly had been blanketed pretty well, at least for the time being. Mick had been on though – he was sharp enough to want to know what the meeting at Lubeck had been all about, but it was still unlikely that he would have known about the closer contact between Armour and Vasilli, not yet anyway.

Armour had decided to bullshit him for a while. Mick knew there was more to it, but didn't push. He thought that Armour was pretty straightforward, had no axe to grind politically, and therefore he felt he could trust him. Armour decided he would probably tell him soon, but he just wanted to have a little more space for a little while longer. He felt it was better that what little control there was of this situation, was his.

He got ready to go to Northampton.

Mac thought Armour was being a bit mysterious. It was a pretty simple message however dramatic. But it was as if Armour had been expecting it. He was certainly not surprised. Maybe he was expecting it. Mac's natural journalistic curiosity started up.

Someone was obviously in trouble, but why did they think Armour could help them. Was it a story Armour was working on – what was he involved in? It seemed very cloak and dagger. Why was the message left with her, there was no real link between her and Armour?

Hopefully Armour would satisfy her curiosity, he would at least owe her that – maybe she could help with the story.

Mac was curious too, of the emotion that reared itself in her. She was quite looking forward to seeing Pete, he was an interesting bloke. She had not had much contact with him in the two months she had been at the paper – perhaps four or five times, and he worked on the subs table, designing pages, and that was in a separate area from the reporters, but only across the room.

They had met a couple of times at the coffee machine. He was 40-ish and had an unusual face – one of round-the-world yachtsman, well-worn and lined crows-footed, lived-in types.

He had a full beard, kept short, but not shaped. She took slightly more than just a passing interest from the time their eyes first met – they were deep, blue, kind, captivating, laughing eyes that raised at the corners when he smiled, in line with the edge of his mouth… and they held her gaze… penetratingly. It was as if he could almost read her mind and was analysing the information that was feeding through. It was one of those moments when two people suddenly realise there could be something between them… if they let themselves. He was obviously intelligent, but also good humoured, and witty when the inclination took him.

He was a big man, and very broad shouldered, but not fat. His clothes were smart and stylish, and although they didn't seem to fit in with any style category, they were never out of place.

The other interesting thing about Armour was that he was always a bit of a loner – a little bit of mystery surrounded him. No one, not even Mart Burricks, who probably had known him as well as anyone at the *Chron*, had any idea what he did in his spare time, except that he was apparently a good skier.

Come to that, no one really knew anything about him. He talked about university in Oxford, but that was about it. Who or where his family came from nobody knew.

Vasilli had left the *Chronicle & Echo* building and this time crossed the road, passed the court building and car parks opposite, towards the bus station.

He started across the road to the path which avoids the bus station and leads to the main Grosvenor shopping centre.

As he stepped up the kerb a large black-window-tinted four-door Ford Scorpio screeched to a halt. Before anyone noticed, or Vasilli could do anything, he was overpowered and strong arms were holding him down in the back of the car, it jerked back into the stream of traffic – he recognised the chemical as the chloroform pad was thrust over his nose and mouth, and he felt rough hands on him for about two seconds, and then his senses drift away.

Chapter Five

Obviously under normal circumstances Armour would not be involved in chasing after people – Military Intelligence had enough 'troops' for that sort of thing, but he had decided very early on to prepare contingency plans. Because things had been going so badly wrong recently and especially because it had been Vasilli. But plans for the next stage depended on circumstances, but this was almost impossible to plan.

He could have kicked himself. He had arranged his own safe house not far away in Warwick, close to where he was renting a cottage.

And now something had messed up Armour's contingency plan and for some reason Burricks was out of it, which made him sick in the pit of his stomach. Had he been the cause of an innocent man's death? ... And now Mac was involved. He was not very happy about that either.

He was not very happy that he had the idea of involving Burricks, but Burricks was sharp. Mac was... too young, too inexperienced, could so easily mess up.

No! What he really meant, as he thought it through, was that she was too beautiful, full of youth, and, yes, sexy, to have her life put in danger through no fault of her own... and he found himself thinking... 'even for Vasilli'.

But he also admonished himself – what was he thinking... he hardly knew the girl, and had hardly thought about her at all, until now.

But he was thinking about her, and apart from the potential danger, was enjoying his mind's eye view of them, heads together, over coffee, talking about Vasilli's message, even though he knew, or thought he knew, what that message said. Really there was no vital need for them to meet. He could ring from a pay phone, which would be safe, and get the message.

Vasilli's message... Vasilli's message – it meant he was at the Grand Hotel in Northampton.

He had just pulled on his tweed jacket, and got to the door when it struck him. He turned on his heel, dropped his car keys on the low coffee table and picked up the radio phone from its base station and first dialled directory inquiries, and then called the hotel.

"The Grand Hotel, Northampton. Good morning, this is Lisa, how may I help you?"

"Hello Lisa," he kept his voice calm, " May I speak to Dieter Schmitt, who I believe is registered there?"

"One moment sir, I'll check and try and connect you," said Lisa, helpfully, but quite quickly she came back on...

"Hello sir?"

"Yes."

"Sir, I'm terribly sorry, but Mr. Schmitt has left the hotel."

"Left the hotel? Are you sure? He checked out?" he quizzed.

"I think so. Hang on sir, I didn't check him out myself, but the person who did is still here, let me enquire?" she said helpfully.

Again she came back.

"Hello sir?"

"Yes?"

"Yes, sir, Mr. Schmitt has left. Two of his colleagues came while he was out. They had his room key, and a note from him saying he was a bit under the weather, would be staying with one of his friends, and it was OK for the colleagues to collected his things. They settled up his bill, collected things from his room, and left, sir. His signature matched with the one he gave when he checked in sir… Sir?"

"Yes? Thank you. Did your colleague get a good look at these two 'friends' by any chance?"

She went off the line again, and when she came back was not very willing to commit herself or her friend… he thanked her… he knew almost as much as he wanted to know, maybe more.

"Shit… Shit… Shit…" said Armour, between clenched teeth as he replaced the phone… the big question was who had got him?

Was it their side or was it ours? And, would it make any difference to Vasilli's life expectancy?

Armour's contingency plan had failed and somebody had nabbed Vasilli… and so quickly, he was annoyed with himself.

If luck was on his side, Vasilli had fallen into the right hands…

Vasilli's head hurt. He had come around two or three minutes earlier and found himself in a small cell. It was not a proper cell as such, and did not have a steel door with viewing hole, but it felt like that to him. It could easily have been a store room in an office, or in the cellar of a house – there was no window, the door was the only way in or out. The light was on, and shone from a single, unshaded bulb.

Vasilli had no idea where he was, or how much time had passed. He would not know if he was still in England, or back in Russia. He was totally disorientated.

There was nothing in the room to give him a clue… he thought the writing on the light bulb might be in Spanish…

The dressing to his wounded shoulder had been removed…and so had a simple gold ring with a black jade inset…and his watch… and his clothing apart from underpants and trousers.

The light went out!

After about three minutes the door unlocked and swung open. Backlit by a powerful halogen, they carried another spotlight, which they plugged in and shone straight in his face.

Vasilli was blinded, but as they questioned him about what happened when the shooting started at Flecknoe, suddenly, there was a crash and the light blew. In the moments between quickly backing out of the room and slamming the door, Vasilli's eyesight recovered just enough to catch the outline of a big man with short silver-grey hair.

Twenty minutes later the lights came on again and the interrogation resumed, and this time there was no nonsense with them.

Vasilli was no hero, and soon had little to hide. He told his captors all they wanted to know, but when he told them he had gone straight to Northampton from Flecknoe, they did not query it…and he knew they did not know about his little trip to Oxford. Nor had they asked any questions about missing documents from the Flecknoe farm – who were they?

If they were KGB it was understandable, and they would come back for more questions, until everything fitted into place.

And if they were British, the same would happen, but they should have known something about the documents, unless they were so taken up with the shooting, that in the confusion it had been overlooked. That was hard to believe unless one or more of the people who had been going over those documents had been killed…?

He was confused, but pleased for the rest when they finally left his cell.

But one thing he felt fairly sure of – if they were Russian he was out of the country and back in the Soviet very soon, never to see the West again… that is, if they didn't shoot him first.

He was hungry, a little cold and did not know how long he had been left on his own. He was strangely comforted by the knowledge that he appeared to have kept something from his captors. At the same time he knew that if they pressed him on the subject he wouldn't be able to resist for very long. In the end, he calculated, why should he?

He did not know how much later it was, but the light was put out, three minutes later the door was flung open and from a backlit figure some clothes were thrown at him. The door slammed shut. The light came on.

The clothes were awful. They consisted of a dark, dank T-shirt; dirty, smelly, socks; some old slip-on shoes which fitted badly, and an old army-style greatcoat…

Vasilli's death was sad and ignominious.

It was late at night and very dark when he was bundled, blindfolded, into a car and taken on a short drive. Out of the car he did not know where he was, although his body would be found later near the Britannia pub on the Bedford Road, not that far from where he had been picked up in Northampton.

He was roughly led, often stumbling, across an area of long grass, to the riverside and he could hear the noise of nearby sluices. The last sound he would hear though was the roaring in his ears as his head was pushed beneath the surface and he fought against the inevitable.

He eventually had to give way as his strength sapped – the strong hands on the back of his neck were vice-like. His lungs were bursting and he gasped and felt the water enter his throat burning in his airways – a sharp pain pierced his temples and lights flashed in the back of his eyes. He tried to force the water out, but only managed to gasp in more. Though the waters were dark, lights flashed across his senses, his arms were flailing, grasping and clawing, but not at anything solid and he could not break free. He knew his eyes opened, but he saw little except that flashing. The water was dark and he did not know whether the lights he saw were actually there or just inside his head. The searing pain, which now spread all across his head and deep into his skull, climaxed and then gave way. He felt no pain, no fear. The strange water bloated his lungs and his body convulsed and went limp… it was over.

Chapter Six

Inspector Richard Banham was having a very bad morning – two bodies on his hands. One he had no clue about, except an Oxford bus ticket in the trouser pockets, but the other victim was only too well known to him, Mart Burricks, News Editor at the *Chron*… and a friend.

He had pulled his clothes on rapidly when he got the call at his home at 5 am. It had woken his wife, who had reached out for the phone and mechanically swung the handset over to him – she was used to this.

He had been called soon after the man's body was spotted floating in the River Nene, near the Britannia on Bedford Road by a fisherman. The man, who was certainly drowned, was a mystery. He looked, and smelt, like a vagrant from his clothes and there was nothing on him to identify him or suggest where he might have come from, and it was assumed already that he had slipped and fallen in the river, and drowned accidentally – it had certainly not been the first time.

But Banham was not so sure. Although not manicured, the 'floater' had tidily cut nails, and the dirt under them was fresh… like from the river bank. He was slightly dark-skinned and he had a slight whiteness circling his little finger where a ring had been.

Basically, he was too 'clean'… except for an Oxford City shuttle bus ticket sodden and screwed up in his trouser pocket. At least it gave them something to work on, and a place to start.

Banham took a slug of semi-cold; sweet coffee, winced, and threw the plastic cup and remaining contents into a wastepaper basket. The coffee on the first floor at Campbell Square was like shit since they had installed that vending machine.

It had been on his return to the police station that he was told that a second body had been found at the back of the Grand Hotel. He was there in a matter of minutes, and he remembered the blood draining from his face as he lifted the lid of the wheelie bin and looked down at the gaping chalky face of Mart Burricks.

The 'floater' could have been suicide, murder or a mistake. Burricks' death was clear. It was murder! A blade about five inches long and very thin had been stuck between his ribs and punctured his heart. Although at first it looked like a mugging, Burricks' death too was also far too 'clean', precise, clinical almost… he dragged the word he was searching for from the back of his mind, and under his breath, it landed on his lips…

'Professional…'

It had been years before, but he recognised the style.

And the 'cleanness' was the only reason Banham had for thinking that the two deaths were somehow linked. And yet the Oxford City bus ticket, that was odd.

If it was professional it was probably a plant. Others would disagree.

It was now 10.30 am. Banham had mobilised detectives and uniformed officers, and then telephoned the editor of the *Chron*, Phil Brown, and told him the bad news and to ask about next of kin. He knew Mart had parents and a sister somewhere but could not recall where. The editor's secretary's files had been helpful. It of course meant that the *Chron* had the story and would splash on it… two deaths, one being the murder of one of their own…

As far as an investigation was concerning, there was very little to go on. Burricks had been found in a skip at the back of the Grand. Obviously there would be a lot of people to question, and he had no doubt that the *Chronicle* would be keen to help with publicity.

It was sad really. He knew Burricks fairly well and they met occasionally for drinks. He liked the guy. He couldn't imagine why anyone would want to kill him. But if he was right and this was a professional hit, it might have been something he had been working on – he would have to speak to Brown again about that.

Banham decided that he would keep his suspicions about 'a hit', to himself for the moment.

He gave priority to the Burricks death – it was an obviously vicious killing, which took place in a busy town centre shopping area. There would be public outcry, and it was a fair bet that the *Chron* would be more than willing to do anything that might help track down this killer. But Banham, as the officer leading the investigation, was the one who was likely to be pilloried by the press, if there was not a fairly quick result.

If it was 'a hit' he knew the chances of a result were pretty slim, and there was no way he could prove it was professional.

If it was 'just a mugging', then it was vital to catch the killer quickly – he was a very dangerous person to have wandering the streets. There was no question that this story was going to raise the level of 'fear of crime' in the community. He had all the men he could spare on it, and some from neighbouring divisions. He put a couple of officers on the 'floater'.

He barked at someone to fetch him another coffee and slumped down at his desk and rubbed his eyes. It was going to be a very, very bad day.

"Bad news I'm afraid, sir," said Blake.

"What's happened?"

"Vasilovski left the hotel at 8.30, and headed straight for the *Chronicle* building. The other team clocked this and we all trooped up to The Mounts. It was almost like a works outing."

"Get on with it, Blake," Staveley-Smythe said irritably, sensing uncommon prevarication and impending bad news.

"It was strange, the Russian was in the foyer of the building, spoke to the receptionist, loitered around for a bit and then left quite quickly. He was heading back to the town centre and was crossing a road when he was snatched by three guys in a Scorpio. We had a car in place, but he was facing the wrong way, and with the amount of traffic passing The Mounts at that time of the day, the silly git of a driver got caught up. We've lost him sir."

"Shit."

"And the other surveillance team have melted away while it was going on."

"Use the usual channels to get a make on that Scorpio, it's a possibility, although there have probably been two switches by now. Start checking the roads in and out again. Get every man on it," said Staveley-Smythe trying to keep calm. He knew Blake was a good man and his own professional code would be twisting the knife in him. He hung up.

"Bryan, what have you done with him?"

"We picked him up, found out what he knew and we have eliminated him. Only what your motley bunch should have done by now."

"Shit. You could have consulted me first. There could still have been a debrief."

"Oh come on Michael, with what he knew he was more of a danger to us than he was to his own side. OK MI5 hasn't gained as much as it might have done, and we are still in danger, but…"

"What do you mean… you did get the papers off him I presume?"

"There you go presuming again Michael. No, we did not get the papers off him, because he did not have them on him, or among his things at the hotel.

"We did not ask him about the papers specifically because I was not about to become personally involved, and I did not want other people to know about them. I simply had my men grill him on precisely what had happened and what he had done since leaving Flecknoe. We did find out why he was at the *Chronicle* building. He was trying to get in touch with Pete Armour, your debriefer man. He works there sometimes doesn't he?"

"Apparently, he's met him before somewhere, somewhere in Germany."

"Yes, they met in Lubeck when he was coming over. Armour was uncomfortable about the operations that had been going wrong and insisted on meeting him before he arrived here. It seemed a little odd, but there didn't seem any harm in it."

"Well," said Calder-Maynes, "Perhaps we should speak to your man Armour and find out a bit more about that meeting."

"Bryan, why did you have the Russian killed?"

With no hesitation Sir Bryan said: "He saw me Michael."

Suddenly, the newsroom fell silent – the editor's secretary had arranged for all calls to be suspended, the editor, Phil

Brown came to the newsdesk which was the 'centre of operations' held up his arms and called for quiet and for everyone to gather round.

With the emotion visibly welling up in him, muttering staffers, who imagined it to be a company announcement, were quickly silenced – this was different, Brown was not normally known for emotional expression, unless it was aggressive.

His voice croaked: "I, eh, I have some very sad news, and I eh, I don't think there is an easy way of telling you…

"The police have just informed me that Mart… Mart Burricks… was found stabbed to death early this morning, and dumped in refuse bins at the back of the Grand Hotel…"

Brown's voice achieved a slight squeak on the word 'dumped', and he completed the sentence with increasing speed, as though he needed to, just in case he retched, which was not far from the truth.

Almost in unison there were sharp intakes of breath, gasps and exclamations of shock.

Brown raised up his arm again in a plea for quiet. He wheezed slightly before speaking again, a result of years of smoking.

"I have managed to speak to relatives, and will be speaking to them again later.

"I, eh, I know Mart had a good many good friends among you, and I know this is going to take some getting over, and believe me there will be time for mourning."

He went on to explain more of what he had heard from Dick Banham, someone he had known for some years. He felt the hearts of his staff sinking deeper and deeper, and his own go with them. Mart had been special and everyone recognised it. Brown himself had seen Mart as a future successor at the paper, he had nurtured him and really grown to like the lad…

Now Brown had to get those other heavy hearts moving, and he had to lift them – it was his job, only he could do it.

"In the meantime," he said, "we will use whatever resources we have to help the police and encourage the public to help us catch his killer or killers, and from here on in it gets harder…

"The one thing I do know is that Mart Burricks was a total professional and above all he would understand what I am going to say now…it is 10.45 am, the next edition is out at 11.50. The whole of Pages One, Three and Five are going to need changing. I want all the stops pulled out on this one. There was another death today we need to work on that one too. I want a meeting of department heads in five minutes, between now and then you can get the wheels in motion. Police statement, what's happening at the scene, backgrounder, etc., get started now, leave the family to me."

He was barking orders like a general on the battlefield. Brown was experienced, and he knew that he could easily have a totally unproductive workforce in a matter of minutes unless he did this right. He knew that afterwards there would be people who would criticise him, claim he was callous, and distasteful, that he was being totally mercenary, selling newspapers on the back of the death of one of his own, but he dismissed this from his mind.

It's not easy being an editor. And Brown, a 48-year-old seasoned hack, knew that people would expect more dramatic treatment. They would be outraged, so the paper would. And he was prepared to make more of it than usual, because Mart was one of his own. There was a proper way to do this and he knew everything that had to be done… even getting a reaction from the family, an unenviable task which he had already assigned himself. He had already gently prepared Mart's mother and father when he spoke to them earlier at their home in Aylesbury.

They actually understood, and they commented that Mart would have wanted it. Brown was always amazed at the way people dealt with death. For the first 18 months of his career, his job on a Monday was to visit the town's two funeral directors and get a list of those that had died. He would then spend the next two days going round to speak with the bereaved families to get an obituary on them, well-known or not.

It prepared him for almost any reaction. Some people were perfectly fine and welcomed the chance to talk about their loved one. Others were too upset to talk. Either way empathy, or sympathy or both were the key to dealing with the situation, and he had become expert in gauging from an initial response, which course of action was needed.

A hardened journalist, he nevertheless needed that five minutes before he would talk to the deputy editor, deputy news editor, the chief sub-editor, features editor and sports editor.

Mac had been helping to produce a backgrounder on Mart. Where he came from, what he had done and the main stories he had worked on during his time at the *Chron*. Mart had been a bit of a rugby player and had turned out for the Saints a few times, but played regularly for the very successful village side Long Buckby. She had completed the task and was sitting, stunned at her desk as others too apparently seemed to be doing.

Armour strode into the editorial department. His first port of call would normally have been to the chief sub's desk or the newsdesk to speak to Mart, but he recognised the shock in people's eyes and walked passed others directly to Mac's side.

She was visibly reddened around the eyes, she had been crying.

"Oh Pete, have you heard about Mart?"

"Yes, I've just heard it on the radio," he told her, and added: "Come on, let me take you for a coffee. Can you get away now?"

She could. The office canteen was probably the safest place in Northampton at the moment for a coffee.

But Pete was not just taking her for a coffee, he was going to have to find her somewhere safe – if she had had contact with Vasilli, then her life could be in danger too. Somehow he was going to have to explain this without giving too much away, or frightening her.

Having collected a couple of freshly ground coffees, they sat behind a green slatted screen that partitioned off the smoking area. Mac lit up and drew a long deep drag.

"It is so hard to believe, and so unbelievably senseless," she said, "I can't imagine Mart not being there, who would want to kill him. Everyone is just so shell-shocked – such a waste of life…"

Armour too was deeply saddened by the loss of his friend, but what was gnawing at him was that he was responsible. It was his fault. There had been no real reason why he should have involved anyone from the *Chron* at the very least he should have warned Burricks of the possible danger. He might have had a chance. OK he was trying to make sure that Vasilli had an escape route in the event of things going wrong, but he should have thought of something else. Some other way of protecting his friend.

Now Mart Burricks was dead and what about Vasilli? And that was when she said it…

"Two deaths in one day – it's just awful"

"What do you mean?" he said, more aggressively than he meant to.

She was struggling not to cry again.

"Another man was found drowned in the Nene. They

think he is a tramp, but they are having difficulty in identifying him. There's going to be a photofit in the paper tonight. The police are hoping someone will know who he is."

She looked at her watch.

"It caught the Town West edition – it should be off the press in about 20 minutes," she said.

Something made Armour feel certain, without hearing any more, that this was Vasilli, and his head dropped – everything had gone wrong.

She saw his reaction and took it to relate to Burricks. She put her hand on his, and the soft warmth of her touch almost made the tear ducts in his eyes prickle, but he maintained control.

Seeing him fighting it, she added the other hand… it was almost too much, and then she suddenly drew them both away, and he felt one of his heartstrings go with them.

"Oh Pete. The message! I almost forgot… "

She showed it to him and he saw how Vasilli had gained Mac's attention, but he stared at the message.

"Do you know who it is from? What does it mean?"

"Yes, I know who it is from, and I am afraid it might mean we are too late…"

But he was puzzled…

"Thane's Excelsior Reserve… that shouldn't be part of it," he said out loud.

"What is any of it? Come on Pete, what's it all about. Stop being so bloodily secretive… Is this anything to do with Mart's death" the strain was beginning to tell on her.

"I can't tell you right now. Come on, let's get a copy of the paper and go."

She followed but did not know why. She was certainly intrigued and he was including her. She did need something to take her mind off Mart. On the way Armour made a brief call on the public phone in the corridor – she was just out of earshot.

Armour Piercing

In the press hall, the Town West edition had just started rolling. The massive press, which was almost as big as a three-storey house, was thundering, and press hands were sliding copies out of the line before putting the stacker on line. They check colour registration, that the print area and folds were good and the inking was right. Press crew were shouting instructions at each other above the din.

Armour retrieved a 'good' waste copy – the photofit of the mystery man was on Page Five

… The Mart Burricks murder dominated Page One, Two and Three…

There was no question, the photofit was of Vasilli.

Armour felt sick.

He felt her presence as Mac came up beside him. His stomach eased, he folded the paper and turned.

"Come on Mac, there are some things I have to tell you, but let's get out of here first," he said, guiding her by the arm.

Outside, he led her to unmistakably the oldest car in the car park – a classic dark blue 1958 Rover 90.

It was a beauty, he had bought in running order, but in desperate need of renovation. It was quite low mileage, but had been left in a garage. He bought it for a song because the brake servo had seized, so when the engine was switched on the brakes came on too…

It had been a fairly simple job to free it, and then it was ready for the road. He wanted the car because it reminded him of the first car he ever had. He had repaired that one himself, but paid a specialist to renovate this vehicle. He remembered being surprised to learn that the original leather that bound the rear suspension and was packed with grease, was still intact. Weighing about two and a half tons it was built like a tank.

It had blue leather upholstery, bench seats, and a wooden

dashboard, and a gleaming upright chrome handbrake that stuck up about two feet from the floor.

"I should let the newsdesk know that I'm out of the office for a while…" she said, slowing up for a second.

"It might be better if they were left wondering…" said Armour urging her forward.

As they got in, he realised he would have to swap vehicles pretty quickly – this was just a little too easy to spot.

The car started first time and he directed it out of the rear entrance of the *Chron* building towards the old Territorial Army drill hall, where he turned right.

"Where do you live?"

"Victoria Promenade. Why?" she asked.

"I want you to get a few things together to last you a couple of days."

"What kind of proposition is that?"

He knew that the only way she was going to believe what he was about to say, was to be as blunt as possible. Pulling over in a side street, he turned sideways on the bench seat and looked her straight in the eyes… they were beautiful… but it didn't stop saying what he had to say.

"Mart Burricks' murder and the death of the man in the river are connected, and so are the shootings at Flecknoe. That was a Military Intelligence cock up. The man in the river was an old friend of mine, a Russian, a defector. He was in contact with Mart and that is why Mart was killed. That is why they are both dead. The message he gave you was not totally the right message, it has an extra element. I don't know what it means or whether Vasilli or someone else put it there.

"Anyway, you, because you had contact with Vasilli, however brief, are in danger, and I have got to get you out of here while I figure out the message and to try and give enough time for the dust to settle a bit."

Her mouth, her beautiful mouth, dropped open bit by bit as he spoke. He gently put his forefinger under her chin. Pushing it up, he slowly closed the parted lips.

He put the Rover back in first gear, glanced in the rearview mirror and gunned it right into Kettering Road, heading towards the town centre. He went right at the island and left opposite the ABC Cinema. In two minutes he hauled the car left into the Homebase car park opposite Victoria Promenade… no one would look in there for his vehicle – they would walk across the road to the house. He did not want them to be more than a couple of minutes at the house… it may not be safe.

The houses were aptly named, and deceptively big Victorian industrial shoe trade properties. The commercial part of Northampton had been built upon this sort of housing and the outworkers that lived in them.

He kept a good look out as they approached the door, but nothing and no one appeared particularly out of place or suspicious. Inside, as she grabbed a pair of jeans, a couple of T-shirts, basic toiletries and some knickers, and stuffed them in a black leather haversack, he noticed that the rooms were comfortably decorated, and stylishly furnished. He was impressed by the incredible difference in the outside appearance which struck him as slightly smutty, to the clean, floral, freshness that pervaded the inside.

Within three minutes they were back out in the street. At the car park, he opened the boot and she threw the bag in. She noticed his bulging lightweight clothes carrier inside.

"You're well prepared – does this sort of thing happen to you every day?" she asked with irony in her voice.

Neither of them could hear the spatter the gun made from 40 yards away, but Armour knew exactly what it was when the bullet buried itself in the boot lid he was holding, and he didn't have to wait for the second.

"In the car, quick!" he yelled. He dropped the lid, slid in the drivers' seat and turned the ignition. It didn't start.

"Shit," he said through clenched teeth. She had skipped in beside him and he turned the motor over again… and the second bullet crashed through the quarter-light on her side of the car and buried itself in the wooden dash.

"Get your head down!" he yelled.

He unceremoniously cupped a hand round the back of her neck and pulled Mac's head into his lap… and simultaneously turned the key again.

The engine fired, he rammed it into first, and the car lurched into motion, and out of the car park, left, and just as the lights turned to red, he ran them.

He crossed the river and carried straight on. He was speeding, but luckily the traffic was light and there were no police around – he would soon be out of town.

He peered in his rear-view mirror, he had not seen anyone following, which he thought a little strange, but in the circumstances, a relief.

He became very conscious of Mac's face in lap. She had made no attempt to move. While his mind was concentrated on other things there was no problem, but he knew he would soon become aroused…

He put his hand down on the side of her face, gave two gentle strokes.

"I… er…", his mouth was a bit dry, "I think it is OK now."

Putting her left hand on his thigh, where her chin had been, she slowly raised her head, but did not remove her hand.

She looked first out of the rear window, and then to the front to see where they were going.

"I'm scared," she said.

"Don't worry, we'll be alright now. It's OK no one

is following us." And despite his poor track record just recently, he tried to comfort her more by saying: "I'll look after you."

She did feel eased by that. If he was scared he was not showing it and he seemed to her to have an inner strength – it made her feel better anyway.

It had been about ten seconds after he had thrust her face in his lap that she became conscious of where her face was. She actually felt quite comfortable and did not mind that it was a rather abrupt way of becoming acquainted, but she had not lied when she said she was scared – she had not been shot at before.

Armour did not know who was shooting at them and it was irrelevant which of them was being shot at, they would stick together from now on. He would not let her out of his sight until this was sorted out one way or another.

But he needed help. He would find somewhere for them that night, and would contact his controller, Mick, in the morning… perhaps.

His first problem was, that he would have to get rid of the car, it was too distinctive, and he had to decide where they were going to spend the night.

Armour's home was a rented cottage on the outskirts of Warwick. It was temporary… well, it had been for about a year, while his own house on the edge of Althorp Estate, near Northampton was being renovated. It would have been nice to have taken Mac back to Leamington that night, and he toyed with the idea, but dismissed it as pretty unwise, considering that he may be running from his own side.

They could just book into a hotel or pub, but there was a fair amount of risk involved in that – at some stage or other, whoever was after them would be ringing round. If it was MI5, they would soon have the police working on that, and a trace on his car.

It suddenly came to him. The car was the answer.

The guy he hired to restore the Rover, Pat Grogan, a big drinking Irishman. He lived in Rugby. Doing up cars was his business, and he loved banger racing – anyway he always seemed to have a lot of cars around the place.

He and Armour had several drinking sessions when it came to negotiating the price of work on the Rover – it tended to last most of the night, involved at least two bottle of Bushmills whiskey, and end with a very sore head. The price fixed was reasonable, and the two guys became sound friends… Armour visiting his place in Leicester Road many times as the work progressed.

It got better and better. Armour recalled that Grogan was also restoring a narrow boat at the marina near Braunston and it was near completion.

Chapter Seven

Armour left Mac in the Rover briefly while he went into the seemingly ramshackle workshop… to a bear-hug from Grogan and a considerable ribbing when he told the big Irishman he wanted to use the narrowboat for a couple of nights maybe.

Mac did not quite understand, but quickly got the gist when she wandered in… not wanting to be left in the car.

Armour took a serious tone about Pat repairing the bullet holes in the Rover, and Pat didn't ask questions – he had had customers like Armour before, nice guys, but with very strange associates.

Grogan was very fond of the women and welcomed Mac taking her hand warmly in both of his. She immediately warmed to his broad smile, rustic brawn, his Irish charm and friendly Dublin accent.

Armour first met Grogan when he went to a stock car meet at Brafield on the eastern side of Northampton. It was not really Armour's scene, but he had a free Sunday afternoon and quite a few of the *Chron* guys tended to pitch up there from time to time.

He didn't see any that he knew, but between races he was wandering through the paddock area and saw the massive

Grogan fighting against the resistance of a five foot crowbar, trying to free the wheel of a crumpled wreck. Another competitor driver was helping him. Off track they are like a brotherhood and will do whatever they can to help each other… on the track they could happily kill anyone in their way.

Grogan cursed as the lever slipped and both he and the other man toppled over the body of the blue 'yellow-top'.

Armour's hand caught the flying bar as it catapulted from Grogan's grip.

As the two were dusting themselves off, Armour looked at the problem and wedged the jemmy in from a different angle, and using a piece of wood that was lying in a nearby trailer as a fulcrum, he prised the metal apart, to allow the wheel to turn freely. Before Grogan had a chance to participate he saw the job done and swung out his meaty paw in Armour's direction, his vision slightly impaired by the glare of the waning sun.

"Grogan's the name – just about anything's the game," he smiled, winked and added, "I might have guessed it was a matter of brains over brawn."

"Come and have a beer," he beckoned Armour, taking an instant liking to the craggy-faced man.

Armour, someone who liked unusual people, went along. The drinking session only got under way when they got Grogan's rig back to his yard – it had virtually been on Armour's way home.

If Armour had a slightly failing, it was good company and Bushmills whiskey, but although there might have been many a laugh and a lot of loud talking, Armour, no matter how much he had to drink, never became aggressive, abusive, or said anything he did not mean. Many could not understand how he could take so much drink and remain relatively 'sober'.

They met several times again, and when Armour bought his Rover, Grogan was the natural choice to do the work on it. Armour found himself at Grogan's yard fairly frequently, even helping with the restoration work.

Grogan joked that it would not bring the agreed price down. Although he never questioned Armour, he had always seemed to be aware that there was more to him than being a freelance journalist. He never could work it out though. Armour seemed to work very strange, flexible and unsocial hours – normal a journalist might argue, but no, there was something else there.

To Grogan the damaged Rover added another piece to the puzzle of Armour, and he had no problem with it. Turning back to him, Grogan agreed to patch up the car, and wanted to share a drink to seal the deal – Armour asked for a 'rain check'.

Before Armour had the chance to ask, it was Grogan who suggested they borrow one of his cars for a week or so, and pointed to a dark blue Alfa Veloce Sprint – a good engine, but dodgy bodywork.

"I bought that last week, it's been tuned and is a real goer, and I will be doing the body soon. I know a guy back in Ireland who loves them – he's got three already and about 50 of those mottled gear knobs. Do you think you can look after it? Please let the only holes be because o' rust. It's not worth much at the moment, but sure, it will be a beauty when I've finished with it."

It was with a nudge and a wink he handed over the keys to the car and to the narrowboat – he said there were some provisions there, but they would have to get fresh stuff if they wanted it. He gave instructions about how to get things started and switch on the gas.

Not wishing to hang around, and with a hundred things going through his mind, Armour shook hands with Grogan, who nodded, winked again and seemed to understand.

Armour and Mac transferred their gear from the Rover, and they drove off in the Alfa, through Rugby, along the Hillmorton Road and into Barby Lane, heading towards Braunston, a distance of about eight miles.

Armour felt better. He could not recall ever speaking to anyone about Grogan by name, so there was little to link them. He and Mac should have a safe car and somewhere safe to stay… at least for a while.

They stopped off at the village store in Braunston which seemed to have a fair spread of the basics and rounded up a few things.

Armour did not have enough cash, so used a cheque rather than Switch – it would give them more time before anyone could trace through the banks that they bought something from Braunston, and realised what area they were in.

Grogan had suggested that Armour let the marina office know they were there, and he said they would attract more attention if he did not, particularly as the people in the office knew Grogan, and that it was his boat. Armour and Mac would be strangers and Grogan did not normally hire or lend his boat to people. Also it would save moorers in neighbouring boats prying… all the gossip came from the marina office.

Armour would have preferred not to have told anyone they were there, but appreciated that the marina was a business, and a community, and they like to know who is wandering around the place. He gave them a false name though.

"OK let's have it," she demanded, "I want the whole story. I have been used, shot at, involved in a car chase, and I appear to be on the run from somebody I don't know, and I haven't done anything. I am tired and hungry and I have been deposited in a dark, damp, floating half-decorated dump. I want to know why…?"

"Oh don't exaggerate… it's not dark," Armour tried unsuccessfully to be funny, and tried to avoid telling his own worst fears.

She hit him hard on the arm with her fist. Despite being tired, her eyes were fiery, and she was angry. She was not being playful. He put his arm up to her shoulder, and she pushed it away.

"I'm sorry," he said.

He realised he was probably going to have to open up if he was going to get any cooperation from her, and he wanted… needed that.

"You are right. You do deserve to know. I'll tell you what I know, but I'm afraid it is going to raise more questions than answers. Sit down while I make some coffee."

There was a bench seat at the side of the cabin and a folddown table attached to it. She sat and watched his rear view as he filled the kettle and put coffee in a couple of mugs.

For her he had a pretty striking frame. He had a good head of hair, greying at the sideburns and into his beard. Broad shoulders tapered down to narrow hips and a rounded, but firm looking bum. He seemed to have strong legs, with very little fat. He was well balanced, and his movements were fluid – he looked agile for a big man. As he turned sideways occasionally and then bent down to get milk from the fridge, she noticed that he carried a little weight on his stomach, but not too much. She fanaticised for a moment on the idea of working it off him.

When he eventually turned to her with two steaming mugs, the anger in her had subsided and there was totally something else in those beautiful eyes. A slight smile played on her minutely parted lips.

He saw the signs and smiled back, but did not know the half of what had been crossing her mind, typical man…?

He sat down raising his left leg onto the bench, and put

his left arm behind her shoulders, but not quite touching her. The last thing he wanted to do was make her feel awkward or uneasy, but he wanted to let her know that he liked her, liked her company, wanted to be friends… wanted her.

He started talking and was looking out of the window, almost at tow-path level, and he felt a little warm as he realised she was still looking at him intently… at his face, his arm, his raised leg… and his crutch.. he didn't know that, but he felt she was…

She knew she was distracting him, and she really did want to know what the hell was going on. She forced herself to stop any overt flirting. Everything apart, she had a few questions that needed to be answered.

What was this all about? What had Mart Burricks got to do with it? It was a good question, and he had some difficulty with it. Justifying Mart Burricks' death was something that was going haunt him for a long time!

Why her? What was Military Intelligence at in all this?… Above all, that was what she wanted to know.

Who was Vasilli, why had he been so important? And what was he to Armour? What was Armour doing, involved with all these shady characters?

Another good one!

Then the big question… What do we do now?

He admitted that for the moment he did not know.

He decided to tell her a lot of what he knew. He minimalised any information that might be sensitive or not especially relevant to what was happening here. He was brief about Vasilli's work, or any procedural data relating to Military Intelligence.

He had to admit to her that he had gone a long way to making the situation worse by his efforts to safeguard Vasilli.

She said she understood why he had tried to get Vasilli away from normal Intel channels, but could not quite understand why he had attempted to use Mart at the *Chron*. She chastised him for his choice and pointed out that it would have been better to have used Grogan – someone who could look after himself, was a loner…

Armour assured her he had looked at every option. Grogan had actually been his first thought. In his own way Grogan was as much an innocent as Mart Burricks. Trouble was he liked his drink, and also had a fiery temper. Mart, though, was a quicker thinker, had a more enquiring mind, would have used his intuition, and in Northampton could have used his influence, contacts, options and local knowledge to greater affect. He was easily the person who was more likely to provide the help that Vasilli needed, even though he had not been fully briefed. He was not supposed to have to actually deal with the situation for more than, say, 24 hours at the most. None of this was actually supposed to be happening. And what was becoming painfully clear, was that Armour did not know the full story, or even who all the players were…

Trying to be more positive he said he knew there was something more to Vasilli's message than there was supposed to be, so that was the obvious thing to work on. He knew that the message had been personalised – it contained the essence of the original, but Vasilli had added a new element, which he clearly thought Armour only would be able to decipher.

After hearing about the crumpled bus ticket, which his killers had managed to miss when they gave his replacement clothing, he knew it had to relate to their time in Oxford all those years ago. Vasilli somehow must have concealed the ticket somewhere during his ordeal.

Armour knew he was going to have to work at deciphering Vasilli's words. On the face of it, they meant absolutely nothing to him.

To remember what he thought was significant at the time was one thing, but to try and imagine what a young Russian, experiencing a new and free country, might believe was significant, was not going to be easy.

'Thane's Excelsior Reserve' that was the out of place phrase.

Thane… a Scottish lord – the most obvious Thane was Shakespeare's *Macbeth*… Thane of Cawdor… it didn't ring any bells with him, no special meaning. Scottish… scotch… Cawdor..?

Nothing was clicking yet.

As Armour started to rack his brain for personal recollections, Mac went to air the bed, in the aft cabin, which had been completely redecorated she was relieved to observe. As she looked down at the bed, although it had not been discussed, she knew that they would be sharing it – she wanted to share it with him. In the circumstances, whether or not there was anything else, she certainly could not be on her own. She needed him close. She needed the reassurance or his inner strength and calmness. She was more scared than she had let him know. This situation was way out of her league and far from her experience… although she did know a bit about the Secret Service, but that was another story and she had not told him anything about it. She did not imagine she ever would.

She cleared the cups and then started to prepare something to eat. The 'dark, dank, dump' had changed – it was now warm, dry and cosy. She watched him as he scribbled notes. And as darkness fell outside Armour and Mac sat close together to eat…

The two men were peas from the same pod. About twelve stone a piece, they had short cropped hair and were wearing similar style dark jeans and dark T-shirts. The only way to tell them apart was that one had designer stubble and a denim jacket, and the other was clean shaven with a black leather jacket.

They were in Leicester Road, Rugby, and the leather jacket was driving the silver-coloured Citroen Xantia which slowly drew up outside Pat Grogan's deserted workshop, lit faintly by a security light above the door to the office.

There had been little need to rush after Armour following the shots that were fired outside Homebase – the 'tracker' had been working perfectly and showed consistent movement. At first it showed that Armour and the girl had travelled south out of Northampton, and then changed direction and speed. They were moving north and fast… probably on the M1.

When they slowed they turned west, and looking at the map, it was obvious they were heading towards Rugby.

The two men followed, but kept several miles distance. Their orders were not to kill Armour, or the girl… just keep after them, keep them under pressure and moving, don't lose them under any circumstances, and report any contacts they make. The two ex-forces men didn't know why, but then, they rarely knew the reason for anything they did, but then it did make life… and death, fairly simple. The money was good, and the law rarely seemed to take excessive interest in their activities, wherever in the world they were.

The guy in denim put the tracking receiver device down on the floor of the car and got out. He crossed the road to the workshop which had an eight foot corrugated tin fence around an uneven gravel earth and patchy tarmac yard, with the building set at the back of the site. The posts of the gates in a square, cut in the tin, were locked with a heavy chain and padlock. A sign on the gate said 'Beware of the Dog', with a picture of an Alsatian.

Sure enough, when the denim man bent to peer through the gap where the padlock was, he almost immediately came face to face with the dog – big and mean. He dodged back but still felt its breath as it leaped up at the gates, snapping and barking viciously.

He bent and looked again, the hound starting to form foaming spittle at the side of powerful jaws and snarled. Sure enough, in the corner of the yard was the 1958 Rover. He ran back across the road to the car and jumped in.

"The car's there – obviously no sign of anyone around, except a bloody big, ugly dog," he said.

It was about 6.30 pm, but it was autumn and the nights were drawing in quickly – it was quite dark.

"Yeah, I heard. Well we've got to know where they are and we need to know now. Get on the mobile and ring the 24-hour number on the sign over the gate. Tell them you were just walking by and you heard the dog yelping, sounding like it was hurt, that should get someone down here," said the leather man, and he got out and crossed the road screwing the silencer home on his automatic.

Making the call, the denim man saw his partner point the gun through the gap in the gate. He heard a faint 'spat', and his partner returned.

"He said he would be right down," he told the leather man. They didn't have to wait for long.

Grogan had not really noticed the Xantia parked in the shadows opposite his yard when he drew up in his old Jaguar Mk10 – he loved old Jags.

He was worried about Jasper. He had only left the yard an hour or so ago… it was far earlier for him than usual.

Grogan, lived on his own apart from the two dogs, Jasper and Gi-Gi, they took turns doing night security at the yard, and spent the day there together with him. They were very well trained. Certainly they would not hassle anyone coming in to the yard during the day. After it had been locked up they could appear quite ferocious.

He had just started to cook something for himself when the call came.

The guy said he had been walking passed the yard and heard the dog yelping, not barking, but yelping. He was on a mobile and would not stay there, or give his name.

Gi-Gi was with Grogan – her head on his leg as he drove along. He left the car door open as he got out, but told her to stay. She was quite happy to oblige.

He had his keys in his hand and as he approached the gate he bent to see through the gap. He sort of expected Jasper to meet him, but there was silence from the yard, and he could not see anything much, despite the night light over the door of the office.

The heavy chain fell away as he entered the yard. Everything seemed secure – there was no sign of anyone having broken in. But where the night light cast a shadow over the main doors to the working bays, he caught a glimpse of Jasper's foreleg.

He called, but there was no response. He walked slowly closer, peering into the gloom, calling gently a couple of times more – still no response. He bent down and touched the fur of the animal as it lay silent, and suddenly felt the warm, wet, stickiness. He drew his hand back quickly and into the light, where his fears were confirmed – it was blood.

He bent down, and dragged the still animal two yards, into the light. Clearly the dog was dead. There was a lot of blood around Jasper's shoulder and as his eyes became more used to the light, he could see a dark patch on the ground against the lighter concrete where he had been. Poor Jasper, what had happened…? He needed better light.

He stood and turned. He did not need the light to see the

two guys, one in denim and one in leather, both at the other end of a silenced gun barrel.

"Let's go in the office shall we mister, said leather man, "and no messing."

Grogan fumbled with his keys. He was big, but he was not stupid.

They walked from the bays towards the light of the office – Grogan followed by the two men… who were followed by Gi-Gi.

Gi-Gi had slipped in after the two men entered, and as they had moved forward, had silently followed… until she found Jasper.

She seemed to understand immediately. She howled, and jumped, almost all at once.

The two men were completely taken by surprise, and had half turned when the large dog landed on the leather man with her strong jaws round his gun wrist, and her hind legs knocking the man in denim slightly off balance.

Grogan, who was not slow, slashed the keys down across denim man's face, and as he curled slightly, brought his knee up into the man's rib cage.

Leather man felt the teeth close around his wrist and pierce his jacket, and as the jaws clamped, the dog's head started to shake. He felt the pain and knew he would never be able to get the animal to release. He managed to grab the barrel of the gun with his left hand.

Fumbling with it in his left hand, and against his body, he managed to grasp the grip.

He rammed the barrel into the dog's ear and the gun spat again, and turned to Grogan and denim man as the animal fell lifeless to the ground.

"That's enough," he shouted at Grogan as he was about to bring his fist down again on the denim man's face.

"Where are Armour and the girl?" said leather man.

They were in the office now and the other guy was trying to regain his senses, and when he had, he found the Bushmills.

"I don't know what you're talking about," Grogan tried, but got the point of a gun jabbed viciously in his ribs.

"His car is outside, so he must have one of yours. What is it and where did they go?"

Grogan knew that these guys were likely to kill him once they knew what they wanted.

He deduced that his best chance, even if it looked as if it might be painful, was to keep going with the question and answer as long as he could… they might drop their guard… the police might come by… they might have too much Bushmills… he wished he could. He thought of Jasper and Gi-Gi lying in the yard. It was going to be a long night.

Armour and Mac had finished their meal, chilli beef with granary bread, helped down with a half bottle of Chianti, when they started to clear the table together.

They had left off talking about their current problem, and Armour had been asking her about herself.

She was born in London, the second of three girls, and her family were currently in Carlisle. She went to university in Oxford. She had been a senior journalist now for just over a year.

"I'll wash," he said, and smiled as she picked up the drying-up cloth and saluted

"Aye-aye Capt'n."

The galley area was very confined, and they could hardly move without touching. And each time they touched, the contact lingered just that little bit longer – it was milliseconds, but significant enough.

It couldn't go on. He dropped the washing up cloth in

the water, turned and grabbed the drying up cloth from her, which left her statue-like with her arms part outstretched. He took the leading left hand with his left hand and pressed it against his lips, while his right hand slipped around her waist.

"Thank God," she said, "I thought for a moment we were going to have to finish the washing up."

By the time she had finished the sentence their lips had closed on each other's, and they tasted, tugged, sucked and nibbled. Their bodies were firmly cemented together, only gently moving occasionally as they kissed, as if there were a tighter way they could fit, and they were desperate to find it.

He had been absorbing wafts of her perfume all day, but now he was immersed in it as his lips were on her neck, and he was gently tugging at the top of her T-shirt.

All the time, as the temperature rose, she could feel his penis growing and pressing hard against her. She writhed and rubbed, and could hardly wait for the moment when she would be able to release it.

Armour backed his way into the aft cabin, with Mac still attached, and fell backwards onto the bed, she toppling on top of him. Wriggling his shoulder blades, and using his heels on the end of the bed, he physically dragged the both of them to the top of the bed, slid his hand up inside her shirt and undid her bra. She curved her body so that when he pulled the shirt up and over her head, her soft perfectly-shaped breasts were lifted and then popped down on to his chest.

He was amazed at the sight, and when her head was clear of the T-shirt, she saw him gazing in awe, as if he had never seen a female chest before, or as if he had seen some miracle.

He handled her so gently at first, and then almost harshly as he kissed and pressed and caressed her breasts and nipples, and then the rest of her.

The urgency almost became blind, as if vital to get the remaining clothes off. And it was extremely difficult for two people to stand together in the cabin.

But she stopped him when he started to unbuckle his belt.

"Oh no," she said, "this is a parcel that I have been waiting so patiently to unwrap, so…" so she took control, although Armour's prick was almost forcing the zipper open by itself.

She did treat it like a child with a Christmas present. Feeling it, squeezing it, even shaking bits. She licked her lips as she slowly undid his belt and flicked the top button undone. She grabbed the top of his zipper, and looked up into his eyes, his hands caressing the back of her head.

She peeled the zipper, and then suddenly forced down his pants and trousers together, so that his penis shot out. She kissed and caressed it, but he wanted to look into those beautiful eyes, and he pulled her up to him and soon they were making love like neither believed they had before, and like it may never happen again.

They explored each other, discovered nearly everything, and when they came, it was as together as you can get, and tears welled with their ecstasy.

Chapter Eight

The Xantia had been parked in the marina car park, not far from the Alfa. The occupants had been there all night. Leather man had been into Daventry briefly at about 10 pm to get burgers and soft drinks.

They had identified out of the many boats, mostly unoccupied, which was Pat Grogan's *Irish Mist*, and they saw a light on. They had been along the opposite towpath, and had just about been able to make out voices.

Using the mobile, they reported in and ordered a clean-up team to Grogan's yard. They decided there was little merit in moving in on the couple that evening, not being ordered to the contrary, they took turns keeping watch – they needed the rest too.

It was 6.30 am when Armour woke. He looked down at Mac. It had been an amazing night – he could not quite believe that such a delectable creature should fancy him. Resting on one elbow for at least ten minutes he just watched and wondered at her beauty. The way her hair fell and the way her cheekbones and nape of her neck were formed.

He slipped the bedclothes from him and towards her and silently rose and made his way into the galley and put the kettle on.

Not awakened, she turned over. He watched her through the opened door as the sheet fell revealing the top half of her body. She was stunning, he could not keep his eyes off her – he lingered as if she was a legendary apparition that might disappear at any moment, and he was the only living human to have seen it.

He was only distracted when the whistle on the kettle started to blow and threaten to wake her. He eased the door closed, made himself coffee, cleared the rest of the dinner things, and spread the notes he had been making earlier last evening.

He was still not much nearer discovering any meaning to 'Thane's Excelsior Reserve'.

Instinct told him that he would most likely find the answer in Oxford. It was the one thing that Vasilli and he had in common that not many people knew about.

If Military Intelligence looked deep enough in his file there might just be something about the two of them, but not necessarily. And whatever information they had on Vasilli would at this stage have been very sketchy they probably did not know he had ever been to Oxford – if things had gone according to plan it would have obviously have come to light.

Armour would probably have told Mick, his controller, long before that.

So, what about Oxford? Armour tried to visualise as many of the people, events and places they had experienced together there. It had been so important to Vasilli to do and see as much as possible in the short time he was in this country – his energy had been inexhaustible. They had been to numerous parties, recitals, the cinema, plays, concerts, rugby and hockey matches, pubs, and punting on the river.

They had been down to London a couple of times – he hoped that this did not relate to those trips… they saw every sight a tourist expects to, and more… from Changing of the

Guard to tasting the cheeses and wines of Le Cafe des Amis du Vin in Covent Garden, where theatregoers and members of the casts would gather after a show – it was a very in place. No, he thought long and hard. Unless something really significant had happened in London, and he could not remember anything, even though it would have been even safer, he had to concentrate on Oxford.

While it appeared to be relatively safe and secluded at Braunston, they could drive over to Oxford each day.

It was about 8.30 am. He started breakfast and when it was ready he opened the aft cabin door and took Mac in a tray with steaming coffee, fruit juice, cereal flakes and toast.

She woke dreamily to see him enter wearing just a jumper which didn't cover all that much.

"Mmm… meat for breakfast, what a treat," she beamed.

"Could be," and he almost blushed.

They ate.

Amour had made up his mind, and he told Mac about his intention that they should go to Oxford, and gave her some more of the back ground.

"And you are saying that from Flecknoe, Vasilli went to Oxford, and on the basis that you and he spent a few weeks there when you were in your twenties? That in your forties, with his defecting, you reckon that is where he would have gone? That after a shootout at a supposed safe house, he would have taken it upon himself to trek around the country in the hope that you would eventually catch up with him? That he would take that risk? OK… I can see it!"

He thought she was taking the piss for a moment.

"No, really," she said, "I think you may well be right. Where else would he go? If he could not find you in Northampton then he would naturally go to where you and he had something in common."

She wasn't taking the piss.

"It is the only place I can think of that he would go," he said, "and besides, there is just one other little thing I have to go on… I spoke to a police friend of mine. When you said that there had been two deaths, I reckoned it might have been Vasilli. I checked with my contact about the other death, whether there was anything to go on, and he said 'nothing… except an Oxford bus ticket'…"

When they made love for the second time, it was not so urgent, but each touch and movement was savoured that little bit more.

Armour had surprised himself. He had not been looking to start anything with Mac. She was a very attractive lady, but until he had properly looked into her eyes, at first sad and red over Mart, and then shocked and scared at being chased and shot at, he had not realised that he felt anything.

She had quite striking features, but it was more than that. He did not understand why, after such a short time and briefest of relationships, he should feel such a strong attraction.

Mac, on the other hand, had been more conscious of something stirring within her. She could not explain it, but being with Armour made her felt reassured and confident. She liked the way he looked, smelled, and exuded confidence and experience. She loved the way he looked at her face and her body, and especially the way he had touched her.

It had been an exquisite start to the day… a day that was to deteriorate very rapidly.

After dressing they went to the marina shop for a few provisions. Armour checked over the car, and then they walked, arms about each other, back towards the boat.

As they neared it, things suddenly went into slow motion.

The roof of the narrowboat and the sides blasted away as a broad pillar of flame shot upwards and outwards. It mushroomed as debris and wreckage flew about them. They were hurled back by the blast and as they fell to the ground pieces of wood and glass hurtled in their direction.

Armour rolled over on to her to shield her from the splinters and shards that were now raining down on them.

He looked up to see a huge plume of black smoke rising and dust and debris settling.

Could it have been a gas leak? He had heard of such things. Was it more sinister?

Armour was not a great believer in coincidence, but if this was a 'hit', it was very sloppy. Come to think of it, a professional shooting at them outside Homebase in broad daylight, misses?

Armour realised in a flash this was a game of cat and mouse.

It meant that Armour probably had time. These people were not trying to kill him. It was unlikely to be fatal until Armour had found the answer to Vasilli's mystery…that was for him, but could not be sure for Mac's safety.

Then again, who were 'these people', and if they were one side, where was the other side?

Amazing what went through Armour's mind in that flash.

"Are you all right Mac" he said, holding her shoulder as she shook her head from one side to the other.

"Yes Pete," she shouted, as people's heads appeared from neighbouring boats and others came running from the marina office. But her head was reeling and there was a loud buzzing rattling her brain… she knew it would subside. He knew what she was suffering, he had the same.

"I think it'll go in a short while," he reassured her. He got up and hauled her to her feet, and they started dusting themselves off

"Are you all right mate," said a man from the office.

He said they were and together they all walked forward to the wreck of the narrowboat.

"Lucky you weren't in there," said the man, "Mind you I saw one of those two guys walking down here earlier."

"Who?" demanded Armour.

"When I arrived this morning there was a car in the car park, with two blokes in it. I thought they looked a bit odd. Well, one of them came down here while the other stayed in the car… talking on one of them mobile phones he was."

"Look," he said," Over there in the car park, at the back. Oh, looks as if they've gone…

"Oh well…anyway, you better come over to the office, and I'll make a cup of tea. You'll be wanting to talk to Mr. Grogan I daresay."

"Yes thanks." said Armour.

The phone at Grogan's yard rang for some time, and Armour assumed he must be out under a car, he let it ring. A man answered, but it was not the familiar friendly Irish lilt.

"Can I speak to Pat please?"

"No. I'm afraid you can't," came the reply.

"Who is this?"

"I'm Detective Inspector John Prime. Who are you?

"What's going on, is everything OK?

"I wouldn't exactly say that sir. What is your name?"

Armour hung up… it was before the introduction of 1471 call checking…

Knowing how journalists get their information sometimes helps. He rang the Warwickshire police media line to see if there was anything on it about an incident there.

There wasn't. He rang a chap on the *Rugby Advertiser* he knew, Ben Larcher.

He kept his voice fairly low, while Mac talked to the marina office man.

"Ben, hi. It's Pete Armour. Have you any idea what's going on at Grogan's garage on the Leicester Road? I have just spoken to someone who has just come past there," he lied, "and they tell me there are police all over the place."

"Yeah, hi Pete. Are you working on this story?"

"No. I'm on a few days off, but I thought I might tip you off."

"Oh thanks. Well, we know something. It appears that Pat Grogan went down there last night and it looks as if he surprised some pretty weird intruders. He's dead… beaten to death. His dogs have been shot, doused in petrol and burned. That old Jag that he drove was burned out too. Really strange…"

Armour was badly shaken. How had they known about him? Either way he had obviously been forced to tell them that he and Mac were at the marina.

How was he going to explain this to Mac. She would soon come to distrust him – anybody he met seemed to end out dead…

"Oh, right…thanks Ben, I look forward to reading your story, bye…" he said and hung up.

He threw the tea down his throat. This was getting very messy. People were dying left, right and centre, and they were all people he knew… and liked. Now though, he was much more worried about Mac than himself. Was it the right time to contact Mick… for help… or would it be death? It seemed he could do little worse. But something made him stop – he would leave it a little longer.

The two guys in the car park must have come to the marina sometime during the night.

He asked the marina man if he could describe the two men. Denim, leather and short hair was about all he got, plus the fact that their car was a new Xantia.

He thanked him and led Mac out.

"What about the boat?" asked the marina man as they left.

"Oh, I'll be back later today," he lied again.

Armour was suddenly sickened and worried. Sickened that a special friend was dead, and because of him. Worried, that Mac, a new and very precious friend was now in extreme danger.

Grogan had been special. That free spirit that Armour had recognised in him was kindred. They were two of a kind. They each had their own interests, but brought together for whatever reason, they were like peas in a pod. They had respected each other, and enjoyed each other's company wholeheartedly. Armour would blame himself for years to come… and not just for Grogan.

Moment by moment, Mac was forming herself into a part of him. That too worried him more than he cared to think. Whatever happened from now on, his prime aim was to ensure that nothing happened to Mac. He… needed her.

Suddenly, Armour's mind was back on the here and now. What were the options?

Was it time to speak with Mick, and get protection? He certainly wanted that for Mac's sake.

Was there anyone else he could go to… without risking their lives? He racked his brains. There was just one place, and he was thinking of his cottage being renovated at Althorp, but even there, after stocking up for a week, they would very soon be vulnerable.

No, he was now sure that their only course was to follow his instincts – to go to Oxford, and find what it was that taken Vasilli there just a few hours before. And Mick would have to wait too.

If the two guys had gone, it seemed likely that they had bugged the Alfa, so he checked it out. Sure enough under the left rear wheel arch was the tracer. He pulled it off, put it in his pocket, after showing it to Mac. He looked around for more, but couldn't find any.

"Let's go," opening up the car.

He pulled the bonnet release as she got in. He climbed out and checked over the engine compartment for anything suspicious and looked along the sills. It was clear.

He started the car and they drove away.

"Hang on, just fucking hang on…" she swore in exasperation, something she rarely did.

They were approaching the outskirts of Daventry.

"OK you've got a sexy body. I'm hooked, but added to the list of things I complained about yesterday, I have now, nearly, been blown up. What do these people want… I don't understand."

He briefly outlined what had happened to Grogan. She repeated that she was scared, and wasn't sure how much more she could take.

Armour felt the same and just had no idea how strongly he felt about Mac… and what if they did anything to her.

The bug he had taken off the Alfa was burning a hole in his pocket, he had to get rid of it quickly, or they would soon be on their tails. Soon he saw his chance.

They came to some temporary traffic lights, and it was their turn to go. In the waiting traffic was a builders' Sherpa pickup, with ladders and buckets on the back. It was last in the line of vehicles, he opened his window and as he passed it, he tossed the bug into the back of the pick-up…hopefully anyone tracking the device would think they turned around and headed in the opposite direction… towards Rugby and Coventry.

He went on a few more miles…

"I hear what you are saying. The trouble is that we don't

know who's after us. One side, or the other, or both. I think we are relatively safe until we find what it is that Vasilli left for me… then, I guess the trouble might begin…"

He rammed the Alfa into fourth as they hit the Towcester bypass.

"Oh great, this, so far, has just been a funfair ride has it – I can't wait. Things are going to hot up… great… stop the car. Stop the car!

"I can't go on," she sobbed as they came to a halt in a lay-by at the side of the A43 road to Brackley.

"Mac, you are so special to me. I care much, much more for you than I ever believed possible. We are in danger, I can't deny that, but I am not going to expose you to more danger than I must. Last night taught me something – it gave me an experience that I thought could not exist again for me – there is no way I am going to put you on the spot.

"Hopefully we have lost our pursuers for the moment – I am going to get you to someone I know. Somewhere you can stay until this all blows over."

She sat in silent for a moment, staring out of the window across fields and hedgerows.

"Mac?"

She kept the silence going while she ran things over in her mind as best she could. Could she stay somewhere, even if it was safe, imagining what was happening to Armour.

"Mac? You'll be safe. And I could move quickly and concentrate better…"

He was not quite sure whether he was trying to persuade himself or her. But he could see her trembling. It wasn't fear this time…

"Oh no! Oh no!" she spoke angrily, "I might be at the end of my tether, or I thought I was. But if this is going to be all there is, then I want to be with you for it. I can't be left out now."

There was something so innocent and beautiful about what she said. She was giving herself to him totally… and possibly at the cost of her life. Maybe, although she was being brave, she failed to understand the gravity, or the possible permanency of what she was saying.

Whatever she was saying, she was committing herself, with him, to what lay ahead… and all because of him. It was sudden – they hardly knew each other, but it didn't seem to matter..

He was no spy. No secret agent. No James Bond… his heart melted at what she had said, and he loved her for it.

He fired up the Alfa, and hit the stream of traffic once again.

Chapter Nine

As he gunned the motor down to third, and overtook a slow moving lorry, they headed west along the A43 towards Oxford, and he shot a glance across at her. She seemed so small. Incredibly compact… in proportion, but… vulnerable. She shot a look back at him, smiled, reached over and squeezed his left hand, which was resting on the gear knob.

He fought off the urge to be totally ridiculous, pull over into the next lay-by and make love to her there and then.

He concentrated on the road for a moment, and then soon his mind wandered back to his meeting with Vasilli in Lubeck…

He had had a fair first briefing – he knew who to expect and the type of initial information Military Intelligence wanted. They would do the more detailed stuff themselves later.

But he had persuaded Mick to let him see his subject before he arrived in England. Mick thought it was strange, even unnecessary, but he had sanctioned it.

Armour first set foot in Germany as he walked down the ramp from the Scandinavian Seaways ship, *The Hamburg*, soon after she docked at the Altstadt terminal just after midday on Monday. It had been a 24-hour crossing.

His idea was to make his visit as touristy as possible, and he was going to make a good couple of days of it.

He knew that Vasilli was not due in Lubeck until the next day and it was only one hour's train journey from the Bahnhof Altona off Max-Brauer-Allee, going via the Hauptbahnhof, the main station in Hamburg – he had plenty of time.

The next day's meeting was to be at the old town of Lubeck, a beautiful medieval settlement with many fine old buildings. He had been to Hamburg several times, and decided he would travel to the ancient city first. Lubeck is on the Baltic, called the 'Gateway to the North', and is on what used to be the border between East and West Germany.

Arriving about 2.15 pm he grabbed a taxi and made his way to the nearby Senator Hotel, recommended to him by Mick. It was a good choice – close to the main town and only a couple of hundred yards from the An der Obertrave, where he would meet Vasilli and go on to a small bar.

Armour had relaxed in his room for a couple of hours, and then went to the town for a couple of beers and a meal of fillet steak and bratkartoffeln, fried potatoes.

The next day was brisk, but sunny, and in the morning he did some sightseeing. When he returned to the Senator at lunchtime there was a sealed envelope waiting for him at reception. He sat in one of the deep leather seats in the foyer before opening it. Inside there was the name of a small bar restaurant – he had noticed the place earlier as he had been walking round – and a time.

He had been wondering how it would be to see Vasilli again. It had been so long since they had last seen each other – he wondered if he would even recognise him.

When it came to it, he recognised Vasilli instantly. Because Armour had the advantage, and Vasilli would need a second or two to assimilate that this slightly weather-beaten face belonged to his old university friend, Armour took his arm and turned him briskly away from the security men and a few yards away.

"Vasilli… it is so good to see you."

"You too my friend. But can you imagine what I thought when they told me that someone called Armour was going to be my debriefer. Do you realise how difficult it was… not to say anything… how are you, you old dog? I had no idea about your work."

"Yes I'm sorry, there was no way I could let you know without letting everyone know. We have been having difficulty with people coming across – things have been very messy. I asked to see you before you arrive in England because I wanted to talk privately first, but also because I wanted to give you instructions in case you should find that things go wrong… And by the way, I didn't know what you were doing either."

"What do you mean exactly.? What has been going wrong, how wrong?"

"Vasilli, my friend, people have been killed, and there has been no explanation."

Two Becks beers arrived at their table. Vasilli had filled out a bit since their university days, but he was obviously still keeping fairly fit. Like Armour he was tall. He had a dark, swarthy complexion, high cheekbones and dark spiky hair, but he was rustically handsome.

They each took a deep draft of the Becks, planted their beers on a beermat in front of them. The mists of time cleared momentarily, and they could have been sitting in a bar in Oxford years and years earlier.

But then the reality swept back and each understood the risks and the dangers, particularly for Vasilli. Vasilli had also been a little overcome at the shock, surprise of suddenly finding his old friend. It was more sudden than he had expected. He had planned to come across, get settled in England, somewhere near Oxford, and then set about finding his old friend Peter Armour. Well Armour himself had forced a change to that plan and Vasilli would have to make the mental adjustments.

"You married…?" Vasilli asked, knowing the answer.

And… a few moments later went on: "I don't know why I am upset about this, but what else don't I know about you Pete…?"

It took only a little time for them to sort out whose was the biggest secret and who, if either of them, had let the other down the most…

It mattered little, and the fact was that as old friends they were now in a position to be of significant help to each other, and perhaps could be friends for a long time in the future… maybe even closer than they had been in the past.

Soon they were reminiscing about the old times.

"Oh Oxford, I miss it so much," said Vasilli. "I will go there the first chance I get. Those days were special."

There was plenty to talk about… plenty that, as far as they were concerned, really mattered. But Pete knew that they did not have a lot of time in Lubeck. Intelligence was very keen to get Vasilli off the street, and into another safe house, and certainly Pete did not want to expose him more than was necessary. He also did not want the Intel agents to become overly aware that they knew each other. This would not normally matter unless at some stage in the future they were interrogated about it.

They chatted for another ten minutes before one of the senior agents moved in and started coughing behind his hand. Armour knew exactly what was meant…so too did Vasilli.

They played it as long as they reasonably could – it was a strange, but somehow very meaningful meeting for both of them, but it was Pete, who took control and who made the first move.

For Armour this was not just another case. This was his old friend, who now was putting every confidence, and his life in Armour's hands. He wanted to made absolutely sure that nothing untoward was going to happen, but how could he be positive? What could he do to guarantee no nasty surprises?

Whilst trying not to alarm Vasilli, he wanted to provide him with an alternative course of action. With a bit of luck, he would perhaps think this was a common precaution, and Armour would not try and disillusion him.

He told Vasilli his secret message and about Mart Burricks.

"Don't worry Vasilli, we will be able to talk for hours once we are there. We will be in a safe house, and there will be no interruptions. But there will be a lot that my bosses want to know. There won't be too much pressure at first, but they will eventually want some serious detail of your work."

"It's OK," said Vasilli, "It is better than I expected. Better than I could have hoped for. I have my best friend to help me… through what will probably be the most stressful time of my life. It is OK my friend…things are good… and will soon be better. Goodbye."

He was gone and Pete and the agent in charge exchanged a few words, and Pete made his way back to the hotel. He sat for an hour in the Piano Bar at the Senator, thinking deeply about Vasilli. The next time he was to see him should have been at the safe house at Flecknoe…

Pete was comfortable with the meeting. He had established the old rapport with Vasilli. He was pleased with the guys who were looking after him – he had known two of them from previous assignments.

Next day, he made his way back to the station and

boarded the train for Hamburg. He would spend a night at the Continental opposite the Hauptbahnhof and then get the ferry back to Harwich at noon the next day.

Suddenly the flashback was gone. He was back behind the wheel of the Alfa and closing in on Oxford.

Mac was slumped down in her seat with her eyes closed. He could tell that she was not deeply asleep… her breathing was too shallow, but she was resting, and that was no bad thing.

He eased off the main drag which by-passed Oxford, and was shortly passing through Summertown. He was heading for Long Wall Street, and eventually to the river, where he and Vasilli went during their spare time in those summer days, years ago.

At that time they have been to so many places in and around Oxford and the surrounding area, but Pete needed a place to start.

He didn't know whether it was the sunlight catching several times from the same angle on the bonnet of the car, three cars behind, that made him realise he was being followed, or maybe he had been expecting it and had been subconsciously aware. Either way he knew that the Vauxhall Cavalier three cars behind was following him. There were two men in it, but that was all he could make out at the moment.

For now, he had no intention of rousing Mac. She did not know where he was heading in the first place, so when he hung a left, and started making his way to the A40 and London, she would not be curious, even if she opened those beautiful eyes and glanced at the landmarks, or at him.

He had no intention of going to London. What he wanted to do was get a little way out of Oxford, perhaps near Thame, cut away into the country and lose the tail. He would then double back, using a different route and go back to Oxford – that was where he had to be to find the answer…

Any turns and changes of speed were mirrored by the Cavalier, keeping a discreet distance away. He turned off the A40, and it was when he turned again onto a little lane that the flash of sunlight glanced off the Cavalier and alerted him to a change.

The two men were now clearly visible, and the car was gunning towards them.

"Hang on Mac, they're on to us," he said squeezing her shoulder twice.

She seemed to know instantly what he meant, and she twisted round in her seat and cursed under her breath.

He slammed the Alfa down to third and booted the accelerator. It was the first time he had asked it to do anything strenuous, and he wondered, although there was not much time for it, whether the old girl, despite her pedigree and a good stable, had it in her.

He was not disappointed – the last thing he expected was wheel-spin in third,

"Wow," he said out loud, "Pat said he had done some work on this… God knows what he put under the bonnet, but it's not production line Alfa."

Quickly the Alfa increased the distance between it and the car in pursuit.

Pete was worried about going so fast on these back lanes – there always seemed to be riders and walkers about, but he was lucky. The road was so twisty that the driving was mostly second and third gear.

Pete was a good driver, he changed down before the bend and powered out of it, but the Cavalier was catching… its driver having the benefit of seeing how Pete set the Alfa up for a corner, and being ready for it. Pete having to keep an eye on the rear-view mirror also slowed him slightly.

Soon they were almost bumper to bumper – there was no need to look in the mirror any more – he swung the back end out for a bend, and a nudge from the Cavalier nearly rolled them into the hedge.

Riding up on to the two nearside wheels along the grass verge, Pete managed to hold it and flick it back onto four just at the right moment. Dust and clumps of earth were flicked up from the tyres and peppered the hedgerows, and the speeding Cavalier.

Mac squealed, but kept her cool. She turned again, her eyes meeting icy, steely glares from the car behind.

"Bastards," she muttered.

But they were not so cool really. Pete's expert diving had caught them slightly unawares. They took the corner slightly wide and bent the front nearside wing on a tree stump which Pete had just managed to miss. Pete accelerated away to the next bend. As he rounded it at full speed an old red Fordson Major tractor emerged from a field gate, its driver looking over his left shoulder at the muck spreader being towed behind – he was not going to stop.

"Oh shi-i-i-i-t," said Pete, as he realised it was going to be extremely tight getting through.

Involuntarily his shoulders narrowed as he felt the Alfa, bodywork sliced by a steel winch attachment protruding from the front of the tractor. But it was not deep and he knew they would get by. The two in the Cavalier were not so lucky. The driver this time misread the fact that Armour had not touched his brakes. It was not a sign of all clear – carrying on at full speed was Armour's only chance.

The Cavalier careered around the corner at full pelt and ploughed heavily into the side and rear of the muck-spreader with a horrible crump and shearing screech of twisting and buckling metal.

Driver and passenger had no chance – neither belted,

both were catapulted from their seats and hurled through the windscreen, blood and skull bone splattering and splintering through the glass and into the spreader. The tortured and twisted bits of car following them, carving crumping and smashing the rest of their bodies into an unrecognisable tableaux of tangled and mangled guts and flesh.

Apart from that, the nearby village of Chalgrove was very peaceful… the birds stopped their calls for an eerie silence, and returned, as if nothing happened.

Pete steadied his nerves and slowed the car, but changed direction for a few miles – they were bound to have radioed where they were and the direction they had been heading.

After another ten or fifteen minutes they made their way easily through Cowley, into Oxford.

"How did they get on to us?" queried Mac with no real idea of what had happened to their pursuers,

'How did they know which way we were heading… I didn't know! Where the hell are we going?"

Armour explained that the most relevant time for Vasilli and he, had been when they were together as students. The real clue had been the Oxford City bus ticket. Others might have dismissed that, considering that only a few hours had elapsed from the Flecknoe farce and when he turned up in Northampton. But obviously Vasilli had made it back here.

Vasilli's message had special meaning for Armour and that too meant Oxford. He had the clue, and the answer was there, waiting to be found… in Oxford.

Calder-Maynes said rather than asked: "O.K., Michael what do you know, this is really proving a pain in the arse."

"Tell me about it, your guys are on the case and every man and his dog has got to hear about it. Surely you did not have to blow up that narrowboat, it wasn't at all necessary, and now we have the local constabulary asking us serious questions, that and the mess in Grogan's yard. Are you enjoying this or what?

"Oh, what are you whining about Michael? My men have got things moving. If Armour has a message from the Russian, you can guess what it is about. It would not just be a cry for help, but 'have you seen these papers?' Maybe Armour already knows the gist of it.

"Remember that your initials are on the top as well. We simply don't have the time to play around. We have to keep the pressure on. We have to be there when Armour picks up the 'evidence'. What I can't understand is why he has this girl Claire Willans in tow. She's a good looking young lady, but he can't be all that concerned about her safety, maybe it would focus Armour's mind if we took her out!"

"OK, OK, I appreciate the urgency, but I still have my men on it, but would you try and make sure that yours don't kill anyone else please. And for God's sake leave the girl alone, I mean it. Someone has to pick up the pieces and try and bullshit some answers, and I am getting fed up with it. By the way I think we turn our attention on Oxford. I think we have wrongly ignored that Oxford bus ticket."

"But he couldn't possibly have got to Oxford and back to Northampton…"

"Well, it looks as if he did, or maybe he got someone else to… I don't know. I'll have men covering the main roads into Oxford… they may be there already of course. I'll have some covering the town centre, and I can't imagine that they would have a great deal of money on them, they left Northampton pretty quickly, we will establish checks on the bank and building society cashpoints, and we will know if they check into a hotel or guest house.

"Now seriously Bryan, no more killing, please," said Staveley-Smythe.

"Look, by now Michael, you know I will do whatever I

have to do to get this matter sorted out… it just can't go on. There is too much at risk. Michael, all I am saying is, you sort it out, or I will."

"The bastard," thought Staveley-Smythe, as he hung up. "In a strange, macabre way he's enjoying this – and he is showing me that he has power. Well he better just watch out."

If the opportunity arose when he could shaft Calder-Maynes, he would, and by God, he would revel in it.

The black phone in Calder-Maynes' plush panelled office rang, and he had the receiver up by the second tone.

His office was rich in memorabilia, a catalogue of military history and a tribute to his own career. Calder-Maynes had produced a tabernacle to his own past. There were pictures of Mountbatten, Montgomery, de Gaulle, Truman and Eisenhower, medals covering every field of conflict and almost every recognition of gallantry and endeavour during first and second world wars, awards, citations, framed letters and pictures, lot and lots of pictures.

Cabinets around the walls held silverware ranging from early athletic awards to engraved plate from grateful luminaries of perhaps sometimes questionable status.

The walls were panelled and the furniture of deep brown leather. The carpet was thick-piled and the very best quality – from the coved ceiling hung ornate crystal chandeliers, and in the corner was a drinks trolley which only carried a decanter of scotch and a jug of water.

"Yes…"

He listened, and then spoke: "Christ… you guys are supposed to be the professionals, the best. How could you let this amateur get away from you?"

He listened again for a moment.

"Lucky? Look Carter, I want them found. I want to know

where they are by tonight," he rattled his orders, "Get what help you need but find them. I would expect them to try and find a bolt hole for tonight. They won't risk a hotel, but maybe a small guest house or hostel. We're buggered if they have got friends in Oxford. We will have to wait until they are on the move again. Look out for that car, it's pretty distinctive. Get back to me when you know anything."

He slammed the phone down.

If it wasn't for the fact that Armour was on the edge of destroying everything Calder-Maynes had been working for in the past year, and perhaps seriously threatening his professional future, and maybe his life, he might have been enjoying this challenge.

Despite the fact that the odds were very much against Armour, he was proving a resilient and resourceful adversary. But no matter how clever he was, Calder-Maynes knew it was only a matter of time before he was caught. But for Calder-Maynes the important thing was damage limitation.

Those papers must not leave Armour's hands… that's if he had them. If he did not they must be destroyed before they fell into someone else's. Armour was tenacious, and dangerous. If he knew the contents of the papers he would have to die…he would have to die anyway and so would the girl. It was almost inevitable.

And frankly, he did not care one way or the other about that.

Chapter Ten

He really hoped that something would come to him, to help him find the answer. Because at the moment there was very little, or so much that it was hard to pick out something that would have been particularly relevant to Vasilli.

He pulled into St. Giles and parked… he was lucky!

It was about midday, so he decided it was time to slow down and eat. He took Mac's arm and turned left into Broad Street, and then right into Turl Street… there was a pub at the end he remembered, that did food… God knows what it was like now.

The Mitre… it was still there, and there was a chalk board outside and they still did bistro-style meals and bar snacks… he had been keeping an eye out behind them – all around in fact, everything seemed in order … they went in.

Mac's nerves were jangled and she had a whiskey. Mac, of course, and, feeling pretty edgy himself, Armour decided on scotch and diet coke.

They each had lasagne and salad.

They didn't talk much. Armour was having difficulty in getting his mind off her body. He watched her. The way she moved. Her look – the way the sun reflected off her skin… it was early, but he wanted to sort out where they were going to stay that evening… he could hardly wait.

She was slightly surprised with herself. Here she was with a guy she would never have considered as a confidante, let alone a lover. A lover, how did that happen…?

In the end, simply, there had been nothing more natural. What was the point of trying to figure it out, or explain it. They were lovers, it had only just begun, but it was great… so far anyway. The big question appeared to be would they live to do it again?

She actually trusted her basic feelings, particularly this time. Maybe Mac wasn't absolutely certain of Armour, but then why should she be?

Strangely, Armour was certain of his feelings. His heart glowed to think that a girl like Mac should want him. He was not expecting anything long term. She was young, and no matter what people claim, age difference does make a difference eventually.

As far as he was concerned it was great though. He would make the most of it. If it finished, it finished, and he hoped there would be no bad feeling.

If it went on and on, then he would be blissfully happy… and he would give up his work for Military Intelligence, finish renovating his cottage on the edge of the Althorp Estate, and maybe write a book… he knew he had one in him.

If he lived that long… he thought to himself.

She had been conscious he was staring at her. She knew it was lovingly, and did not look up in case it embarrassed him. She was also aware when the trance was broken, and she caught his returning glance and smiled.

"Now what?" she asked, "I've always liked Oxford… nice shops, pubs and night life. I used to come here quite a lot at one time."

"The message Vasilli gave you was exactly the message I told him to send me if he got into trouble, except, that is, he added three words… 'Thane's Excelsior Reserve'… it is a message to me, that at the moment means very little. It is a message in itself, or maybe it is a place that I will find the real message. Vasilli was highly intelligent, and very sharp. This clue is going to be relevant only to me, and therefore the information is only retrievable by me.

"It seems that at least some of the people who are following us realise that, but we are still being pushed along. Perhaps what they don't realise is that I am still trying to work out the answer. They might think I am playing for time, and at the same time trying to escape the tail.

"Mac, the situation is confusing. There may be some people out there trying to give us some protection, help even, if we get in a fix. Then, obviously there are people on our trail who don't actually care whether we find the information or not… they just want to stop us.

"And to cap it all, I don't know which side is which, and can't even rely on my old contacts to help out. I don't know who I can trust."

Armour had his foot up on a stool opposite him, and it started to slide away. He pulled it back and he carried on.

"So we have got to stay one step ahead of the game all the time, and for the moment that means staying on our own. For now, I feel it is the safest thing to do. And we can't stay in one place too long. We have to work out a plan."

The bar was slowly emptying as they were talking and Armour kept a wary eye on those coming and going. He thought he might spot anyone who was paying them more than the normal amount of attention.

"Oh," she said, "How do we formulate this plan, and what do we do first?"

"Well, any plan is going to have to be based on my recollections of the time Vasilli was in Oxford, and perhaps the best way to do that is to find some lodgings first, that are as private as possible, and talk."

He reached forward with his right hand, and gently clenched her chin between his forefinger and thumb.

"You're the reporter … you can ask me questions and perhaps something will spring to mind. And even though we both know the town, we could also do with a good street map.

"So let's find somewhere to stay…there used to be quite few places out on the Botley Road that provided rooms, let's try there…"

Armour knew this game was getting serious and he was not actually as comfortable, or casual, as the impression he was trying to convey to Mac. He was particularly worried about being out on the streets where they could easily be spotted and get a tail put on them that they would never see. While they were out in the open they would have to keep moving, cutting back, twisting and turning, so the likelihood of someone following them might be more easily spotted. He worried about how easy finding somewhere to stay was going to be.

Guesthouses and B&Bs were the best. For anyone to check all those would take ages, some of them were not registered anywhere – it would give them time, and that, at the moment, was what they needed most. Time was getting on and they would need to get moving.

They had finished their meal, and he was about to head off, when she caught his arm.

"I think I can help here," she beamed… "My uncle is a professor at Merton College, I reckon he would be able to get us rooms…"

His agile mind was immediately back on course, if somewhat abruptly so.

"Think again Mac… people are already dying, think of Pat Grogan, and we are dealing with MI5 here. When you said you knew Oxford well, I didn't think it was because you had family here. They will have checked out all known family and friends by now, and they will know about your uncle – he will be being watched already… maybe even bugged. He would be too close. Going to him would be very risky, for him and for us. But maybe if there was someone else you know who could help us, someone not obviously close… and someone who won't be easily connected."

She slightly flushed for a moment at how naive her suggestion had been, and disappointed that her idea was ill thought out – it had been on the spur of the moment, and she could have kicked herself. He must think she was stupid she thought. He didn't. His reply had not been with any air of cleverness and he certainly had not been trying to put her down – but it was obvious he was used to thinking in terms of betrayal, spying, chasing, information gathering, spy technology, danger, risking lives, and all that.

She suddenly realised that her life was so small, maybe insignificant, and she was frail – the tears started to well in her eyes.

Armour spotted her face redden, and then in moments, the tears appeared at the side of her eyes – and it was like a dagger in his side, twisting in his flesh.

How bloody stupid could he be? How unsympathetic? How unthinking? How brutal? He had not recognised the stress she was under, and then he had treated her like an agency recruit who had got a shiny new gun licence, but had not engaged his brain.

She got up from where they were sitting in the pub and walked out into High Street, wiping the tears from her eyes.

He followed and caught up with her, turned her, moved her sideways into a doorway out of the way of passing shoppers and tourists.

One hand held her shoulder and the other her face, and his steely eyes were fixed on to hers.

"I'm sorry…" he said perhaps more firmly than he had intended. "… I love you," he stammered, and then crashed his lips on to hers.

Initially, she was a little stunned… he was fast. She pulled away a little but liked the warmth she felt of his face on hers, and the fact was she wanted to melt into his body, and she gave in.

Walking on through the streets, they both realised the need to get somewhere to stay was becoming vital.

Mac was to come up trumps.

"I just need to make a phone call," she said and as they walked back to St. Giles, they diverted to a public phone booth.

She made her call, while he waited… not knowing, but trusting her now… she knew the possible dangers.

They waited outside the phone booth for about ten minutes, and the call came back. Mac knew the address, and they hurried back to the Alfa… Armour decided that when they got there he would dump the car somewhere… it was time to find something else.

They drove away from the town centre back towards Summertown, and turned right into Bardwell Road, and checked the address. It looked ideal, and there seemed to be a lot of student accommodation in the area.

They drove to the Summertown shopping area and after a round the houses route, put the Alfa in the corner of a car park near the Radio Oxford building. Mac popped into a chemist for a few things and they stopped off at a mini-market for some provisions, then make their way back to the house.

Armour was certain they were not being followed, he had checked pretty thoroughly.

It was a large redbrick house that had been converted into apartments and flats. Others in the street were similarly converted.

Mac's instructions were to go down an alleyway at the left hand side of the building and use a rear entrance to the building.

Looking around Armour noted that the door area was secluded and not overlooked at all.

When they got to the door, Mac moved a heavy concrete pot. Then in the wall behind, removed a loose brick, and brought out a set of keys.

"It belongs to an old friend… don't worry no one, and I mean no one, could make a connection, and this place is about as safe as you can get," she said.

Armour, although he wanted to know more, felt that he shouldn't question her again on this subject, but he found it difficult, he was more used to being in control in 'safe house' situations. But he didn't want to make two major cock-ups on the same day, he would have to trust her.

Inside the door it was dark, and they nearly tripped over two mountain bikes… that sorted out the transport question, and what better in Oxford, at least they would not be too obvious.

The fuse box switch was high on the wall and could just be seen by the daylight through the frosted glass above the door. He reached up and flipped the switch, the light in the corridor came on, and he heard a fridge motor start to whirr in what he reasonably assumed must be the kitchen, a short flight of steps above them.

Armour got to the top, he was very surprised. He had expected something studenty, basic, averagely furnished, but a bit unkempt… he thought they would have to air the place.

This place was very smart, very clean. The kitchen had every facility you could imagine, and it was all the latest equipment. The lighting was very tasteful, and everything was in cream and beige and wood. There were two strippine doors in the wall in front of them and each lead to a large sitting room, dimmed because of the closed heavy curtains.

Mac slipped passed him and went to open them.

"I guess it might be an idea to leave those closed," he said, but she ignored him and drew the curtains. He was relieved to see the curtains were heavily netted, but allowed in the light… but then she obviously knew that.

Another door on the right led to a large and sumptuous bedroom, again in beiges and creams. A huge king-sized bed with velvet covered headboard and billowing valance dominated, and uplighters, drapes, and very thick shag carpet complete the incredibly luxuriant feel.

Mac moved through another door on the right and inside, again carpeted was a heavily mirrored bathroom with a massive double-width bath… she turned on the taps.

Armour's mind going ten to the dozen. He did not think the owner of the apartment could be a member of the security forces, that would be too much of a coincidence, and foolhardy for Mac to have contacted. But the only other people who might want obscurity, sometimes at least, are celebrities. He wondered, not judgmentally, which celebrity Mac knew this well.

There were no photographs around, or anything to give a hint.

It was obvious that the rooms were regularly attended to, though possibly not regularly used. In fact that was the feeling he had. This place was not used but kept in readiness, for the moment when it would be… very strange, who could afford to do that. Why would they want to do that. Anyone who could afford this would surely want to stay in one of the top hotels in town… The Randolph for example… unless of course, they did not want the fuss, or they did not want to be seen.

His thoughts were interrupted by Mac's hands sliding under his arms and over his chest.

He felt her breasts meet the middle of his back, and her face gently press against his shoulder blades. He dropped his right shoulder and twisted round, and he looked down into her eyes.

"I think we should be safe here," she said, and he did not argue… and he certainly did not have a better idea.

"It's amazing," he said. "Whose is it?"

"I can't tell you Pete, and it's not really important… Let's have that bath!"

It was her turn to be secretive and anyway, he thought, too good an idea to mess up with silly conversation.

There was no need to rush to see who got the tap end, because they were in the middle, but their clothes came off pretty quickly anyway.

Armour was amazed again at her beauty. She was thin and small, but in perfect proportion. Her breasts were round and firm, her nipples small, but protruding… provocatively, mischievously he thought.

Her waist was narrow and her bottom rounded and … the texture of her skin caught his eye. It seemed to catch the light with a faint shimmer – he just wanted to touch…

Mac had added some bath oil, and the surface of the bath seemed a little slippery, but it made their touching more exquisite – he stroked her body as she lay between his legs and her back against his stomach. Her head fell back gently onto his left shoulder and she groaned slightly as his hands passed erogenous parts. His memory was brilliant and he recalled some from their night on the barge and he made a mental note of others as he went along.

She was impressed… he really knew how to move. And his timing was extraordinary… how did he know that? She eased open her legs as his fingers moved closer to her mound.

She was relaxed, and he was taking the lead, and she could feel herself getting very warm… and wet.

But the opulence of the flat, the warmth of the bath, his confident, controlling movements, and the fact that he was not making any demands… with his voice or his body, let her gently 'absorb' him. And the pressures of the day were taking their toll. She was tired… very tired, and she needed at least a little rest, and gently her eyes drooped.

Armour felt her muscles slowly drop too. The conversation had slowed and he knew she was falling asleep.

He brought his right hand to rest just below her left breast and his left hand at the base of her stomach – he only moved occasionally to add a little hot water.

After a while he eased himself from under her, using the weightlessness created by the water, and then lifted her from the bath, wrapping her in bath towels, he laid her on the bed. He padded her dry, and he assumed she was well asleep… and in a way she was. She knew what he was doing, but it was a half sleep, and she was happy to let it happen. When she was dry, he pulled back the duvet, and rolled her under it… within a few moments she was totally asleep.

She had had perhaps the most traumatic days of her life… little did she know.

But he understood. He lay with her for 20 minutes and then got up. He went to the sitting room, and noticed that on the far side of the room was a wall of books.. strange that he had not particular noticed them earlier…

He scanned the various literary pieces, and picked out a few local publications on the bottom shelf, sat down on the floor, leaning against the thick padded sofa.

His eyes glanced over a few lines, and similarly over another book and then a leaflet… Soon his eyes were heavy and he lolled into a half sleep.

When he came suddenly to his senses he appraised his situation very quickly, and got to his feet. He knew Mac would be hungry when she woke. They had a choice. Either he cooked something from what they bought earlier, or they went to a restaurant fairly close by.

The serious question was, how big were the risks?

He reckoned that for the first couple of nights they would be OK, but however well they blended in, he knew Oxford would be swarming with agents, probably with more tomorrow.

Whilst someone was on their tail, manpower could be kept fairly low, once they disappeared, finding them became a top priority.

He guessed that the first inkling that anyone would have of their rough position, was when they found the Alfa in Summertown… but they would have one hell of job after that to pin them down to the flat they were in.

He had noticed a small Italian restaurant in their walk through Summertown. It might be their last chance – he hated to think of that.. He decided it was worth a try. He gave them a ring and booked a table for about 10 pm. He wanted it to be dark when they went out. Tonight of all nights he wanted no unwelcome interruption, or visitors.

He woke Mac about 9 pm, knowing that it would only take her about 20 minutes to get ready. She wore very little makeup, and actually wore very few clothes – he wondered if he had made a mistake and they should have eaten, very simply, in.

Mac's reaction told him that he was right to go for eating out. Fact is, Mac wanted anything that might take her mind off what was happening outside… just for tonight.

She hoped it was in their best interest to find whatever it was Vasilli had left for Armour, but she did not want to think about it tonight… there would be time.

In a large cupboard near the back door were a couple of large wax jackets, so they borrowed them. They would help to disguise them – they were big and no one would be looking for a couple with matching clothes. They still kept to the shadows, without being obvious, and within ten minutes they were at the restaurant.

He had already figured that he had enough cash for the night. He thought he would be alright cashing money at a hole in the wall, in town in the morning, as long as he got away from the area pretty quick, and organised a good escape route – he doubted they would try to freeze his account… they needed him to do the spade work.

When the work was over… that was the worrying moment. He wiped the thought from his mind. Like Mac he wanted to clear his mind of it for a while.

Chapter Eleven

He had mentioned that they wanted a quiet corner table, preferably away from the door, and the result of his request was perfect. The restaurant was not particularly busy, probably just over half full.

Shortly after taking their seats Armour decided to check the place out. He did not tell Mac what he was doing. He made to go to the toilet which was next to the kitchen door and that was the door he took. People saw him enter and he apologised as if he had mistaken it for the toilet door, backed out, and then entered the men's room.

In that short time he had sussed the shortest route through the large shiny steel units of the kitchen, to the back door, which had a quick escape push-bar latch. He knew that there was one chef and two assistants. The sinks were over to the left and out of the way.

The three cookers were on the right, and people at them, could get in the way if they were in a rush. There were two windows above the cookers which were both open, and steam rising from a huge pot of spaghetti was spewing out into the darkness. Near the back door, cloths were hanging over a radiator to dry.

The toilet was one cubicle and one urinal. The small frosted glass window was too small for anyone to go in or out, even Mac.

He returned to the table. He had only been gone a minute or two. He had not wanted to leave Mac too long. She looked, smiled and took his hands as he sat down. It was a special moment.

They ate and talked about each other. She told him about her background. She left a couple of significant episodes out, still, this wasn't the full life story. And he felt obliged to tell her about his very strange little side-line, but skated around the situation leading to Vasilli's arrival in the country.

They were soon paying and leaving the restaurant. He with his arm around her shoulder and her with her arm around his waist, they made their way back to the apartment.

As casually as he possibly could, Armour checked up and down the street as they turned into the alleyway although he was sure they would not have ruled it out, he guessed that at this stage, although they might be close friends, he would not imagine that any possible agent spotting them would have expected them to be this close… lovers, and it was obvious to any onlookers that they were …she gave no hint of noticing that he was checking the street.

Inside, she ran up the steps and into the lounge. She dived into one of the deep sofas, chuckling, and he was soon after her. He didn't land on the sofa, but on the floor beside her, He ran his hands along the outside of her leg and thigh… her waist and torso, and then sideways on to her left breast. She wriggled so that her right breast was also available, and he brought his head down on her neck. He could smell her perfume, but he could also smell the natural aroma of her skin.

His hands were now roving all over her body and, gently, but firmly, he was pulling her to him, and he was undoing her blouse… her left breast sprang out into his eager hand, and then the right – his hand moved between the two with considerable skill. And then he moved down her body and undid her jeans and with a helpful roll, they were eased around her buttocks and down her legs… and then she went in search of his body and what she could find. He helped her eagerly. It had only been last night, but he missed her so much.

He rose to his knees and he slipped his hands under her body and lifted her gently, and carried her to the bedroom.

The circumstances allowed it… he brought his lips up to her ears and whispered: "You are amazing… I love you."

Her body, involuntarily, shivered with ecstasy, and she searched his body. She moved her fingers skilfully and he groaned.

She pulled him towards her and helped him inside her warm wetness. It was going to be a long and sexy night. Mac already felt more fulfilled than she had ever been. Armour was amazed. He had never felt anything like this is his life. It was not just the sex. It was far, far more than he felt he deserved.

Just touching her was tantalising…and that night he touched like she had never been touched before – it was as good for him as it was for her…

Sunlight broke through the netting – she didn't notice it, but he did. Ruffling his hair, to try and make it make some acceptable style – he couldn't – he made his way to the kitchen. Feeling the weight of the kettle, and finding it half full he emptied it and refilled it with fresh water, he flipped the switch, and turned to look around the flat. He was still intrigued by it, but felt sure that whatever guess he came up with, he was probably going to be wrong. He decided, that for the moment, perhaps the best bet was to concentrate on the matter in hand.

He sat on the arm or the sofa and looked back into the bedroom. His eyes were closely focussed on her, and whatever he thought about the previous night, he only seemed to home in on her eyes.

Mac's eyes were amazing. They sparkled, yes of course, but the irises were rimmed by an incredible steely line, which seemed to give a marble quality, but it was almost as if those eyes could drill deep into your soul… he found them mesmerising. You had to see it to appreciate it. Those who saw it, usually fell in love with it. But that alone was something he had not come in close contact with before. He was captivated, and with a lot more about Mac – she was… all he had ever wanted and the last thing he had ever expected.

But sitting on the edge of that sofa, he realised that if they ever had a hope of a future together, he would have to find an answer to the problem… and maybe they were running out of time.

He sat down into the cushions and looked once again at the books and leaflets about Oxford. He was aware that the answer was here… even if the path to it was not.

Thane? The only Thane he heard of was, *Macbeth* – Thane of Cawdor Mac…beth,

Mac..beth, Mac.beth

He dashed into the bedroom. He gently shook her, then more firmly.

"Mac… Mac…Mac, your middle name…is it Elizabeth?"

She turned over and smiled, gently rousing from her slumbers.

"How did you know that?" she asked.

"Just a guess…" he said and slumped down to the floor.

Vasilli, he thought to himself, that's very clever, and one third of the riddle. He could not begin to imagine how Vasilli had got his information, and so quickly, it did not really matter, but it also gave an indication of the type of clues Armour could expect from the message. The one thing he knew was that it was a personal message, direct and personal.

He thought that, in a way, the second and third parts of the riddle should be easier.

Perhaps he even knew how Vasilli got his information. Armour knew that the *Chronicle* produced a booklet about the paper, its staff, and aims, which included a code of practice, and this leaflet, which was kept updated regularly was available in the foyer of the newspaper office. It would have had some basic information about Mac… Not much, but whatever it said, it may well lead to the second part of the riddle. He needed to know what it said… he was going to have to wake her.

He went to the kitchen, and prepared breakfast for two… orange juice, flakes, boiled egg, toast and big pot of coffee. They had bought most of it the previous evening, except for the coffee. He had found fresh beans in a Dutch-packeted foil bag. He found a grinder and prepared the coffee using an old-style coffee peculator taken from a cupboard.

In the bedroom Mac heard him moving about and soon smelled the rich aroma of freshly ground coffee. She stretched, and then as he came in, sat up, revealing those beautiful breasts as she turned to fluff up her pillows and sit up straight, and she caught him looking at her. She liked it and smiled to herself – it gave her a warm, wanted feeling, made her feel sexy.

"Hey, this is a great. Two mornings in a row. I am being spoilt."

She: "Mmmm-ed," as he set the packed tray on the bed beside her.

"At you service Marm," he mocked lightly.

She giggled at first and then said: "Why do you say that?" surprising him by taking on a sterner look and tone than he expected.

"No particularly reason, why?" he asked. He was curious.

"Oh it's OK, it's nothing important…" She shrugged her shoulders, curled her lip and pulled a face.

"You asked me about my middle name earlier, was that particularly relevant to anything?"

"Glad you mentioned that," he said, "In fact it was very important – you appear to be part of Vasilli's clue. Vasilli was quite well up on Shakespeare. He mentioned Thane in his message, which was not part of what I told him to say. The only Thane that I can think of, although there must be others, is the reference in *Macbeth*. Macbeth was the Thane of Cawdor… Mac … beth, your nickname, and an abbreviation of your middle name – Vasilli knew that much and probably more about you."

"How?" she said, "If this is all linked to the thing at Flecknoe, he didn't have much time to swot up on biographies or even who… who the hell I was for that matter…"

"It must have been that 'All About Us' booklet in the foyer at the *Chron*. There was a new one out a couple of weeks ago, it must have had some details about you in it. Do you know exactly what?"

"I'm not sure. I remember soon after I joined the *Chron*, Mart Burricks asked me to do a short bio and give it to the editor's secretary for the booklet."

"Try, it would be really helpful to know… word for word would be even more useful…"

He understood this might be difficult, but that was what Vasilli had been working on – they really needed to know.

"Tell you what, we need some money. I could go down to Cornmarket Street and use the cashpoint, and you could give that some thought while I'm out," he said.

"There are cashpoints in Summertown… it's much nearer," she advised, wracking her brains over what she had written about herself. She was slightly spooked by the fact that Vasilli had included her in his cryptic clue.

"Yes I know, I saw them last night. Fact is, whoever is after us will be pretty sure that we are in Oxford, and they might guess that we are short of money. They will almost certainly be monitoring the cashpoints of our banks in Oxford for when we try and use them. Then they will move in. I don't think they want to stop us… yet, they just want to know where we are, so they will probably let me have the cash, but then have a tail on me, but obviously I don't want to lead them back here, so I want to use one away from here, and then I will have to move fast to get free of a tail."

"Will it be dangerous?" she sat forward quickly.

"No, of course not," he said…

Chapter Twelve

The wax mack hung open, and her naked body hung tightly to him. He gripped round her waist and back, and almost decided not to go. There was a feeling inside him that nagged him saying: 'You had better make the most of this because it can never last…look at the age difference.. what happens when you are a bit older, a bit slower?'

Through his own clothes he felt her outline, the wax mack fell to the floor, and she felt him stirring.

"You had better go, or you better stay, I'd like you to stay, but you better make up your mind," she teased.

Very gently he broke away, and he slapped her gorgeous backside as she turned back towards the bedroom.

He dropped easily down the steps to the corridor and back door. He opened it and unhooked the larger of the two bikes, and picked up a chain with a combination lock – it was open and he noted the number.

Outside, the early morning sun had been overtaken by a thin cloud, but it was still bright. He make his way towards the town centre, using the bus lane. One car, a sporty blue Renault 19 16-valve with its characteristic bonnet vent, came a little too close to him, and he couldn't see the people inside, but he decided to start a random route. This actually had another purpose, other than trying to confuse pursuers, and that was to try and stir his memory – getting him to remember what it was like, here, with Vasilli.

While he had been looking at leaflets in the apartment he had found a town centre plan and had refreshed his memory. He knew that many of the universities, for example, were open to the public all year round, and that he could easily use the labyrinth of colleges for an escape route, particularly on a bike or on foot.

He found himself passing the Pitt Rivers and University Museums. One hundred yards on, he decided not to turn directly into Broad Street, towards St. Giles, but carried on a little further and turned right in to Brasenose Lane, off Radcliffe Square.

Then crossing Turl Street, close to where they had lunched the day before, he entered Market Street, and then Cornmarket Street, which was very busy. He swung his leg over the saddle and stepped to the ground, and pushed the bike beside him – no one would reckon him to be a student, but he could easily be a tutor or professor, and anyway lots of residents had bikes too, it was the sensible way to travel in the city. Parking is always appalling, and usually it involves walking some way before you are where you want to be.

It is completely different and much more convenient to use a bike.

He saw his cashpoint, and looked round.

The fact is that they may not have closed in as much as he feared, after all if he had about £50, he could probably use his cheque book, and not need any more cash than that for a week or so.

Armour was 'banking' now, on getting as much cash as he could, as quickly as possible. They would have to be frugal, and then use cheques for food shopping at different places. It would be sensible to eat in, and he had to make sure that they protected their 'safe house' as long as possible.

It the next day or so, he would have to seek out a possible alternative, just in case.

The fact that Armour was sticking round Oxford would soon become apparent to those after them. They would suss that Vasilli's message was not a clear and simple instruction… perhaps it would have been better if it had, but they would then have time to find him… it was only a matter of time.

He kept an eye on the area of the cashpoint, scanning people moving about, but more so the people who were in the same position, or only moving a few feet. The street was busy already.

He reckoned on about £200 on his Visa card. He knew the route he would take.

The card went in, he punched in the pin number, pressed 'withdraw', and input £200.

He waited… was it longer than normal?… but it was more than he would usually withdraw… does it take longer the larger the amount? He waited, and looked around, all seemed calm.

In a moment, the card popped out and the whirring started. He looked around and the cash came out. Quickly he snatched it out, stuffed it in his pocket.

His right foot on the pedal he scootered three steps, swung his foot over and pedalled in amongst the crowd of shoppers.

He thought he saw a guy in a brown leather bomber jacket, who had his hands in the pockets, pull them out quickly, and right himself from leaning against a door. He thought the move was too quick, and he shot a glance in that direction. The guy was looking at him, but stayed where he was. Another, on the other side of the road had a mobile phone to his ear, he was talking, but not looking towards him. He felt decidedly vulnerable, but he knew he had a good escape route, and it would take a big team to keep tabs on him. He weaved his way right, in to Queen Street, and then cut left into the indoor shopping centre. There were at least four exits, but he did not want to attract too much attention, so dropped from the riding position to scooting the bike. He cut left again and out through the Pembroke Street exit, into Pembroke Street, right in St. Aldate's and then immediately left through the impressive college gates of Christ Church.

He stopped, took off the wax mac and stuffed it into the saddlebag

The grass quad had a gravel path cut round the edge and in a circular path and a cross path. He took the circular path, back on the bike, to the left, and he heard footsteps stamp through the gate area and onto the gravel.

Quickly he made his way to the door on the left hand corner, jumped from the bike, lifted it to his shoulder, ran up the steps and as he reach the doorway stopped to glance over his shoulder… it was a mistake. A silenced bullet smashed into the stone near his face, sending splinters of rock flying. A piece of grit stung his face.

"Wow, they're fast," he thought as he crashed through the door, up more steps, along and down and right, then left and out. He quickly appraised his position, and then back on the bike he turned to his right by Oriel, and sped along a path and then grass, through trees at Corpus Christi, left and then right, and as expected he found himself in Merton Street, with the 13th century college on the right, he had forgotten it was cobbled. He cut left towards University College, and kept snatching a view behind him… it seemed clear, but he entered the university building, crossed the small quad and through the building on the other side.

Before going out onto High Street, he stopped in the doorway. The sun was out again, but he was in the shadows. He looked up and down the street, left the bike, back-tracked to the quad, it was still clear and then back to the bike.

It was still clear. He went right and then left into Queen's Lane and then stopped in an alleyway leading through to Holywell Street, and then off down Parks Road. He cut left and right several times and even stopped, buried his bike among a pile of others and watched from a shop window to see if anyone suspicious came along, but it looked as if he had lost them.

Keeping to the quieter roads he made his way back to Bardwell Road, and before entering the pathway to the back of the house he had a good look around. He knocked softly at the door, and was surprised by the swiftness with which Mac swung open the door.

"You've been ages, I was really worried, what happened, your face is cut?" and she put her hand up the mark made by the piece of grit that hit him.

It was not a cut, and had not bled, but was very red… it did not hurt.

"Well I was a bit over-enthusiastic in my getaway, and tripped. It's nothing."

She knew he was lying. It was not just the mark on his face. He had been sweating, she could smell and recognised the mustiness of it.

"Look, are we in this together. Don't you think you can trust me? Or do you think I can't handle it? What happened? Come on Armour tell me…"

He decided to be open with her from now on. There were all kinds of things going through his mind, and, truthfully, he did not want to frighten her, so he would keep much of this to himself, but there was no reason to keep her in the dark.

"OK I was spotted at the cashpoint, but got away. I skipped through a college, but just as I got through, someone shot at me and hit the doorway where I was standing… a bit of rock hit me. Again I got away, and shook the tail…look I didn't think they would be shooting at me. I think something has gone very wrong. The shooting at Flecknoe… if that involved some internal treachery in Military Intelligence, and I think it might have, it could explain a lot…"

He actually found talking it out quite useful.

As he went on they moved into the kitchen, she made a cup of coffee and they went through to the lounge and sat down.

"You see I can't understand, at the moment, why else anyone would actually want to kill us. I work for British Military Intelligence… MI6, why should they be aggressive to me? The Russian defector is dead already, their problem is over, why should they be upset, unless they think we have something sensitive with us? If that was the case though, they might chase…but they would expect us to give it straight to Military Intelligence they wouldn't get involved in killing. But they have obviously seen our guys chasing me. Something has been going wrong with some of the defections recently… this is not the first. It would appear that some people here have foreign masters. My guess would be that Vasilli got his hands on something that is particularly sensitive, otherwise he would not have run away from Flecknoe, why should he?

"Basically Mac, we could effectively have three agencies after us – we really need some answers, or at least a pretty good idea what we are looking for before we go wandering round the streets," he said.

"You have obviously been in this business for some time, isn't there anyone out there you can trust. Isn't there someone who can help us?" she asked with just a little desperation in her voice.

"Maybe, but you have to understand that I was very

much a special case, and a little bit on the outside. This was not my full time job, and I reckon there were probably quite a few who do not trust me either. I was certainly not involved in any internal politics. I only ever knew the people involved in each case. I knew a few of the 'troops' on the ground, because they had been involved as minders on two or more of my cases, and of course my boss Mick. We mostly made arrangements on the phone. I knew him from way back, but I've actually only met him about a dozen times since I joined.

"He had always seemed pretty straight with me, and I know he is quite involved high up sometimes. I guess that doesn't necessarily mean much, but, since you ask, I have been considering contacting him… that would certainly bring things to a head… and right out of my hands. No matter what we do, I can't guarantee our safety… so you see the problem."

In the time he had been talking she had stroked his head and then his arm, sat by his feet and sat beside him on the sofa.

He noticed her movements… and he loved her for them. It was a sign she cared. And she did care. He had been out, and had risked everything to help them find an answer. She knew by now that he was not just finding an answer for himself, but for them, their future, so they could be together. It made her heart swell. She was so proud that this mature, experienced man, who could have any woman he wanted, had chosen her. She sort of felt that the circumstances had contributed, but, what the hell… he was special, and he loved her… he had said as much.

"Have you had a chance to remember your bio stuff?" he asked, almost nonchalantly, but noticing her fresh showered glow.

"I think so, yes. I'm not sure I've got it word for word, but I don't think it can be far off," she told him. She explained that the *Chron* guidebook was laid out with the various departments, starting off with editorial, and started to read from the notes she had made while he had been out.

> 'Claire Elizabeth Willans(27) – senior reporter. Born in London and educated in Oxford, Claire, known to her friends as 'Mac', joined the *Bury Free Press* as a trainee.
>
> After three years, she returned to Oxford and worked for the *Oxford Mail* for two years, taking a special interest in education and the arts. Claire joined us at the *Chronicle & Echo* a few months ago, covering education and crime. Her hobbies and interests include the theatre, music, botany, history, windsurfing and skiing.'

"I think that was it. We were encouraged to keep the bios short," she said, "but I can't see anything there that could be of any help, can you?"

"No, not immediately, but there has to be something…"

Mac went to the kitchen. From the lounge, Armour heard the kettle flick on and he called "Yes" to her offer of a ham sandwich. He was still studying the piece of paper when she returned with the food and coffee.

"We are going to have to go out. I need something to jog my memory. You know the clues and the town pretty well, so together we should be able to come up with an answer.

"I suggest though, that we go out later, just before it starts to get dark. Whoever is after us will have had a tired, fruitless day and they will be looking to scale down for the night, but we will still have to be careful."

Mac picked a crumb from the front of his shirt… and adopted a cheeky smirk

"What are we going to do till then may I ask? She questioned… raising an eyebrow, and bringing her hand up along the inside of his thigh.

He looked down at her hand, back up into her face and then back down to her hand…

"I was just thinking of going through some of those town street maps, and …"

They were both laughing as she crashed her lips into his and they rolled off the sofa and on the luxuriously thick pile carpet.

She was on top of him and she set about unbuttoning first his shirt and then his trousers. She was only wearing a baggy T-shirt and knickers, so his hands were quickly up inside the shirt kneading her gorgeous breasts and he gently, but then more firmly squeezed her nipples between forefinger and thumb… and she whimpered.

She had been caressing his chest, but broke away to drag his trousers, and underpants, clear of his feet, and he raised himself up on his elbows to watch her.

His 'response' had already become very obvious and she smiled. He groaned as she grabbed him with both hands, kissed all around, and then took him in her mouth.

She worked expertly and ecstasy though it was, he pulled up his body, but she kept her mouth against his skin, slurping and squelching all the way, until their faces came closer… and their groins began to meet. She raised her head and looked deep and longingly, down into his eyes.

He rolled her over, teasing her with his prick, and then he picked her up and put her on the sofa.

"Don't move," he said and walked to the kitchen and the fridge. He removed a bottle of Chardonnay and two glasses. He uncorked the bottle and returned to the sitting room.

Mac was sat upright. Her head rested on her left shoulder and then rolled forward, her hand was between her thighs.

Armour Piercing

He put down the drink, went round to the back of the sofa and brought his hands over her shoulders and down into her groin… and quickly finding her clitoris.

She moaned and reaching up and behind his head and pulling him to her mouth again. Moments later he was over the back of the sofa and their bodies were meshed together, writhing and grinding…

"I took a shot at him, yeah, there was no danger of hitting him," he lied, "and I was able to get a tail on him. I know where they are. He was clever, and he took some chasing, but he didn't clock me. What do you want me to do sir?" Carter waited for instructions.

Initially a grin spread maliciously across his face, and then dropped as quickly as it had appeared.

He said: "Yes sir," hung up, kicked open the door of the telephone kiosk and swore.

But he was a professional, and he organised himself and his back-up team, two of which had been waiting along Bardwell Road.

Chapter Thirteen

They had had one glass of wine after making love and another each as they bathed.

When they left the apartment, they both had their wax macs on and led their bikes out onto Bardwell Road.

Armour had a good look up and down the street and also at the surrounding houses – nothing seemed out of place or suspicious, No one seemed to be hanging around. They mounted their bikes and set off towards the city centre.

With only four main routes into the town centre, from Abingdon; from Swindon; from Stratford, Buckingham and Banbury, through Summertown, and London and Maidenhead, over the Magdalen Bridge, Armour guessed that each approach would be well monitored, and the simple fact they were a man and a woman, would mean they would be scrutinised more closely. He reckoned that it was probably going to be almost impossible to totally elude their pursuers in any case.

What he was concerned about was initially not to reveal where they were staying, which they had been lucky about and lucky to have kept secret this long, and more importantly, when they finally knew what they were going after and where, it would be good if they had a head start and some time – if they were lucky, it might just give them the chance to get away.

As they approached St. Giles, he led them in through the portals of St. John's College, to cut through to Parks Road – in the busy town it would help him to spot anyone on their tail. Everything seemed normal as they turned right under the famous replica of the Venetian Bridge of Sighs, and in to New College Lane.

A couple of turns and he nearly fell off his bike. He glanced up and had to steady himself on the pavement before stopping.

Mac came up on the outside and put a hand on his shoulder.

"What's up Pete, are you OK?"

"Yeah," he said looking up to the walls in the now rapidly dimming light, "You see the gargoyles up there. I remember Vasilli talking about them, particularly the one which has field mice eating the wheat that supports their nest, look at the second one along. He told me that was what he felt Russia was like. The regime had become corrupt and the rulers were taking advantage of the people in their lust for power, and determination to line their own pockets. He pointed at that gargoyle and said: 'They will bring themselves down,' and the way things are going in the east, he might well be right."

They pushed on, under the other arch of New College, into Queen's Lane. They turned left towards Magdalen.

Mac was in front and Armour was close behind. He heard the car engine steady about 30 yards behind them. There was nothing coming the other way. He glanced round, putting his hand out in an overtaking manner, and drew up alongside Mac.

The road with odd shops and offices on the left and college buildings on the right curved slightly to the right as it approached Magdalen Bridge.

"Get ready to turn left at the last moment into Longwall

Street," he said wobbling the bike again, as he looked up and added: "Christ, I think I've got it!"

Before he had a chance to explain any more the black Merc he had spotted a moment before sprang forward, a short screech emitted from the tyres as they momentarily lost traction. The engine revs rose menacingly with the acceleration. Both bikes wobbled.

The bullets that crashed into the right front fork, and tore through two spokes, ricocheting off the pavement, were obviously not meant to kill Armour, but he was not so sure about the one that just missed Mac's head.

Anyway, the idea was obviously to get Armour focussing on the job, and to remind him that they were on his tail again.

He knew that the fact the Mercedes had overtaken and sped off over Magdalen Bridge did not mean that they were now safe, or that their pursuers had in anyway lost interest. A new tail was now on them for sure.

And it was just as well that they had not been intent on killing them because Longwall Street was like a shooting gallery – a 150 yard quiet stretch of road with the high wall of Magdalen College on the right and solid buildings on the left with no apparent breaks, no alleyways or paths.

Pedalling for all they were worth, Armour was pleased when they were out of it, turning right and right again, and drawing up in the trees and college parkland just over the bridge across the River Cherwell.

Her bike thrown to the ground, Mac ran over to him and threw her arms around his neck. Dropping his machine, he grabbed her.

"It's OK… it's OK, we're safe," he tried to calm her shaking body.

"Safe…" she forced out the word in an abnormally high voice, "What makes you think that?"

He was stroking her back and the back of her head, and holding her closely.

"Because those were professionals and I know it's little consolation, but if we were supposed to be dead, we would have been by now." It was a pretty vain attempt to reassure her.

He felt he was trying to convince himself as well as her, but it was a logical argument.

That of course was not to say that at any time someone else, with a different motive, might take pot-shots and mean them to be lethal. They were having to fly by the seat of their pants, there was no other way. He had to keep Mac and himself mentally together, but he realised their quest would have to continue. Backing out and leaving Oxford now would not halt the pursuit, and in fact, might be a fatal error.

He was sickened by the continuous threat of danger to Mac. He was sure that Vasilli would not have expected this to happen. He had been in a desperate situation too, and would have presumed that having simply given the message to Armour, Mac would have been out of it. Armour would have known better. But then, it would have been better if Armour had kept Burricks and people from the *Chron* out of it altogether. He had to admit to himself that he seriously cocked up with his attempt to provide Vasilli with an alternative escape plan. But then one could not have foreseen the shoot-out at Flecknoe, or a host of other things that had happened.

Mac's body sagged into his. He sat her down on the grass and folded himself around her.

"Anyway," he said, when he thought she was ready, "I think I have got a lead on the next part of the clue."

She pulled her head back, and looked into his eyes.

"Yes … botany! It just struck me as we turned into Longwall Street… I looked up and saw the signs for the Botanic Gardens they're just before the bridge on the right, and on your details at the *Chron*, it says one of your interests is botany. Vasilli and I used to get a punt from just below Magdalen Bridge and go along by the Botanic Gardens. Maybe `Excelsior Reserve' is there, and we just have to go and look for it. It has to be that. I even remember Vasilli and I going there once or twice."

"Well that seems reasonable," she said, having calmed pretty quickly from her fright.

"I have been to the Botanic Gardens quite few times… it is possible that something there has a name like Excelsior Reserve. Excelsior is a fairly common name. But we won't be able to go there tonight, it'll have to be tomorrow."

They agreed that they would be there as soon as it opened in the morning. The main job now was to take some food back to the apartment, and try to lose the tail that was now bound to be on them. Armour had a few ideas.

Armour said he thought it would be reasonably safe to walk some of the way up towards St. Giles, but he was not sure and kept a wary eye out.

People were coming towards them away from the main shopping centre, and behind them was a sophisticated middle-aged woman with one of those bags on wheels it appears mainly middle-aged women use for shopping.

They approached St. Giles and turned right.

Two men in their path just stood there. Two swarthy, unshaven men in their thirties, wearing black leather jackets and jeans.

Armour and Mac stopped… they were about fifteen yards from the two men.

Armour was slightly sickened when things started to go into slow motion. Things went bad when that happened. He saw the hands go into their jackets chest high, and he knew what was going to come out. From this distance and now relying on street lighting, he could not tell the type of weapons they had, but he could see them being raised to shoulder height in front of them. This was it… he grabbed Mac and turned her away with his back to the men… he waited for the bang.

But what he actually heard was two tell-tale 'phutts' that are characteristic of a gun with a silencer and what he also heard was the unique breath of a bullet, then another, passing within a couple of inches of his ear.

He was turned away from the two men, but when he opened his eyes, he saw that sophisticated middle-aged woman pointing a silenced automatic.

"Better run," she hissed at him.

He looked round to see both of the assailants lying on the pavement. He looked back at the woman, but she had already turned on her heel and walk back the way she came.

Somewhat stiffly, but sure-footedly, Armour picked up their two bikes, forced the smaller into Mac's hands and turned her, so that they crossed briskly, and without turning back, into Beaumont Street, and down passed the Randolph Hotel and the Playhouse Theatre.

They heard a scream and the gabble of a gathering crowd behind them… they kept going.

Through gritted teeth, and in low tones, she said: "I thought you said they weren't trying to kill us… what is happening?

He stopped and turned, leaning the bike so the cross-bar rested against his backside.

He took hold of her shoulders.

"Someone was trying to kill us, and someone is protecting us. But at least now, there are two less of those trying to kill us"

"You are not trying to be funny, are you?" she quizzed.

"No! The fact is, we are still in danger, but I wish I knew

which people were on our side. Even if I rang my controller, and let's say, for instance, he was one of those who just tried to finish us off, he would obviously say that the reverse was true, that I could trust him and that we could come in out of the cold. And if he was on our side, he would say the same, so we have still got to try and go it alone. It is the only way at the moment…Come on, let's move."

She could see he was right. She just wanted to get back to the apartment. She felt safe there.

They turned right, and then a little later right again into Little Clarendon Street. Armour couldn't see anyone follow, but knew that they must be. He doubled them back and then turned right again – no one had changed direction with them… smarter than that.

He quickened the pace slightly, and said: "Ready to ride?" it was more like an order.

"Follow me close."

Any question of food seem totally irrelevant by now… they would make do with what they had in the apartment.

She agreed and they set off.

He cut right into an alleyway, out over a road and left. He scoured the right hand side and then suddenly stopped, peering through the darkness. He turned into the drive of a very large house, which looked if it was split into student flats. She followed as they pedalled alongside the house, through the back garden to a low wall. They hitched the bikes over the wall and carried along another alleyway. They crossed the Woodstock Road, along a bit and then again into someone's garden…

This was not as crazy or haphazard as it appeared, as Mac found out later, Armour had sussed out this route earlier, eyeballing part of it, and getting the rest from the map he had found in the apartment.

Soon they were at Bardwell Road, and Armour was more

careful than ever as they approached the apartment. Just as they entered the path alongside the house, Armour noticed someone cross the junction at the end of the road… it could have been anyone.

Soon they were inside.

Before switching any lights on, Armour was at the window, peering out into the darkness, but all seemed quiet. He made sure the heavy drapes were securely in place before flicking the switches.

Mac fell into his arms, and then stiffened as they heard a soft knock at the back door.

She stood, with just her head peering round the living room door as Armour stepped through the kitchen towards the back door… on his way, he picked up a small grocery knife that lay on the work surface, reached down and slid it in his sock.

"Who's there?" he called through the closed door.

"I've got a message from Mick… open up, mate…"

"Mick who?"

"Oh come on mate, stop fucking about, you know damn well Mick who!"

He opened the door. He reasoned that he had little choice. They knew where they were now, this guy would only come back with a small army, and anyway, he might just be on the right side… abrasive though he was.

He backed away from the door and the man entered. They all look the same he thought though this guy wore a heavy wax jacket, black roll-neck jumper and jeans, edged in to the hall. He was thin and wiry, and had tense nervous eyes, that took in everything at a glance.

The hand that he had behind him, he brought in front of him, and it contained a small automatic.

"What's the message?" Armour demanded without retreating further. He did not want this guy in the place.

"Nice gaff, mate," said Calder-Maynes' man in his south London accent – he pushed Armour back up the steps and into the kitchen.

"Look," Armour said, trying to appear assertive and in control, "What's the message? Tell me and get out of here."

"In a moment, not so fast, unless you hadn't noticed, mate, I'm the one holding the piece." Carter leered in Mac's direction.

"Nice" he said again, " I can see why you are taking your time over this and getting everyone worked up. Nice gaff, smart bird, people protecting you. We did well for you today, didn't we?" he lied, "So whose side are you on? Mick can't understand why you're sticking on your own… I do, but Mick doesn't. He thinks you are either now working for yourself, or the other side… so which is it? Whether I shoot you and the little lady now depends on your answer," said Carter.

Armour was well ahead of this guy. He had no sanction to kill them right then, he was just trying to scare. Mick just wanted to know whether he had any information, or was about to have, if indeed he was working for Mick. Armour decided the truth would ring truest.

"I know that Vasilli came to Oxford before he was killed in Northampton. The police found an Oxford bus ticket on him."

"So why bring the girl?"

"Because he gave her a clue, meant for me, only I can't decipher it."

"We could help," Carter waved the gun from side to side.

"I don't think so, it was obviously meant for me, and I am going to have to work it out. If Mick really is looking after me then he will let me run with this. I'm not stupid. I know there are people out there trying to kill us. It's obvious there is a mole in the organisation – look at all the things that have gone wrong over the past two or three years. The real opposition would not be risking so much over this. It has to be the people who have gone bad on us, whoever they are. So give Mick my message. Leave it with me.

"Maybe we will have it sorted in the next day or so, but I appreciate the protection anyway…"

This seemed to settle the man and he relaxed, and best of all, he did not come any further in.

"OK I'll be back in the morning. I'll see what Mick has to say, and I guess he would like me with you from now on. I'll be close by anyway, so don't try anything stupid, remember we're keeping this gaff cased," and he backed away to the door, opened it behind him, and went out into the darkness.

"Yes Bryan, what can I do for you…?," he said and then heard the familiar, but louder and rougher bark than usual down the earpiece.

"Calm down Bryan, it's hard to make out what you are saying, this is a bad line anyway," said Staveley-Smythe… at last he had done it!

It had been Calder-Maynes' men who had approached Armour and Willans in the Street, but it was one of his agents who had taken them out. It was great. And what was Calder-Maynes going to say he wondered.

"Staveley-fucking-shitface-Smythe," Calder-Maynes spat his venom and spittle through his teeth as he spoke, "I have not taken any of your guys out, the odd civilian, but never one of your own. Are you trying to declare war on me!"

"It would have been very constructive to kill Armour and the girl in the street would it?" said Staveley-Smythe with condescending irony.

"You sometimes amaze me Bryan, with your 'bull in a china shop' approach to some things. How could you allow your men to go this far. None of us would have ever be sure about the documents and what has happened to them if you start taking out key players.

Those dummies deserved what they got, and I would do it again. I really think you are bloody losing it sometimes, Bryan."

"Fuck you, you weak willed little wanker, you better be careful," blasted Calder-Maynes with very real and heartfelt threat. His face red and his eyes bulging, he slammed the phone down in its cradle so hard it flew out again. He retrieved it and slammed it down again and again – the line was long since dead.

It suddenly struck Staveley-Smythe that Calder-Maynes might have truly flipped. He would be dangerous, and unpredictable.

The old warrior spent some time on the phone to others who had been at the Flecknoe meeting. The conversations were long and involved and at times heated.

When he came off the phone, Calder-Maynes had been livid. His face was flushed and he headed for the drinks cabinet and poured himself a generous portion of scotch and swilled it down. As it hit the back of his throat with a familiar bite and the warmth filtered through his chest and into his stomach, he slowly calmed. The men he had lost were unknown to him personally, but it was the principle. And he did have difficulty in condoning their action in broad daylight in a busy street. It was pretty silly, and he would have to speak severely to Carter about the people he was using. He was not happy that Staveley-Smythe's people had made him look stupid, but it was not worth getting worked up about any more. The only thing that mattered was the right result, and what happened might just shake Armour up enough to get on with it. He did understand now, from Carter that Armour did not know what the papers contained or where they were. But he was on the trail. They would have to keep close tabs on him from now on in.

"Two things," said Mac, who seemed strong and assertive – Carter's visit having the opposite effect to that which Armour had expected,

"We are not unprotected, and secondly, I could probably arrange another place like this in Oxford, and just as safe. It would take them a little while to find it."

Mac actually felt she could do something useful, and that again made her feel good. It was OK for Pete to take control in situations, but she had found them this place. She had the contact, and could do it again. She knew she could, but she would still not be able to tell Armour about it. That would probably gnaw at him, but she knew she could not reveal anything about that, not as things were anyway… it depended in the future, if there was one, and on Armour himself… if only he knew it.

"Er…what exactly do you mean… we are not unprotected?

She smiled. He loved that. She crooked her forefinger and beckoned him to follow. She led him to a bookcase, the base of which was part of the wall… or so he had thought.

She felt along the rim of the base of the bookcase and pressed a hidden button.

Armour's mouth dropped open as he gazed on a shelf of weaponry.

There was a Walther PPK, a Smith and Wesson, a 357 Magnum, and a disassembled high-powered rifle.

"There's bullets in the compartment below," said Mac.

"Listen Mac, I know you don't want to talk about this, but promise me that some day you'll tell me the full story about this, because I can't wait to hear it…"

Although not a gun expert, Armour had experience of various kinds of weaponry, and these matters often cropped up in debrief situations. He knew his way around most of these pieces.

"I hope we don't have to use any of this stuff," he told Mac, "I'm no expert…"

She said she was glad to hear it. Armour did not pursue the matter of finding other accommodation, because he had his own ideas.

She thought he might. She had her own plan, and decided not to pursue the matter at that moment.

Armour picked up the Magnum, loaded it, made sure the safety was on and swung it round his forefinger like a cowboy's six-gun.

"Just let that little shit come back and I'll show him," he said.

There was a knock at the door…

Armour checked the chamber, released the safety and went to the back door, This time he was the one with his right arm behind his back.

The security chain was on, so when he unlocked the Yale, it only opened three inches.

A PPK poked through – he recognised it.

"Let me in mate, or it is going to be a cold night for me. You wouldn't want that would you?"

The Magnum came from behind his back and he pushed it through the gap…

"Fuck you, asshole," came the reply from Armour, as the barrel jerked under the leather jacketed guy's nostril, and made his eyes water.

"Christ…where did that come from…we didn't think you were armed…?

"Just go away sonny…come back in the morning, not too early, let's say nine-thirty, and maybe we can talk…would that suit you?" he asked jabbing the gun more firmly into Carter's face

"Seems more than good to me" he said and turned, bravely on his heel and walked away… he felt he had done well to survive.

Armour shut the door firmly, and returned to the lounge where Mac was waiting.

"He just called to say goodnight and sleep well, and that he would see us in the morning, said Armour.

"Pete, you used the Magnum, and if there was anyone who does not need a penis extension it is you…"

"Yeah, I couldn't help it."

Her soft small brown nipples puckered as his lips swept slowly over first the left and then right, with his tongue flicking out making them glisten with cold wetness.

They were soon naked in the dim cosiness of the lounge. Armour had replaced the Magnum in the secret compartment, but it still lay open.

His feeling was strange and exciting. There was no doubt that he had been excited, exhilarated even, by his encounter with the gunman. It was something to do with ancient tribal, warrior or hunting instincts…and Mac felt it too. Not just in herself, but now in the way Armour moved, held her and caressed her.

He dominated physically. He lifted her, moved her, turned her, rolled her and controlled her. She did not have to do anything, and it was bliss. He had all the right moves and touched all the right places at the right time.

She whimpered as he rolled them off the sofa where she had been on top, onto the pillows on the floor, and he came down on top, ramming into her even deeper as they hit.

It was then fast and furious, and she felt as though the top of her head would blow with sheer sexual ecstasy. She could feel by his pace and the tensions rippling through his body that they were reaching a massive climax… and she was there too. Her head was swimming and she saw stars and flashing lights, and she slapped his buttocks almost brutally, and drew him in so deep when his muscles contracted wildly and uncontrollably, shaking her as much as him, although, at the same time, she could hear herself calling out, but strangely couldn't focus on the words.

Over wine and a snack they talked and worked out a plan for the morning. They had an early start. Mac decided that her's would start slightly earlier… with a phone call…

Mac couldn't help going over the happenings of the past 24 hours – it swung from beautiful dream through thrill and excitement to… nightmare.

One minute she was making love with the first man that had really meant anything to her, and the next she watched two men die at her feet. She had trouble coming to terms with that. She had not checked with Armour, but she hoped that this was not the sort of thing that happened to him all the time in his 'second job'.

Surely, if she survived this ordeal, and stayed with him, which is what she would like, she wouldn't always have to live in fear? She wanted him, but did not think she could cope with too much of that. It would be a mad roller-coaster – no one could live that way.

She slept fitfully, each time she woke, she reached out to make sure he was there, the one thing she would not cope with in these circumstances was if Armour was not there.

He was her strength. Fact is, he was more than that. He was her heart and soul. Right at that moment, he was more to her than she was to her-self… if that made sense…

She woke, and reached across the bed. It was warm, but he was not there. She sat bolt upright and listened… and she heard a movement in the sitting room, the door was open.

Reaching for the PPK that Armour had loaded and put on the floor by the head of the bed where he had been sleeping, she flicked the safety off as he had shown her. She pushed the duvet aside and went to the door and peered around, he was at the window watching the street.

He heard her movement and threw the curtain aside and raised the Magnum, lowering it again instantly.

"It's 1.30 am, and I know what you need…" she said.

Fact was it was what she needed too, and it got them both to sleep.

Her body clock, which many times she had been able to rely upon, woke her at 5 am, and she went to the kitchen and made herself instant coffee. She drank and thought long and hard, then made the call…

Her explanation had been concise but complete, as far as it could be… her life was threatened.

She need not have said any more, the voice on the other end of the line was calm and gentle… she had always found it so. But the instructions he gave were clear, they would have to move fast.

Mac ran to the bedroom.

"Pete, Pete," she said as she shook him awake. "Pete, do you trust me."

"Yes, of course I do."

"Then get up and get ready. We have a way out of here, and we have somewhere to stay, but we have got to be ready in fifteen minutes… a car is coming for us."

"Mac, that's great," he uttered and questioned, "but aren't they going to spot a car pulling up outside?"

"No, that's just it, they won't see a car pulling up outside. Trust me, come on, get ready."

It actually didn't take them all that long… they didn't have that much with them anyway. She quickly made a sandwich and they had half each with a slurp of coffee, and she led the way out the back door. Armour had picked up the PPK.

The small courtyard at the rear of the property was surrounded by a high wall, which ensured that the back door was not overlooked. In one corner, a huge, thick, ivy creeper clung to the wall, from top to bottom. She led them to it and started pulling it away from the wall. It was not actually attached to the wall there, only near the top. Behind, there was a small door, not rusty and stuck, but clean and well maintained. She turned and pushed the door which opened inwards and she went through, he followed and closed the door behind him.

They found themselves in a large garage workshop, with room for two cars, and apart from the large up-and-over door there was a small ordinary door at the side near the front. There were tools, equipment, and a small settee. The up and over door had two small portholes at head height.

Armour walked forward to check the side door, it was locked, but there was a key in it.

"We must wait here for a few minutes. The area is being checked, and a car will be here shortly," she said.

"Did you know about this before?"

"No. The apartment, yes, but this way out, no."

"So who is helping us Mac, and why?"

"I can't tell you Pete. Certainly not at the moment. Believe me I have been sworn to secrecy, and I will honour that. It is something to do with the time I lived here, nothing bad, more …sensitive."

"Well, this sensitive bloke has some class, I'll say that for him."

"Oh yes, that is certainly true."

"OK Mac, I said I trust you, and I do. I won't pry," but he was not used to this feeling, and he was itching to know who was behind this set up. Luxury apartments, secret exits, checking the area, cars ready to pick up at a moment's notice.

"Can I ask who is checking the area?"

"It will be the driver. There are companies that provide a driver and complete security. They are highly trained for all situations."

"Mac, this kind of 'service' comes very highly priced, who?"

"Pete, I love you, but I am not telling, so don't try to turn this into Twenty Questions. Let's leave it."

And with that a large black Jag with slightly smoked windows pulled quietly up outside, and a black guy in a smart suit got out and came to the side door and knocked three times then a gap and knocked again.

"Let him in Pete,"

He turned the key and let the man in.

He was about 5ft11 and only slightly more stocky than average. He moved easily and looked Armour up and down, and then to Mac.

He addressed his comments to her without titles or pleasantries: "The name's William. We have got to move fast. There are cars cruising and people watching the front of Bardwell Road. I need you to get in the back of the car and keep low until I say."

They did as he said. He locked the garage door and slid the key back underneath. The car door nearest to them was open and they all got in.

He drove off calmly, not wanting to attract unnecessary attention. His eyes narrowed as he peered in the rear view mirror, and saw a black Mercedes slowly round the bend, then suddenly pick up speed.

"Shit," he said through his teeth, "We must have been made by someone on the roof somewhere."

He gunned the car up to about 60 mph, and the Merc was coming up fast. He mounted a drop kerb using the pavement to make a left. The Merc was close.

William swung the car first left and then full lock right, off the accelerator, on with the handbrake, into second gear, off with the handbrake, foot on the juice.

In this manoeuvre, he had completed a 180 degree turn, with the Merc passing them midway through. Before the Merc driver realised it wasn't an accident, they were in another road.

William pulled into a driveway and round to the back of a house.

"Quick, get into that BMW," he said, and obediently they got into the back of the metallic grey five series BMW, with dark glass windows.

As they drove calmly out of the driveway they saw the Merc screech past. William turned sedately in the opposite direction.

"That was some driving William," said Armour.

"Yeah," was all he would say, but he had a small satisfied smile on his face.

'It sure was," he thought to himself, 'sometimes the pursuit car suddenly goes the wrong way and broadsides you midway through that manoeuvre... messy and expensive, but that one had been sweet as pie...'

He drove silently on. Mac and Armour looked at each other, and Armour put his hand over Mac's and squeezed it, motions not missed by William.

He cut back across the Banbury Road and passed the University and Pitt Rivers Museum, along St. Cross Road, along that stretch of Longwall Street, and left over the Magdalen Bridge, round the island and a short way along Iffley Road. He took a left and left again to the rear of some four and five storey homes, and then right into a mews-style road. Outside one of them, William pressed a remote and drove the car into a garage which magically opened, and then closed behind them.

He got out, flipped the light switch, and then opened the car door for Mac.

He went to a small cupboard by a door to the house, took out a key and opened the door to the house, and then handed her the key, an envelope and the remote.

"Just as you go in, if you would be so kind, could you trip the remote to let me out, and again to close it."

"Yes of course," she said and smiled, "and thanks William."

"No worries," he said, and Mac watched the car disappear before re-closing the garage door with the remote. Again there was transportation… two Honda 90s, each slightly bigger than a moped. The helmets were on a shelf above.

"Blake, Blake, what the hell is going on?" asked Staveley-Smythe

"Not quite clear sir. Since Randell, dressed as a middle-aged woman took out the two mechanics it has become very warm around here. We have come across other teams we recognise…some we have worked with before. I saw a bloke called Carter, an ex-mercenary and a particularly nasty piece of work. I heard he had got out of minor wars and into private hits. Have you got more men involved sir? You should have told me"

"No, I haven't Blake, but I know who has."

"Do you require action?"

"Not unless your men, or Armour or the girl are directly threatened."

"That's another thing sir. We had a lead on them through one of the other teams. And in fact very briefly we saw them early this morning being driven by a coloured guy in a big black Jag. We gave chase, but we lost them. We think there might have been a car switch, but that would have required some heavy duty outside help. I thought they were pretty much on their own?"

"Christ, I underestimated Armour," said Staveley-Smythe out loud, knowing that the longer this went on, the harder it was going to be to keep him alive, although he was almost beginning to think it would be cleaner if he were terminated. Certainly they could not afford for the papers to get into the wrong hands.

"Look, try and get back on their tails. They are likely to be picking up a package soon, and time is running out. We need to have them under surveillance when they make the pick-up… it's vital Blake. Do you need more men?"

"Well, the more men the more eyes I suppose."

"I'll arrange it. Report in this evening, about six-thirty."

"Right sir," said Blake, pushing his way out of a telephone box in Little Clarendon Street, and climbing into a basic Sierra L, which just happened to have a Cosworth engine under the bonnet.

"Bryan, tell me straight, did your guys pick up Armour and the girl this morning?"

"I wish to God they did!"

"Who did then?"

"I don't know. It means there is another player in the game. And that means that someone else probably knows what the game is about, which means that it is definitely going to get messy unless we can clean up quickly."

Calder-Maynes went on: "It would almost be safer to terminate them as soon as we spot them."

"Not clever Bryan. What if there are copies, and what if those copies are on the way to the Home Office or the newspapers.

"I'm not too worried about that. I think I might be able to control that to some degree, even if the papers are found. The problem is allowing them to back it up by telling their stories. And especially now that there would appear to be someone else involved. I don't like that."

"Who could that be though?"

"I don't know Michael. We knew where they were, we had a flat surrounded this morning and we are having difficulty finding out who owns it… or rather, who really owns it. Then, all of sudden they are spotted jumping into a Jag and driving off at speed.

"The flat had a small courtyard at the back, with a secret door behind climbing ivy, leading to a garage on another street – almost a purpose-built getaway route."

"My God, and you say you don't know who owns the building?"

"Well, we have traced it to a property company, but they handle hundreds of properties up and down the country for all kinds of people, and some of them are very private."

"Perhaps you might have better luck," said Sir Bryan, giving Staveley-Smythe details of the address.

He added: "It is important to find out who this is, because it is pretty obvious that they will have been moved to another pretty secure house, or if they are really clever, well away from Oxford altogether. So, once we know who owns the place the more chance we can close in to the next likely address."

"OK Bryan, we should be able to sort this out fairly quickly. I'll get back to you," said Staveley-Smythe and he hung up. He lifted the receiver again and dialled a number.

Chapter Fourteen

Armour made a quick survey, taking special notice of the possible entries and exits, and whether or not they were overlooked from any direction… they weren't.

Again, luxury was not in question… the decor, furnishing and facilities were outstanding. The property was quite small, but no expense was spared in making it comfortable. Again it had been impeccably looked after, if not necessarily used all the time.

But it was still early morning and Armour did not want to stay around the house when vital work needed sorting.

One good thing was that they were actually quite close to the Botanic Gardens.

They stood in the garage looking down at the Honda 90s.

"Do you know how to handle one of these things?" Mac asked Armour, and went on,

"They're dead simple, I had one when I worked on the *Mail* – best way to get around, like a bicycle, but faster."

"Well, I have to say that I prefer four wheels to two, but I have ridden bikes… I had an old Norton Commando with cow-handles."

"What are they?"

"Handle-bars which stuck up like cow horns… very high in street-cred in the Sixties I'll have you know."

Armour Piercing

It took them just five minutes to cross back over Magdalen Bridge and turn left in front of the gardens. There was no admission charge and they started walking through stopping momentarily by a plinth which had a simple map and explanation of what was being grown in which areas. It was obvious that the beds in the front section were in a regular grid layout, but behind that were less formal herbaceous borders and rock gardens, and then lining the river's edge were glasshouses containing more exotic plants.

There was virtually no one about. They had been wandering for about ten minutes...

"I know it is supposed to do with Scotch, so my guess is the rock gardens and heathers might be a good place to start," suggested Mac, and she headed off, and Armour followed, but lagged behind as he thought of the times he and Vasilli had hired a punt from under the bridge, and made their way beside Christ Church meadow, or having rounded the island, made their way back passed Magdalen College.

Vasilli had taken to this pastime on warm afternoons packing a picnic, and bottle of wine. He particularly enjoyed it because some of the female students, attracted by his Eastern European accent and strong features, seemed eager companions for he and Pete.

As they worked their way round with Mac checking plant names, Armour kept his eye out on the entrance and watched people on the bridge, particularly anyone who loitered – he could see nothing out of place.

As they wandered around, separated from the river by a high wall, Armour spotted a gnarled old tree about 15 feet high in the corner, and he recognised it.

Another couple entered the gardens and slowly made their way to the greenhouse area next to the river, and just the other side of the wall.

He quickened his step until he was close to Mac.

"Hey, you see that old tree. Vasilli and I walked through here one time with a couple of girls, heading for the punts… and he reached up, and put his hand into one of those holes in the trunk and brought out a bottle of Côtes du Rhône, as if by magic it certainly impressed the girls.

"I'll bet you two did. Did you do any work while you were 'studying' here," said Mac, and added, "That's an ash tree, Fraxinus … probably … EX..CEL..SIOR, of course!!!"

Sure enough, a label tacked on to the tree, just above eye level confirmed what Mac has said, helpfully adding 'Pendula' and 'c.1800'.

There were several openings in the dark bark, but only one was really accessible, and it would be quite a stretch.

Armour looked around and then reached up and into the bowels of the tree. At first there was nothing except the dampness of the bark, and his fingers touched what he guessed were a few slugs and woodlice, but then he felt something man-made and familiar… polythene.

He gripped his find and it came free from the tree. A polythene bag with some papers inside. Without looking too closely, Armour wiped away some wet bark, droplets of water and shook off a slug, and slipped the package under his jumper, lodging it under his belt.

Quickly, and somewhat furtively, he looked around to see if anyone had spotted his unusual behaviour.

He led Mac through a gap in the wall so they were on the river side, but quickly they made their way towards the bridge and the entrance to the gardens.

The safest bet was to get back to the house. They put on their helmets, they would be the best disguises they could have at the moment. They led their 90s up the slope to the main road, kicked them into life and waiting for a gap in the busy traffic turned right towards Iffley Road, and the mews house.

As Armour sorted out the remote and stowed away the bikes, Mac had gone through to the kitchen and flipped on the kettle.

Armour came in and threw the documents onto the table… somehow not eager to read what was in them. Would it simply lead them into more trouble? Would it mean more danger for Mac? He didn't want that. Above all he did not want her hurt.

She sensed his reluctance and watched as he left to go to the toilet.

When he returned she had already opened the bag and was staring at the documents.

One didn't have to be very sharp to get the relevance, she held them out to him.

"I guess this is pretty important. If this is true, our Vasilli certainly opened up one big can of worms," she said.

Armour read over her shoulder, and was slightly surprised that none of this material bore the familiar 'top secret', plus a classification number, for the level of 'eyes only' it was meant to have. There was nothing.

But then as he worked his way through he realised why that was.

The main lead-in document read:

PURPOSE: The governments of the world, major conglomerates, top companies and organisations, and even influential and affluent individuals, are prepared to pay for the information and services your organisation resources, processes and executes… with minor alterations. For the decisions you have to make, there is a ready market, often simply based on timing. You have been carefully, vetted, selected, and notified of this meeting because you have expressed an interest in the commercial potential of our expertise.

FAO.: Cmdr. J.H.P

CC: Sir B. C-M; M. S-S; C.C.; M. McM; Cdr. B F-S; Mjr. J.K.; Capt. J.G.D.; H.R.F.; and J.M.C.'

There were a few auxiliary notes with dates and venues qualifications and responsibilities of the names above, and finally to a question:

The Way Ahead?'

The second document was a backgrounder detailing some of the latest operations where there had been a profit to be made, and Armour recognised at least two of them were defections where a liquidation had taken place, and deep shit had hit the internal fan at MI6. They had regarded it as something going drastically, but coincidentally, wrong.

There were also several operations which had gone according to plan, but where the timing had been changed, either delayed or brought forward – in each case, at short notice.

Another document outlined various 'hot spots' around the world, including Northern Ireland, the Middle East, North and South Korea, China, and various sub-Saharan places around the African continent. There was speculation about political situations and who with a little help, and a 'hit' or two, would be able to pay large amounts, probably in diamonds or gold. There was even a sort of business plan showing a profit and loss projection for the first five years, which included major expansion of the group – there were no losses, very few costs, and the projected profit line was astronomical.

These guys, and it would appear Mick was among them, were prepared to not only use government resources for their own ends, but actually create scenarios, mainly in underdeveloped, Second or Third World countries, where the group could have involvement manipulate the situation to someone's benefit, and rake it in.

It was developing a commercial spy world within the spy world… as if it wasn't complicated enough.

At the base of the page it said in bold type: 'This document must not leave the meeting room – it will be retained for shredding.'

How had Vasilli got a copy? There must have been a meeting of the group of names at the top of the paper, at the Flecknoe safe house the day before Armour was due there.

Vasilli must have come across the meeting room when the shooting started, read the documents and pinched a copy. He obviously realised the importance, took them, possibly for 'insurance', and then decided to hide it for Armour to pick up later if things went wrong… and they certainly had.

The other trouble was, who else was involved. Who were these other names at the top of the paper?

Armour was now worried about the time element. Once people knew that the documents had been found, and somehow, they would, things would really start to hot up. He hoped that they had not be spotted coming back to the mews, but the moment he and Mac left Oxford people would know that the game was over. Time would run out very quickly for them.

So, the other thing he needed to sort out with Mac was what they were going to do. He was worried about her. She did not need to be involved any further – he doubted they were going to get out of this alive.

This was going to be difficult to explain.

The larder at the mews had been well-stocked and they did not have to go out again.

Mac had been quiet since they found the documents, and now busied herself, making food, while Armour sipped wine and browsed through the Vasilli's bombshell papers.

Peter Aengenheister

There was a serious problem. Whilst the discussion document made a statement, and an investigator, given the names at the top, would have plenty to work on, on the other hand, there was not too much to read. It was all typed… no handwritten notes even, and all unverified. It was not proof of anything. In fact it could simply be someone's notes for a spy thriller. But it was one hell of an idea, and even if Armour didn't know those other initials, or names at the top, someone surely would.

If this was not a fake document, one had to suppose that whoever initiated this, had good reason to think that the people mentioned would go ahead.

And if that was the case there was good reason to assume that they were also already collaborators in other enterprises.

The determination of some people to get their hands on these documents had led to the deaths of five people in the past couple of days Vasilli, Burricks, Grogan, and the two gunmen in St. Giles. It certainly gave weight the theory that the documents were authentic.

Armour knew that he was going to have to go high-up to sort this out, and even if he found someone to listen to him, how would he know they were high enough?

They could now leave Oxford, which was a worry, because if they were seen doing so, it would mean they had found what they came for and probably had it on them.

He guessed, probably correctly, that those after them, in those circumstances would be expected to get the evidence, and that he and Mac would no longer be relevant… and considering they knew the contents of the documents, should be disposed of.

He was pleased he had not contacted Mick… his sixth sense had probably saved them.

Armour shared his thoughts with Mac… even his fears about their expendability.

Chapter Fifteen

Calder-Maynes had been wracking his brain, trying to sort out the possible implications of their new 'player'. Could it have been the Russians? His men had seen known agents in the area. That was not particularly unusual and they would certainly have an interest.

But that would have declined since Vasilovski's death. Calder-Maynes' men had reported their presence, but that they had maintained a very low profile.

The trouble was they did not know what friends that Armour and the Willans girl had. They could be important, or they could just have money, or be very influential. Either way it was a worrying twist, no longer a simple cat-and-mouse game.

Calder-Maynes was still deep in thought when the phone went, and it rang three rings before he lifted it from the cradle.

"Yes," he said. He never used his name, which irritated many people, not least Staveley-Smythe, although the deep tones of his voice were unmistakable.

"Bryan, we could be in a spot of bother, and this could turn messier than we ever imagined."

"Just fucking tell me." Calder-Maynes hated drama-builders.

"The nearest we could get to an actual name is 'the estate of the Duchy of Cornwall'."

"Jesus H. You don't mean they've got the bloody Prince of Wales, the fucking next monarch of this country, helping them. Oh my God."

"I didn't actually say that Bryan, but it could be. It is possible…"

"Well, does the Duchy own any other properties in the vicinity?"

"As a matter of fact it does, a mews place off the Cowley Road. We are on the way there to, check it out," said Staveley-Smythe, giving him the address, but avoiding telling Sir Bryan that he had given his men a good three quarters of an hour before his call.

They should be there now!

Who do you go to when you reckon members of your country's secret service have gone into business for themselves?

Mac reasoned that the only course of action which guarantees a result, is to go right to the top…

"What, you mean head of the secret service? Or do you mean Cieran Carmichael, the Home Secretary?" he asked.

"Well, if you go any lower, they might be involved. I mean, do you know who this Sir B. C-M might be?

"Well, there is General Sir Bryan Calder-Maynes, who acts as a consultant to the MoD, on strategic policy and planning. He would certainly have top security clearance."

But if he were involved it would mean that in this country, it was not just MI5 or the security services, that were working this, it could be far broader – he looked again at the names and the piece which showed their area of responsibility. Some general references could have meant forces involvement, others were more vague, and some had not specific area of responsibility.

It was a little after midday and they went into the kitchen. He sat on a bar stool at the breakfast unit as she warmed up a ready meal.

"I have to say, I think, whatever we do," he looked up from the papers and gazed out of the window. "We have got to make our move by tomorrow... considering the possible scale and importance. Time is running out, and the fact that they probably haven't got a tail on us at the moment, might mean that those involved will bring all their resources to bear.

"Whilst this," he added, holding up the documents, "is not proof, it would certainly be embarrassing to some very important people – shit will hit the fan," and then in a softly mocking, but not malicious way, he added, "... I don't suppose you happen to know where the Home Secretary might be tomorrow, it would be awfully decent if he could spare us a few moments of his time?"

As he said this he was walking towards the front door. He had seen a small duffle bag there and taking it from the hook walked back, pulling the drawstrings open. He picked up the papers, replaced them in Vasilli's polythene cover, slipped them into the bag and threw it onto the sofa.

"No I don't," she said, "But I think I know someone who does."

"... And can help?"

"Yes, I think so."

She went to the phone, lifted the receiver, and dialled. Armour, whilst trying not to appear too obvious, craned his neck to get a glimpse of the number she was calling, but had missed the first four digits, the code, but mentally noted the last six numbers.

"Hello... yes, it's me. Yes, I'm safe at the moment, but it's vital now that I... we, see you as soon as possible, something of the utmost importance... importance to the country."

She was silent and listening as she gradually turned and lifted her eyes to him.

"Yes, he is with me…" she listened once more, "Yes, he is very important to me."

Slightly embarrassed, and because this part of the conversation was about him, Armour rose and went to the kitchen, lifted the kettle to check there was water in it, flicked on the switch and got two cups down from a shelf.

He could hear her muted conversation, and in a way was desperate to hear what they were saying.

On the other hand he knew that he was the important one. he could read it in her eyes, feel it in her body language. He had no reason to feel insecure about Mac. She loved him, and even if this was a former lover, it was clear it was over between them, however close they remained as friends.

In a way Armour felt happier about their mystery friend than he had been since they arrived in Oxford, which he had to remember, was only two days before. Mac listened again for a few moments and then added: "I would like to, if you really don't mind… I did promise, and I will stick to our agr…thanks."

Armour heard her say: "Yes… yes… yes, right… yes… OK" and then a few moments later the conversation came to an end and he heard the click as she replaced the receiver.

Chapter Sixteen

She came into the kitchen and smiling, she picked up her coffee and led him back into the lounge.

"Thank you Pete, you are a beautiful man, and I love you."

He was not used to being called that and he flushed.

"I love you… as I have loved no other," she said and he knew she meant it, and then she added, "Because he knows how we are, because I told him how we are, and because it looks as if you will have to meet him, he has said he believes it would be 'appropriate' for me to tell you now, who he is and about me and him."

Armour, at first, did not like the sound of this… it was more than a little daunting.

Who was this eminent, almost unmentionable in the same breath as other mortals, person that seemed to have some sort of hold on Mac, not threatening, but controlling…

He clearly seemed to have extraordinary wealth, power, and resources at his disposals, and had been using it to Mac and Armour's benefit, and… unstintingly.

Mac led him back to the lounge, in the circumstances, the bedroom was not appropriate, and sat him down. She sat by his feet and gently stroked his thighs as she told the story. It was long, complicated and quite, quite, amazing.

When she had completed it, Mac went to the kitchen, where she had noticed some scotch earlier, and poured a healthy portion for each of them.

When she re-entered the lounge he was in the same position on the sofa, but his head was lolling back on the cushions and he was rubbing his temples, but he looked up and smiled. Just momentarily she felt a pang of pain as she felt that something between them had been lost perhaps, but it quickly diffused as she realised that he was perfectly OK, but had other things on his mind.

He had been fascinated by Mac's story. It had been one of coincidence, some fairy-tale, but genuine feeling and deep affection. With the personalities involved Armour should perhaps not have been too surprised… in fact there were probably quite a few young women in Mac's unique 'club'…a little disapproval clouded Armour's thoughts, but he was a realist and it cleared quickly.

And the fact was that this long past, but strangely never likely to be totally dead relationship, was proving incredibly, and now understandably useful to them both.

Armour had always been pragmatic, and certainly had no problems with the past, less so if it was going to help them now.

He was as sure as he ever was going to be, of his relationship with Mac. And even with 'His' help, they were still going to take some saving from their current dilemma.

"So what happens now Mac? I heard you seem to take down instructions. Has he a way to help us out of this… that was what the call was for in the first place, wasn't it? And you did say we were likely to meet."

Armour had to accept that he had a personal fascination in meeting the man. He was known and respected the world over…and ridiculed by some. But he had always kept his head above it all.

"Yes…we have to use the old Honda 90s. We haven't got far to go, but we need to leave as soon as night falls… he will…"

Mac's words were being punctuated, first by glass smashing in the kitchen, then by bullets thudding into the front door that they had never used, then more through the glass lights above the door.

Armour was in the air and, arms about Mac, he dropped them both to the floor – it took the wind right out of Mac's lungs, and she was gasping… she had never felt pain like it.

Armour rolled her over on her back and with his right hand on her solar plexus, he gently pressed and lifted. Someone had told him once that it helped when someone was winded and it seemed to ease her back into the normal breathing pattern quite quickly, although she would feel the knot in her chest for some time.

The bullets were coming from the front of the house, and although the hail was extensive, the noise was isolated to the breaking glass and hammering on the door…the weapons were silenced.

And even though everything was coming from the front, and he could not rule out that the back was covered, Armour chose to head for the back. It may be a trap, but the odds were against them either way… and in fact Armour had taken a good look out the back, and felt there was slightly more cover in that route…using the Hondas was totally out of the question.

If they were able to get clear, they would have to fend for themselves.

Armour assumed they had been spotted retrieving the documents from the Botanic Gardens, and the game was up as far as the opposition was concerned… finishing the job and getting those documents was all that mattered now.

Instead of using the back door though, Armour grabbed

the duffle bag quickly passing his right arm and head through the straps he slung it on his back. He led them through to a rear bedroom and undid the window latch, the window was large enough for them to climb out, but they would be forced to drop ten feet or so into a short alley. If a gunman was in the right position, they were dead, they would be right in his sights with nowhere to go.

He dropped first and looked in the line of fire he had anticipated would be the worst for them, and there was no one there. The first hurdle was cleared.

He beckoned quickly to Mac to join him. She dropped into his up-reached arms and was quickly crouched by his side. Armour swivelled and headed along the narrow alleyway.

At the entrance he stopped and eyed the terrain… he guessed there were a number of places a gunman could hide.

He edged into a corner to get a better view over a wider angle… and felt the cold steel of a gun barrel touch the bone of his skull just behind his right ear. He knew better than to make a fast move, but was allowed to turn just enough to see the scrawny face of Carter, the one he thought was Mick's man, he did not know it, but that did not make much difference now..

"I have to say, mate, that this is not our move. This is all turning out very messy and certainly not my style… well, I like a bit of mess, but not this sort. He lifted a two-way radio to his lips as Armour, and by now Mac too huddled down.

Armour knew he could not trust this man, but was not too sure what he was going to do about it.

It was obvious that they had got on to them very quickly, and Armour hoped they had not had time to tap the phones, otherwise their almost certain route to safety would be useless.

"Ace, how you doing out there?" Mick's man asked.

There was a crackle, and lot of hissing, and the tension showed on the main muscle along his jaw line.

"Ace, what's going on?" he called, moving slightly to tap his transmitter.

The movement, and the slight loss of concentration was enough for Armour. His left hand jarred the guy's gun wrist into the air, where a silenced round was let off and spat brick dust off the wall above his head. In the same moment, Armour's other hand clenched into a fist and was rammed up and under the man's ribcage, and then as the wind left his body and he crouched forward, Armour's then raised arm came down hard on the back of his head. He was out cold…

Armour took the guy's gun, pushed him aside and looked out of the alleyway. He could not safely see anything, and was very reluctant to stick his head out any more than was absolutely necessary. He looked back along the alley to see Mac pulling the guy along the ground a few feet, to get him out of the way.

She moved up alongside him and whispered.

"Only a few moments more…"

"Only a few more moments and what?"

"The last thing he said on the phone was that he would send William as a back-up until we reached him. He would not interfere unless there was trouble. Now I don't imagine he would have thought it would have happened this quickly, but he would be able to handle it… I guess…"

Almost as if it was it was part of an elaborate script, Armour heard an engine, and arching his neck he caught a glimpse of that silver-grey BMW.

What happened next was truly amazing…

The BMW screeched up and the back end slid round. It clipped a wheelie bin, tossing it to the other side of the alley entrance. Suddenly, Armour and Mac were provided with cover from one side by the car, and from the other by the bin. Although they had to be quick and nimble, they had a clear run to the car doors, which William had already swung open.

"Going my way?" he yelled coolly, as rounds thumped into the other side of the bullet-proof vehicle.

They took no second asking… they ran and dived into the back seat, Armour pulling the door closed behind him, and William screeched away from the mews.

"Well, you really are a hot couple, but you've got good friends, and I mean good," said William over his shoulder, as they took a corner almost on two wheels, and soon they were out towards Botley.

William kept off the main road and cut through onto the B4044 towards Eynsham… it looked to Armour as if they would head towards Burford. A frown started to grow across the driver's face.

'What is it William?" asked Armour who had spotted the expression through the rear-view mirror.

"Ugh, it's just that I was kind of expecting a tail. There were quite a few troops around that flat. I would have thought they would have been on our backs for a while, but I haven't seen anyone."

Armour, who had been turning a few times every now and then to see if they were being followed voiced his agreement, but then added: "We did leave very quickly – and they would have had to gather and get back to their cars…"

Sounded plausible…

They had been travelling for about fifteen minutes since any apparent chasers were lost.

They were weaving along a fairly narrow lane with tall hedges along either side, and they had not seen much traffic since they had turned off the main roads out of the city.

Still a little uneasy Armour and Mac sat hand in hand, grimly watching the road.

Mac had been 20 at the time, with another year to go at university. She loved Oxford, and fully appreciated the privilege of student life there. The spring had been warm and the summer looked as it might be long and hot.

One of her best friends – Mac was popular, always friendly, helpful, a good listener, was not prone to gossip and rely on cliques – was a deb called Annie. Annie was unlike many of her social class. She was not a total airhead. She mixed with the best of them, loved champagne, rode to hounds, attended the right balls, went skiing in Klosters, summered in the south of France, and was totally at the home with influential or just obscenely rich people. She was attractive and slim, but was actually very intelligent and quite cultured.

Annie was how she was known to friends, her full name being Annabel Powbright-Hawkesby, and her father, when he worked, was 'something in the city' and brother to a title.

Much during student days was assumed, and many undergraduates purposely played down or simply did not say anything about their backgrounds, money or status.

Annie and Mac just seemed to click. Annie did not try to get Mac too involved with her society friends, wanting to keep her apart as a special friend.

This suited Mac, who was not too keen to get involved with them – anyway, most of the boys seemed to be the pasty, blotchy-faced types with uncontrollable hair. That was a bit of a generalisation of course, but a fair observation about some of the louder, more extreme examples.

Occasionally when the group was more select, possibly a soiree after a musical recital,

Annie would suggest Mac would like to come. Annie never took it to heart if Mac declined.

Mac had a house off the Woodstock Road which she shared with three other girls and a flock of attentive boyfriends who seemed to flow in and out. Mac, who although had boyfriends, was unattached most of the time, and had some difficulty keeping tabs on who was with who. Half the time it didn't actually seem to matter that much.

Annie was a regular visitor, and one Sunday afternoon, in white T-shirt and baggy jeans, breezed brightly in, to find the house quite quiet for a change, but Mac was curled in one of their voluminous comfy sofas near the opened French windows to the back garden, the sun, and the warmth of its rays streaming into the room. She was deep in a book.

"Hello dear thing," she said, and flopped down into the sofa, smiling.

"Hi Annie," Mac returned, "how are you?"

"I'm lovely, and you?"

"You're very perky today. Not that you're normally dull, but you are decidedly…up. What's going on?"

"Well yes, it is true. I am a bit excited. I don't know if you remember me mention one of my cousins, Guy, well, he's having a small party for a few family and friends at his parents' house just outside Beaconsfield this coming Wednesday evening. He's heard me talk about you and he's invited us both. It'll be great. Are you OK for that?"

"Oh I don't know Annie, I've got a lot of work to do this week. Thanks, but I don't think…"

"No, wait Mac. Let me explain. This is not a bash, this is going to be very special, and there will be some very important people there – you said that you were going to be a journalist one day, you never know who you might meet!"

She was right there.

In Annie's bright red MGB Roadster they had taken the old A40 south towards London. They turned off left towards Chesham after passing through High Wycombe and Beaconsfield itself. A mile or so later Annie turned right into the high hedged and tree-lined lanes, passing Seer Green and left to Jordans.

Annie double declutched from third to second (a move she was delighted to have perfected), and pulled into a private lane screened by tall firs. The lane turned gravel drive and the firs on the left suddenly stopped and a huge turn of the century country red brick and beamed house with gables and pitched roofs, terraced lawns and summerhouse, was revealed. The drive actually took them past the side of the house to the front. which had a huge turning circle wide flower beds with rhododendrons, and manicured lawns, leading 50 yards to high hedges, beeches and more firs. Parked on the turning circle were eight cars. One Rolls Royce, two large Jags, a BMW, a red Ferrari Dino, a Mercedes SLK Sports, a black Ford Grenada and a Range Rover.

They parked next to the latter and climbed out of the Roadster.

Having been told that it was a pretty posh do, Mac decided to wear a simple, but very fetching black cocktail dress to just above the knee, and pearls. Annie had gone long, also in black, with a deep blue and gold tasselled wrap – they crunched across the drive to the huge studded oak door, which almost mysteriously opened as they reached it. They walked into a large be-rugged hallway which housed a massive stairway with carved balustrade which rose and then cut across to the right and then back upon itself and out of sight.

A tall, dark man of about 30 walked briskly towards them with an extended hand out towards Annie

"Welcome young Annie," said the man in a rich deep voice, his eyes flitting across to Mac's smile. Annie kissed the air both side of the man's face.

"Guy, how wonderful to see you and thanks for inviting us. This is my good friend Claire Willans."

"Hello Claire, Welcome to my home, I feel I know you, Annie talks so much about you."

"All good I hope," she said, feeling the warmth in his hand, "but please, my friends call me Mac."

"Well Mac, Annie, come through, everyone's here now, except for our guest of honour, so come and meet them – it is all very informal, so please relax and enjoy yourself," he said and turned on his heel, gestured with his hand, passed the dark wood panelling to an opened door to the right and they followed him.

Annie knew most of the gathered throng – some were names that Mac had heard of, two politicians particularly, and their wives, or were they their wives? An eminent honorary surgeon to the Queen Mother and his wife, also a leading surgeon. A city stock broker and his wife, a barrister and her artist husband, and the rest, three young men who worked in Hatton Gardens in the diamond trade, and their wives. The atmosphere was relaxed and very soon there was comfortable chat. Guy was unmarried, but going out with a very attractive young, struggling actress, who had been on screen in a few small parts in television plays. She and Guy saw to the drinks.

"Who is the guest of honour?" Mac whispered to Annie.

"I don't know," she said "I spoke to Guy on Monday and he said it was likely someone special would be here, but wouldn't say who, but he was quite excited. He said everyone else knew who it would be, but he wanted to surprise us. He's a swine that way – he's been playing tricks on me for as long as I can remember."

"Well let's ask then,"

"No", she put a hand on Mac's arm, "we would look silly and anyway I sort of like the idea of a surprise – it'll probably be Elton John or Rod Stewart, or with a bit of luck, Richard Gere."

Just then the door open and a young man in a waiter's outfit beckoned discreetly to Guy, who had been watching the door, and he followed the young man out. The others in the room fell silent and then spoke in murmurs and whispers and people were visible checking and straightening their clothes.

Mac felt her throat going dry. Others were putting their drinks down – Mac took a good slug of her Martini. Unlike Annie, Mac did not particularly like surprises of this kind, but she had little time to think about it.

The door opened and Guy led him in and started introducing his guests to Charles, the Prince of Wales.

Mac felt her jaw drop open, she forced it closed.

The Prince was smiling and laughing and said loudly enough for everyone to hear that it would give him immense pleasure if everyone would be so good as to dispense any and all formality. He seemed very relaxed, unlike he was often seem on television. He had obviously met some of the assembly before because he greeted them with both hands – the Queen Mother's surgeon especially.

The Prince was in a smart lightweight browny-green suit, white shirt and red and green and gold paisley tie – as he spoke his right hand played with the gold and jade link on his left cuff.

Annie and Mac were last in line to be introduced, the Prince having had a quick few words with everyone.

And Guy looked towards them and then back to the Prince…

"And let me lastly introduce you to my lovely cousin Annie Powbright-Hawkesby and her equally lovely friend Claire Willans, otherwise known to her friends as Mac."

The Prince, at the time the most eligible bachelor in the world, smiled again.

To Annie he said: "Hello my dear, I eh, the name, eh, your father, he was a colonel in the Blue and Royals?"

Annie could not forget her upbringing and in addressing him slipped in the 'Your Royal Highness' title, somehow because she thought she should and to help Mac whom she thought ought to address him formally.

"That's right Your Royal Highness, he retired last year to the family patch in Norfolk. What a brilliant memory you must have – I remember he said he met you several times, but not recently."

"Oh, not really," he said, " I remember because we had a long discussion over dinner about the Battle of Waterloo. He has a brilliant military mind."

And then he moved onto Mac extending his hand, and she made a slight curtsey, but he scowled with mock disapproval at her.

"Now now, Miss Willans, I insist, none of that stuff, please. If you can bring yourself to, please call me Charles, and might I be considered a friend, and be so bold as to call you, Mac."

"It would be a great honour if you would call me that," and she felt her cheeks flush.

"Well, perhaps we can talk more over dinner," he said, and allowed Guy to draw him away to the others who now talked freely, and he was given a glass of Chardonnay.

Unbeknown to Mac at the time, Guy, as if acting on a secret password, whispered to a waiter to rearrange dinner placings so that Mac was positioned to the right of the Prince.

Although the conversation around the dinner table was light and afterwards the Prince mixed and chatted and people walked in the gardens, she felt his eyes falling on her – there was always a twinkle and a slight smile.

Outside one could hardly fail to spot officers of the Royal

Protection Squad all around, but the prince behaved as if there was no one there.

As Mac sipped coffee in the doorway of the garden house, watching Annie and Guy playing on the crochet lawn, she suddenly became aware of his presence behind her.

"I, eh, I'm sorry, I didn't mean to startle you. I wondered if you would care to join me in a walk around the garden."

She flushed slightly, and looked around, but no one was taking particular attention, well, not overtly.

"I would love to, thank you," she said, and put the coffee down on a low table. Charles outstretched a guiding hand to her, to lead the way and she stepped out through the French windows.

They actually made three circuits of the gardens while engrossed in their conversation.

He wanted to know all about her. He was gentle and caring, and when he knew she was at Oxford he suggested that they might meet. She could hardly say 'no', but when they did meet it was for a private recital by a string quartet followed by a meal at the home of an affluent friend of the Prince. Afterwards they were left on their own.

Several similar 'liaisons' happened over the next six months, and it was only after the fourth that Mac became aware that he was physically closer to her, kissed her hand when they met, and lingered longer with his touches. She knew something more serious could be happening. She was not stupid and knew perfectly well that there would never be, never could be, anything much more significant than a gentle affair.

Despite the secrecy, which Mac found no real problem, and the fact that their relationship could never really be anything more, was acceptable. She would enjoy the friendship while it lasted. But the thing she really found hard to get her mind around was that he had other women, and especially one other long-term relationship which he, not so much talked about, but occasionally alluded to.

She never said anything or challenged the situation – it was pointless. In fact she knew it was the way of kings, queens and princes for hundreds of years. But finally, it was she who brought it to an end and told him she could not carry on.

He was genuinely upset, but said he understood.

He said he hoped that she would not harbour his any bad feelings. She equally genuinely said she did not. They parted while real affection still remained, and he said that she would always hold a special place in his heart, and if she ever needed help she should contact him – she believed him.

All three saw it at the same, a farm tractor and hay cart half way out into the road. It was on a long straight section of road and William slowed the vehicle well before coming close to the tractor. The tractor driver was just getting down from the machine and lifted a side panel on the engine.

William hissed as he noticed that on either side of the road were deep ditches before the hedges, and it meant that he had no chance to get by. As he stopped he immediately slapped the car into reverse and eyed the rear-view mirror. As his eyes dropped back to the scene in front of him he saw a pair of legs beneath the tractor, on the other side… wearing suit trousers… walking towards the front of the tractor.

It was enough for him. He rammed his foot down on the gas and let the clutch spring up. The BMW shot backwards…

Neither he, nor Armour or Mac saw the grenade rolling towards the middle of the road, as if synchronised so that it and the car would meet… as they did. A second grenade closely followed the first.

When the two booms happened it was with incredible

force and noise, and the front of the car shot upwards, first one way, and then slightly turned in another, tilted first by one impact and then the other.

Unprepared, Mac and Armour had been thrown forwards and on to the floor in the back of the vehicle by the force of the reversing… it was lucky for them. The floor of the car was reinforced, but as it landed on its roof, William who had been twisted round and over the rear of the front seats to ease his vision… was crushed between the buckled metal and a seat. Blood was flowing freely from his mouth, and probably other places, but his shoulders and head were all that Mac and Armour could see for the moment.

"Are you hurt?" he asked Mac, although he could see she was conscious and not seemingly in pain,

"Uh… yeah… I think so… poor William…oh how awful…" and she whimpered, not through fear, or pain, but genuine grief, like for the loss of a good friend.

All had seemly gone sickeningly quiet, except for a trickling sound, which Armour knew had to be petrol. He felt drops beneath his torso, which he wiped. It was blood, but he was not sure it was his. He knew the silence would not be for long. On the other hand he did not like the thought of being trapped in the car, and that it might suddenly explode.

He pulled the door catch and pushed, and at first nothing happened. He gave it a kick, and feeling OK he forced his body and pulled Mac through a tight gap and to freedom.

They were close to the deep ditch at the side of the road, and pulling Mac with him, Armour dropped into the bottom of it. They were out of sight unless someone happened to be standing in line with the ditch and looking along it. Armour looked in both directions and could not see anyone. He took the lead and they crawled along it for about 20 yards… just waiting for the bullets to thud into the ground around them and eventually eat them up. Two seconds later the car exploded in a massive mushroom of flames and black smoke.

Only glancing back for a second Mac and Armour scrambled under the cover of the blast, into a gateway, tumbled about 30 yards and landed face down in a field of mature barley. They lay still, again waiting for the noise of guns to erupt, they surely must have been seen…

After what seemed like ages they heard voices, and saw some movement, but kept their heads down, and very quickly they heard cars driving away. The BMW was still an inferno… there was no way anyone could survive it. Maybe that was what the ambushers had assumed, perhaps a little too readily.

But soon a school bus and other cars approached, and people ran towards the burning car. Edging up, Armour could just see thorough the gateway, a man on a mobile phone. He looked very excited and was obviously onto the emergency services.

Hardly believing that those who would have killed them had just gone, Armour coaxed Mac to her feet and they made their way along the side of the field with cover from the hedgerow, and then into another field.

Night was gradually beginning to fall, and on the other side of the field Armour could make out a fairly large barn, and they headed for it.

"We'll wait here for a few hours, and then we should make our way on foot… I reckon it will be about an hour's walk back to Oxford, if we take the most direct route possible," he said, and Mac did not argue… even though she knew that was not the way they should be going.

She was quiet. They had had some shocks, and William took the death toll to six. Armour took her in his arms and held her, and she seemed to melt into the contours of his body.

Occasionally he would gently but firmly rub a part of her body he thought might be feeling the cold, like her shoulders or the small of her back. Amazingly, she slept. He could not.

Armour did not know the territory. He had little knowledge of which direction to head next. He knew he might only have a chance if they got back to the road, but he realised that they would have to get off the road every time a car came. They could not afford to be spotted now by anyone. He felt their luck had run out.

He might have been dozing, but suddenly he was wide awake. Armour glanced at his watch and angled it to the moonlight to catch the hands. It was 10 pm.

He began to massage Mac, to bring her gently back to consciousness, and she stirred.

And then suddenly sat bolt upright.

"It's OK it's OK no worries, but we will have to get a move on soon," he soothed.

She relaxed.

"Do you know the way from here?" she asked.

"Not from this spot, but take me back to the road and I think I could find our way out of here."

They had not had the chance to discuss exactly where they were going.

"We were sort of going in the right direction."

"What, to the A40 and then towards Cheltenham?"

"Yes, to the A40, but not towards Cheltenham… we need to cross the main road and make for Bladon."

"I've seen that on the map… it's up towards Woodstock," said Armour, thinking aloud, and working it out on his own, "Woodstock… of course… Blenheim Palace… how are they going to let us in there?

"Don't worry they will," she said confidently, "Our problem now is getting there."

Armour agreed, and particularly as by now there was a fair chance that the wreckage of the car had been searched, and only one body had been found.

They set off, away from the where the car had burned and had only gone about 300 yards when the lights of a car lit the hedgerow on their left hand side. Even though there was no chance whatever of any occupants seeing them through the undergrowth, they crouched down, and when it had gone, they climbed a gate dropped onto the road.

They soon found themselves adjacent to the road skirting Eynsham, and followed a quiet road which signposted Cassington and Bladon. They crossed the busy A40, passed through Cassington, and trudged on for three quarters of an hour, occasionally dodging down into the ditch or hedge to avoid any cars that came along. They were fairly confident they had not been spotted.

When they reached the Bicester to Witney road, they quickly crossed over, seeing the lights of Bladon a short way off to their right.

They scaled a seven foot wall and were now on the Blenheim estate. As they dropped to the ground Armour stayed crouched… Mac stood upright trying to see in the dark.

Armour grabbed her sleeve and pulled her down.

There were a number of trees in what seemed to be parkland. The ground slowly dipped away, and could be seen to rise steeply again about half a mile away.

"Look… over there…" he hissed as he pointed a little way off to their left.

A Range Rover was parked in the dark by a tree and partially obscured. Armour had only seen it because he had spotted the occasional brightening glow of someone inside smoking a cigarette.

"It's OK, they are waiting for us," said Mac.

"I don't doubt that Mac, but who are 'they'…?"

"Don't worry, it was part of the instructions I was given. He said there would be someone waiting for us just inside the wall, and to look out for a Range Rover. Come on let's go," she said and made to set off.

Armour pulled her down again.

"We have come this far, and frankly have been amazingly lucky. Bear with me. Can we take this next step just a little carefully."

"Alright, but I don't see the problem."

Armour too hoped there was not a problem, but somehow he felt a bit uneasy. They were on the estate now, so why was the Range Rover not at least on sidelights, so they would be able to see it.

He reasoned also that by now those after them may have managed to find a link between the safe houses they had been using and their lofty Samaritan. That and the direction they had been heading may have rung alarm bells with someone, who had put two and two together…

Maybe he was being pessimistic, but anyway, he motioned for her to stay close behind him and raised his right forefinger to his lips so she did not speak, and he readjusted the duffle bag which was still strapped to his back.

They moved from tree to tree and were approaching the vehicle from its left rear quarter. Still some 40 yards away and keeping low, he circled them round to the rear of it.

He stopped suddenly when, in the brightening moonlight, he saw steam rising from the base of a tree between them and the Range Rover, and then as he tilted his head he managed to catch the occasional splashing sound of someone pissing against the bark.

This guy too had a cigarette, which, after pulling up his zip, he took from his mouth and expelled a huge cloud of smoke. He turned back towards the vehicle, took one more lungful, dropped the cigarette on the ground and stepped and twisted his foot on it. He climbed into the passenger seat.

As Armour looked around he caught sight of a row of sheep troughs. At first he carried on scanning round as something, out of place, made him swing back to the feeders.

Moving away from the vehicle and round to the other side of the troughs he suddenly saw it. The round dark shape at one end of the first trough was a man's foot, and now Armour could see the body of the man, lying on his back with his arms down by his side.

Considering the way he was lying, there was little doubt in Armour's mind that he was at the very least unconscious, and more probably dead. Was this number seven?

Their best bet now was to give the Range Rover a wide berth. Mac had seen what Armour had, and even in the darkness seemed to go pale.

Armour squeezed her shoulder and hunched his own.

They did not have to talk to jointly understand that this was probably the man that had been sent to collect them, and the two in the vehicle were agents of some kind.

They were now behind the Range Rover, which was facing the wall. Armour considered that they now could do nothing but run the gauntlet between there and the palace. Armour sort of had his bearings. There was some cover for a good part of the way, but once they got nearer to the building and the ground rising to it, there would be very little. Armour remembered this from a visit there once, a few years back.

Whatever they did, it was better to do it now under the cover of darkness. Once it was light they would be totally exposed.

Armour was worried. Inside the estate at least some of the opposition were already stationed. How many more of them would there be, and what sort of resistance might they come up against in the short distance between there and the palace. He began to wonder if the whole thing was a trap, although he had to doubt it.

They had only gone about a quarter of a mile when they suddenly saw the huge dark shadow of the palace. They were now to the east of it and facing the rear of the building.

They could just about see some lights on the far right. They scurried as low as they could across the open land. Armour knew that someone with a night sight could pick them off easily – he relied of Mac's ignorance of this as they ran over the steadily rising ground.

Chapter Seventeen

It seemed remarkable. They were approaching the private apartments of Blenheim Palace, and they had come across little security and no opposition agents. As they wended their way through ornamental gardens they found a gate marked 'PRIVATE'.

The padlock was undone and they soon found a door, and knocked.

Their eyes blinked as the light streamed out… they could not quite see who had opened the door.

"Good Lord, Claire. Where's Hobbs? My, you two look awful, are you alright?"

She, her eyes not yet focussed, fell forward into his welcoming arms. He was strong and he cushioned her weight and held her comfortably.

He was obviously relieved to see her and it was a few seconds before his eyes turned up to meet Armour's.

He smiled, and then momentarily held out his hand.

"Welcome," he said, "I would imagine that you could do with a drink."

Armour was astonished that they had not been first met by armed bodyguards and security – that was not to say they were not around, but even the Prince seemed shocked that his man Hobbs was not with them.

The door closed behind them, and with their eyes becoming accustomed to the light, they were able to see him properly.

He was dressed casually in cords and a beige check shirt, and he smiled warmly.

Armour said about the man at the sheep trough. The Prince was very concerned to hear that Hobbs might have been hurt. He picked up a phone and quickly dispatched security men and Royal Protection officers to check out the Range Rover.

After that Armour felt a little awkward. He and Mac obviously had things to say to each other, but he took Armour by the arm and despite their bedraggled state, sat him next to Mac in the comfort of an exquisite and deep soft sofa. He handed them both a scotch, Mac's with a healthy dash of Stone's Ginger Wine… he had remembered, and then sat in a single high-backed chair.

Strangely, he had never been able to bring himself to call her Mac, despite the fact that is what friends were expected to call her. He actually preferred Claire and always called her it.

He urged Armour to address him by his first name only. Armour somehow knew he would have difficulty with that, but would try. Both Armour and Mac also felt a little uncomfortable because they were still dirty even though they had washed their hands and faces in the kitchen soon after coming in.

Armour felt more awkward because, even though he accepted there was no rivalry, he would have liked to have been at his best when he first met the Prince. He felt that perhaps the Prince was taken aback by Armour's age. He perhaps had expected a far younger man.

Their host recognised their discomfort and said not to worry, but from what Mac had said it was more important for them to talk if he was to make further arrangements, and he particularly made Armour relax.

"Claire, although briefly, told me on the phone how important you are to her. She is very special to me also… so I will do whatever I possibly can to help you both, in this current… eh… predicament. Claire, if I might know the nature of the danger, might be able to assist."

She glanced to Armour, shifting the onus of reply on to him, and he took it up immediately… not least because Mac was looking very tired.

Armour spent the next half hour, and two more scotches to tell him the story so far, and explained the documents that they had found in the Botanic Gardens in Oxford.

"This is indeed disturbing, and Claire was right, perhaps the Home Secretary is the right person to approach about this. I would like to help personally, but I have to be in London tomorrow, and I know the Home Secretary is in Stamford in the morning, for a meeting with leading Lincolnshire businessmen I have been told. But I will get a message to him to say you are on the way, and I will arrange transportation to get you to Stamford."

Trust did not come into it. There was no question. For the first time both Armour and Mac each felt totally safe… for the time being at least.

The conversation stopped when a security man came back with a report about the Range Rover, but before listening to it, the Prince had them shown them to a suite of rooms on the first floor.

He told them that in half an hour someone would be along with something for them to eat, and they would get a call in the morning at 8.30, and they would have from 9.30 till 10 am, to discuss arrangements. He wished them a good night. His smile was warm and gracious to them both.

The decor was what one might expect for one of the country's most famous palaces, kept at the standard one might expect.

The private apartments were beautiful, and luxurious, full of strangely familiar hand-painted portraits of long past people, but the place, despite someone else's ghosts, was easily liveable in – even cozy.

When Armour and Mac bathed together, it was pretty much in silence. She moulded into his shape as much as possible… her back against his chest. For a long time they just sat, gently caressed and steadily steamed.

And afterwards they dried each other off, checked out the food that had been brought, picked at a few things, had a cocoa, and went to bed.

Under any other circumstances the surroundings they found themselves in would have been the subject of awe and excitement, but too much had happened.

They found the room quite warm, and threw off the bedclothes and this time he wound the front of his body round the back of hers. She was comforted by the warmth and firmness of his body. He was stirred by the beautiful lines and smooth curves of hers … but battered by the day's events, they both quickly fell into a long deep sleep.

The mists started to clear and the thirteen-year-old boy stood at the side of the grave, not crying. In customary black, a few relatives and friends parting and moving away, the formal part of the ceremony over.

Although he felt the form of his loving aunt remain supportively behind him, he now wished that she too would leave.

It was like he stood on the pinnacle of a tall isolated chimney of rock, the winds and skies and clouds whooshing by him. His balance on that rock was precarious, but he was the only one who was ever going to control what happened next.

He looked down at the top of the oak casks that lay before

him, and then felt the sting in the corner of his eyes… God he wished his aunt would go off with the others.

The first he had heard of the tragic crash which killed his parents was when the head teacher walked into his class at school and whispered in the ear of his teacher.

It was the first time ever he had seen such a look on her face, it had never been used on any of his classmates.

He was ushered out of the room, which held all his friends – they were told to carry on working on a special project. He was taken to the head teacher's office where he and his teacher ceremonially prepared him.

He felt the moisture go from his mouth, and the nausea rise in his throat. At the same time his stomach churned, felt his anal sphincter quiver, but he did not disgrace himself.

He knew the news about to be dealt to him was cataclysmic, but they were waiting for the arrival of his aunt…

He was thirteen, and he smelled the perfume of his aunt's neck and cleavage and, for the first time did not finding it smothering or offensive. There was comfort there, and he soon needed it.

They seemed to expect him to break down on hearing the news, but after they had told him he just sat down, calmly as tears slowly welled in his eyes and trickled down his cheek. The adults turned and talked amongst themselves.

It was hard to appreciate. His mother and father were dead, killed in a car accident, and he would never see them again…

As he sat there, he turned his head to the window. Snow started to fall… well, it was Easter and somehow that seemed inevitable to him…

His aunt, Jean, and husband Len were childless, but very special. How could they possibly know how he felt, but they always seemed to, and then they treated him as their own. They always had made him feel special. While they were fit and health they did everything they could to broaden his knowledge, and helped and encouraged him with travel and they made his life at university easier than it was for many students in Oxford.

A year after graduating, and within a year of each other, he saw them wither and die, one, his uncle, of cancer and the other, Jean, of a broken heart.

Over the years, Armour had developed into a highly self-sufficient person. It was not so much that he did not need people, but that he was usually just as happy on his own.

He liked people, but equally he liked his own space, and certainly did not seek out the crowd as some people seem to need to do.

He also revelled in his self-sufficiency, he was his own master, but as so many people had told him, he did not show or express his emotion… at least not enough for them.

Some of his friends, and particularly women, found it very attractive at first, but irritating in a long-term relationship.

But Armour was OK, he was not sure what he could do about their problem, but basically he was as good as on his own, so why worry? He would have liked to have been able to express what they wanted, but how can you, how can you?

He woke with a start… Mac was still there. Her perfect form right by his left hand. He felt her even breathing and the tiredness once again engulfed him. They had their morning call and breakfast was brought, and in the lounge area of their suite they found new clean clothes, all at the correct sizes. After breakfast they descended a broad staircase with huge leaded window from top to bottom, and walked into the sitting room where they were the previous night.

There he was, pacing… and furious!

Although he was trying to keep calm. One of his security consultants was close at hand.

"Hobbs was a bloody good man. Damn and blast! I want to know who has done this. If this has anything to do with Calder-Maynes, I'll have his guts for garters," he swore another oath and turned to see them enter the room.

His scowl melted, the ridges in his forehead faded, and the anger in his eyes softened.

With a gentle gesture to the security man he dismissed him, and turned back to them.

"Forgive me," he said, with obviously nothing to forgive, but embarrassed at being caught in an unguarded moment.

But in the next breath he explained that the man they had seen by the sheep troughs was in fact dead. His neck had been professionally snapped.

Hobbs made seven.

He was one of the prince's trusted old retainers and the prince was deeply upset. Who could blame him? He was renowned for the way he cared for his people.

Mac moved forward and touched his arm tenderly. She knew what he was like. He stroked her hand, but moved away for a moment and stared out of the window.

To the Prince, what had happened to Hobbs was an indicator, proof even, not that he had doubted Armour and Mac's story, but that what was being dealt with here, was very serious indeed, and the people involved would stop at nothing. He had to admit to himself he had not expected anyone to take any action against him, his property or his people, But what about William? He had been wrong, and had underestimated the danger that was involved. He was angry with himself for sending Hobbs, an untrained man to do what the security people probably would have done simply and successfully, but also relieved that William, although lost, was a good man who had saved Mac and Armour the previous day.

Armour had mentioned Calder-Maynes the previous night, but the Prince had not reacted to the name, not shown any hint of recognition.

This morning, he used his name as if he was someone he had dealt with, or knew well.

Armour knew he would probably not get the chance to ask again, so quizzed the prince on Calder-Maynes.

When the Prince turned back to them, Armour said: "I know he is a defence consultant, but who exactly is Sir Bryan Calder-Maynes, and just how important is he?"

"Not easy to say, precisely," said the prince, frowning, and rubbing a ring on his finger.

He went on: "I have met him quite a few times, and heard him mentioned on many occasions. For many years, he served with Uncle Louis, Lord Mountbatten, and that is how I got to know him. He was always ambitious, and being with dear Uncle Louis he was in the right place most of the time – he was a very young officer, but he was even there when the Japanese surrendered at the end of the Second World War… I never really liked the man, and have never known anything about his personal life.

"He rose pretty quickly through ranks and now, as you say, he acts as a consultant, not only for our government, but several others in Europe and even, I understand, the Americans, and the Israelis from time to time. He has many contacts. I have seen him now and again, at diplomatic events, but not to speak to."

They went on to discuss the fact that he was in a perfect position to coordinate a lucrative sub-business based on the activities of many 'secret' government agencies around the world.

The Prince was talking with an authoritative air. He knew what he was talking about, and obviously his experience in the Royal Navy gave him a confidence that Armour had not really expected.

Much of the press coverage about the Prince was about his eligibility and wild speculation about whom he would marry. His name over the past few years had been linked with almost every unmarried female in all the noble families of Europe… and beyond.

Charles himself said very little and never fuelled the speculation, that seemed to happen all by itself, with almost everyone he met – even Barbra Streisand and at least a third of The Three Degrees.

But here he was talking about military and security matters with knowledge, experience and even expertise.

Although he had no wish to see the documents in Armour's possession, he readily gave his opinion about what Armour had told him of the general outline.

"What I am not clear about is how these documents fell into this Soviet fellow's possession," said the Prince and Armour explained not only that, but the fact that he had known Vasilli since his university days.

"OK so they are at Blenheim Palace. They are probably with someone very important, look don't worry Michael, this is kind of out of your hands. It is now in my field of jurisdiction, diplomacy and politics, so just forget what has been happening. I will deal with it. I'll keep you informed, but the ball is now in my court," Calder-Maynes said to Staveley-Smythe, and the latter was now relieved to have the burden lifted from his shoulders. Calder-Maynes was right, it was out of his league, and he had to admit that if anything went wrong, he was happy that there was someone else who would get the flak. He was a little uneasy because he did not quite believe that Calder-Maynes would readily accept the flak for anyone, and he was not sure he was going to let him.

He would keep his men pretty close to the game. He had

a stake in it as well, and certainly his career and reputation hinged on it as much as Calder-Maynes'.

"If there is anything I can do Bryan, let me know," he said and hung up.

Calder-Maynes stared at the phone which buzzed at him and slowly put it down in its holder.

"Fuck the useless little arsehole," said the old warrior to himself, and his thoughts added: 'If the world wasn't so full of little wankers…' but his venom was wasted… only he heard it.

He knew that the whole future of his business and the plan for the group now hung on his abilities to organise, and his influence with members of the government, not least the Defence Secretary and the Home Secretary. It was not going to be easy, but just as he had enjoyed the game so far, he was confident he could run the distance. He was not ready for early retirement, he would give it a damn good go!

Chapter Eighteen

The Prince had arranged for a helicopter to fly them to Stoke Rochford Hall, a large old country mansion which served as the National Union of Teachers training centre about three or four miles south of Grantham. There, a fast car would meet them and take them the 15 miles south along the A1 to Stamford.

"I'm afraid that with the Home Secretary in the area and whatever, we could only get clearance at this short notice to fly into the park at Stoke Rochford… it's not far though from there to Stamford. I have managed to get a message to the Home Secretary, and he knows you are coming and he understands it is very important.

"Mr. Carmichael will be lunching at The George in Stamford, and that is where the car will take you. Good luck, the helicopter will be ready in about ten minutes. My pilot will come and get you when he is ready… I wish I could help you more," he said holding out his hand to Armour, and adding: "I hope the clothes fit, I had to guess the size.

"Good to meet…" he interrupted himself, "look after Claire won't you?"

He said of course he would. He could see the helicopter at the back of the main palace.

205

The Prince obviously knew Mac's size, because the clothes left for her were a perfect fit, and she looked radiant again.

She and the Prince stood opposite each other and he held out his arms. She walked forward into them and they hugged for almost a full ten seconds… it seemed like an age to Armour, but he was OK…

"Good to see you Claire. Let's hope that next time we have a bit more time to talk.

"Take care," he said, tightening his squeeze momentarily and then let go.

She thanked him for everything he had done.

He picked up a bag that was by the door, and through the open door handed it to his personal detective who stowed it in the boot of a large Jaguar waiting on the gravel outside.

He turned before leaving, waved, smiled and was gone.

They had moved through to a kitchen and Mac flicked the kettle switch, and made coffee, and then with their free arms, his left and her right, around each other they drank and watched the pilot while he made a few checks under the engine cowling, and then close it. He then made his way to the private apartments, knocked on the door and opened it…

He was about 29 or 30, blond-haired, medium build and fresh-faced. His eyes were bright, she noticed, and he had a breezy smile.

"I'm George, ready whenever you are," he said. "It's 10.15 now, there's a slight westerly breeze which should help us, so we should be there in about three quarters of an hour."

"OK, we're ready… let's go," said Armour, he and Mac downing the last of the coffee.

He slipped his right arm and head through the cords of the duffle bag again and swung it onto his back. They put the cups in the sink and they made their way out to the chopper.

It was a five-seater, and George directed them into the back. He belted them in, and told them that if they wanted to speak to him they would have to put on the headphones that hung on the hook above their seats.

It took only a moment to go through final checks, the blades picked up speed, took the weight and then they were off the ground. They had been moving forward as they rose, but George then dipped the nose slightly more which took them faster forward and up, and then he banked away to the left. They were away over the parkland, and they could see Bladon beneath them and Oxford sprawling away in the distance to their right.

The sun was rising in front of them and a slight haze made visibility a little difficult. George was OK, he had his dark Ray-Ban Aviator glasses on. Armour and Mac could see well out the sides.

As he shaded his eyes, Armour saw the compass heading change from east-north-east to north-east, which if geography served him right, should have taken them back over Northampton, then Corby, and over Rutland Water… he would recognise many landmarks and roads when he saw them.

As they climbed some more, Mac reached out and grasped Armour's hand and squeezed it. He returned the gesture and smiled.

For 20 minutes or so it was pleasant to sit back, relax and enjoy the scenery. They had just passed Northampton. Mac wished she had had a camera to do a few aerial shots, they always do well in the paper, generate a lot of interest and bump up the number of reprint orders for that edition.

It must have been the fact they were looking down on the town that she realised it was the first time she had thought about work, it had only been days since this all started, but it seemed like an age. She also realised she had not been in a position to let work know that she was not coming in for a while. She guessed that in the light of what had happened to Mart Burricks, they might well be worrying.

Mac came back to the present suddenly when she realised that the grip Armour had on her hand was beginning to hurt.

He was looking down. She loosened her seatbelt and lifted herself close to him so she could see. The shift in weight, light though she was, obviously made a slight difference to the helicopter's handling because George glanced round, and then turned back to follow their gaze.

All three were looking at a black helicopter, similar to theirs climbing fast in their direction, on an intercept course. There was no doubt that the pilot of the black chopper knew they were in his path. As it approached, the nose was turned slight to one side and it became very obvious they were the target, the side door had been removed, and there was a marksman lashed to the side, standing with one foot on the runner.

"Oh shit," said Armour as he saw the man lift an automatic rifle into position, and he put on a pair of the headphones, Mac did the same.

"Time for evasive action," said George, as he dived the chopper down on the offside of the rising aircraft, so the gunman could not get a shot.

He went on, although Armour was not sure if George was talking to himself or to him: "It might be a reasonable idea to reduce height in case we are hit, but just keep enough room to manoeuvre."

It was a sound suggestion. In the next moment, out of nowhere, the black chopper, its windows shaded out, screamed down in front of them, it was sickeningly close. It came out of its dive in front of them and then turned as it moved so the gunman could get a shot.

But that was all he did get as George dived and shifted left. The shot that came seemed to ricochet off one of the rotor blades, but miraculously caused no vital damage.

The black aircraft swooped again like a bird of prey… it was only a matter of time before the game would be up. The two choppers were similar and they were either going to get shot down or run out of fuel even if George could keep up the twists and turns. He was doing well, and the gunman was having difficulty in getting a clear shot. They could see his frustration as he waved and was obviously shouting at his pilot, through his headset. Armour could see Rutland Water in the near distance, there was not that far to go really.

He said encouraging things to George, who did not seem all that fazed at what was happening.

"Did a bit of this in darker parts of Africa a while back," he said as if answering a question.

But the black hunter came around again, and in the next moment was directly in front of them, the gun was in position and tell-tale flashes were appearing from its muzzle.

He was sweeping the gun from side to side, and a shot slammed into the windscreen hitting George in the shoulder… their chopper lurched to one side, but George was still in control.

"Don't suppose either of you know how to fly one of these things…?" he asked, kind of guessing the answer, "I thought not… this could get a bit bumpy."

He had climbed above the other craft in avoiding it, but then dived again.

Mac and Armour were thankful for that. Somehow being nearer to the ground seemed safer, but the fact was if they crashed they had little hope of survival.

But George wanted them to follow him. He twisted and turned, but not too much. The cat-and-mouse game was continuing and they were getting closer and closer, and their altitude was dropping.

Another shot smashed in the chopper and chopped a fuel line. George noticed the needle on the fuel gauge starting to drop.

"Just a little longer," he said, to himself, but Armour and Mac heard it through the headsets.

He was hammering along at full pelt, and the black chopper was close on his tail.

George could now see his target. He skimmed the ground, and latched on to the edge of a line of trees, the tops of which were higher than his rotor blades. The aircraft was angled sharply forward to maximise speed… the black chopper followed closely in their wake, the gunman leaning precariously out, trying to get off another blast.

The line of trees angled round to the right and George kept close to it, and then suddenly swung the body of the helicopter first one way, then the other and used the left hand outswing to pull the craft sharply round a cut in the trees.

But the manoeuvre had been telegraphed and their pursuer copied the procedure, as the gunman blasted… it proved fatal… doubly deadly.

As George made the turn it was almost as if he made the aircraft rear up on hind legs, like a horse. The jolt forced Armour and Mac forward. In that moment a round from the rifle slammed through the back of the cockpit and smashing into George's back.

Caught up by the chase the black chopper's pilot failed to see what George had planned for them… until it was too late.

He had played them hook, line and sinker… as George rose sharply the black chopper ploughed plumb square into the spire of a church, and exploded in a ball of flames.

But George did not live to talk of the incredible airmanship that had saved Armour and Mac.

The chopper, in the air about 150 feet, started to rotate and gently lose altitude. That brought them to about 75 feet and then George slumped forward. Armour had been expecting that… the wound in George's back was gaping.

Armour had kept quiet while George seemed to maintain control.

Now that he had slumped forward they started dropping faster. Mac and Armour could see the ground coming up fast, and there wasn't a thing they could do. They were going round and round but keeping upright.

"Tighten your seatbelt and get your head down," he barked at Mac, and she quickly complied.

A picture of the explosion of the other chopper raced through Armour's brain. He knew that when they hit the deck there was likely to be a blast. They would have to get out, and fast.

When she gauged that they were going to crash, Mac closed her eyes, and thought of Armour's strong face… strangely she felt safe.

The impact jarred every bone in their bodies and the wind went out of Mac's lungs.

Luckily, the chopper landed in the upright position, another tribute to George's skills, but much as he tried Armour could not open the door.

As Mac gasped for breath, Armour leaned over, amazed he was still in one piece, and kicked the door.

It was one of those moments of desperation that give people incredible strength. The door pinged off as if sprung, he slammed the release on Mac's belt harness, and dragged her tumbling from the aircraft.

Twenty yards away, it was not enough, they fell to the ground and waited as silence surrounded them… As the

Armour Piercing

seconds ticked by nothing happened …they couldn't know that there was no fuel left in the machine.

Mac, desperate for air, kept her eyes screwed shut… she knew the blast should come soon, and that it should be devastating.

A full minute seemed like an age, especially for Mac who still fought for breath – Armour realised that she was badly winded, but miraculously they had walked, or run, away from a crash that should have ended in an inferno – that had not happened… who was he to argue with fate?

Instead of the blast there was silence and then the birds started twittering.

Armour raised himself from the ground, and in another second was running, he meant it to take as little time as possible, he sprinted to the aircraft and put his fingers against George's throat. He felt nothing, and at that moment the crumpled and bleeding pilot's head lolled towards Armour, his eyes staring blankly into space.

George made eight.

Armour ran back to Mac, and for the first time surveyed their surroundings. At the same time he turned Mac away from the stricken craft and quietly: "He's dead… come on let's get away from here."

Suddenly, his head swimming, Armour tottered, grabbed Mac's shoulder and fell to a sitting position.

"Pete, Pete, what is it. Are you OK?"

Instinctively Mac knew he was not.

Armour suddenly felt a searing pain at the back of his left arm, and at the same moment, Mac saw blood staining the fibres of his beige Arran jumper.

"Take that jumper off," she barked uncharacteristically, and she got up and dashed to the chopper – she knew there must be a first aid kit. Sure enough, strapped to the bulkhead behind the front passenger seat was the kit she sought.

She ripped it from its position and also picked up a jumper with chamois shoulder pads stitched into it. It had been on the back seat of the helicopter at the start of their flight and she took it to be George's. She dashed back to Pete.

He had removed the jumper, but was now lying down. His vital signs were alright, but he was light-headed. Mac looked around.

They were in fallow fields on slightly raised ground with rolling scenery all around them, but there were no villages or roads that they could see. Cattle grazed in an adjoining field.

Even if their aircraft had not exploded, the other one had, and police, agents and all kinds, would be swarming all over the place in a very short time Mac rightly gauged.

She inspected his wound, and although not being trained, was able to assess the damage.

Along the back of Armour's left arm ran a bright red trench, perhaps just a half a centimetre or so, deep and three inches long.. It was bad enough for Armour to feel considerable pain and for him to have lost some blood. But it was not serious, and as long as she was able to stop the bleeding, he would soon be OK, if a little sore.

She cleaned and guessed the best way to stop the bleeding was an Elastoplast which she tenderly administered.

She then dashed back to the helicopter – she had seen George swig from a bottle of cola, and reckoned that raising Armour's sugar levels would do no harm. She tried to avert her eyes from George's lifeless stare, but could not. She then surprised herself by doing what she had seen done in a thousand films, but never for a moment thought she would bring herself to do even presented with the unlikely situation – she reached up and put her fingers over his eyes and closed the lids…

She checked… gulped and swallowed to halt the retch

rising in her throat, as she saw the blood from the corner of his mouth. She grabbed the cola which was strapped in a side compartment, and ran back from the horror scene.

Ten minutes was all she felt she could allow Armour. She was sure that people would suddenly descend on them, even though there had been no explosion and they seemed sheltered from prying eyes. She felt certain someone must have seen the aircraft come down.

Armour said he was feeling better and she helped pull him to a standing position. The truth was, he was still slightly giddy.

There were still close to the trees that George had been following, but were now the other side of them. If their luck held out, it might take a little time before their chopper was spotted – most of the attention would be focused on the blast and on the severely damaged church, and that was at least half a mile away.

Listening to police radio bands would probably bring their pursuers all the quicker.

They walked along the line of trees and when they were able to see open land on the other side, they entered the copse as it, and the field, curved round to the left. Emerging on the other side Armour recognised the great expanse of Rutland Water. As his eyes scrutinised the shores of the lake, he murmured that it was very busy… there were lots of people around, walking, cycling and fishing.

Calder-Maynes had his mobile car phone with him, and only certain people had this number. It was one of the new digital models, so he could still make sensitive calls without fear of being monitored.

He had just turned his Land Rover Discovery north onto the A1 when it rang, and he grabbed it from the holder.

"Yes," he barked.

"They are in the air over Oxford in a north-easterly direction. Don't know where they are heading, but we have one of our own in the air close by with orders to terminate."

"Good, I know where they are heading, I had a call earlier from Ceiran Carmichael about it. He wants to see me in Stamford just before lunch. Ironically that is where they are heading. Hopefully now they are not going to make it. Let me know when you have confirmation Michael, would you?"

He agreed and the line went dead.

Calder-Maynes was about ten miles from Stamford and it was coming up to 11am when the phone rang again, he acknowledged and just listened. It took only a few moments for the blood to start draining from his face, and his eyes flickered skyward.

It was Staveley-Smythe in a pretty excited state, and understandably.

"Our chopper is down, smashed into a church. I believe there's was damaged and is probably down, but we are not sure. It's a total fucking mess. All four of our guys in the chopper are dead. Teams on the ground are searching for them, and I have another chopper in the air making a sweep, but we don't know which way they went."

"My guess would be to concentrate in the direction of Stamford, and order 'shoot to kill'," said Calder-Maynes and he hung up.

All was not lost, even if they got to Carmichael. He and Carmichael were close, and Carmichael had an interest in Calder-Maynes' little project. He would be able to control the situation.

He was almost at Stamford, turning off the A1 and rolling down into the town past the Lady Anne Hotel on the right. He pictured the possibility that he might have to do the dirty work himself if necessary. He found it hard to believe that Armour and the girl had got so far. It showed how vulnerable they could be.

"What day is it…?" he asked, as they continued walking towards the water's edge.

It was almost the first time either of them had considered the question.

"It's… Thurs… no… Friday!" She said having seriously to think about it.

There were a lot of people around.

"It must be the school holidays…well that might just be a good thing for us. It shouldn't be too difficult to merge with the people around the lake. The only trouble… it is nearly 11.45 am and we haven't got much time to get to Stamford. I know the way, and it is only about eight miles away, but we need transport,"

Even though they had been on the move, the adrenalin seemed to have taken over.

Armour was feeling better and reasoning well.

They were dressed quite casually and certainly did not look out of place with others enjoying the scenery. Armour's wound was properly dressed and he was wearing George's blue jumper with the chamois-pad shoulders.

They came to a picnic area, and saw a signpost pointing the way to Barnsdale Lodge on the northern shore.

Armour decided to take this route. It led to the A606 Oakham to Stamford road. As they left the edge of the lake, they spotted a young couple in loosened leather, asleep on a large tartan blanket. Just above their heads was a food hamper, open and with the remains of an early lunch. Just a few yards ahead of that was a Harley Davison with extended front forks.

"Blimey," he said, almost under his breath, but loud

enough for Mac to hear, "That certainly brings back old memories."

It was the look though – this bike was not an original from the Sixties, but a new version… still a very nice bit of kit, and it had a very special name.

Armour looked around and could see no one close by. He spotted two helmets by the footrest and the keys of the bike by the lid of the food hamper.

Mac could read Armour's mind, and she too looked round, trying not to look too furtive.

It was not going to be easy, lift the keys without making any noise, and then they would have to move the bike as silently as they could, at least forty yards away before trying to start it.

The biker looked a big guy, and Armour had no wish to have to engage in any form of combat with him unless it was absolutely necessary, but time certainly was running out.

The couple did not stir on their approach. The girl was small thin with reddish hair and very attractive, Armour noticed, but he soon fixed his attention on the guy as Mac moved toward the bike, and he stealthily moved in on the keys, which were perhaps only three yards from the snoozing couple.

Rather than lift the keys, he muted any sound, by covering them with his hand and closing his grasp quickly… still they did not stir. He looked to Mac who had been keeping lookout, and her eyes, while still saying it was all clear, urged him to get a move on. He moved away from the couple and towards the bike.

Slipping the keys into the ignition, he lifted the machine from its rest. It was too heavy to push up hill, and he did not want to go downhill, so he followed the contours of the hillside as best he could. He did not look back. Mac was doing that and walking backwards, keeping Armour within arm's reach. She was ready to give the warning… in the end she did not need to.

Incredibly, they were soon almost 150 yards away and well out of sight of the couple. Both put on the helmets.

Armour swung his leg over the seat and turned the key. It was well behaved and started first time, but Armour avoided unnecessary revving.

Mac climbed aboard and put her hands on his waist. He kicked the machine into gear, and they pulled away up the hill and soon re-joined the track they had been using. At the road, with the Barnsdale Lodge across from them, they turned right, heading for Stamford.

If the couple had discovered their loss within a few minutes and then spent some time trying to get to a phone, they would have covered the eight miles to Stamford before the alarm and the police could be notified. It would be enough.

Armour was very conscious of the closeness of Mac's body, and the over-revving on a couple of initial gear changes was not totally down to his rustiness in riding a big machine.

The passenger seat was about three inches higher than his own. Mac's legs therefore hugged him high on his waist, and then her hands were wedges above but also slightly between her thighs and his body.

He promised himself, as this particular journey was only going to last a few minutes, that if they ever go through this thing, he would arrange a long motorcycling tour with Mac, as soon as was practicable. To him, this was the way to enjoy a trip.

The contact was not missed by Mac either. She was becoming a bit blasé about the fact that everything, however dangerous, had worked out, and they were still alive, they had even stolen a motorbike right from underneath the noses of the owner and got away with it… and even though she remembered the people who had died along the way, mainly while helping them, she no longer felt scared.

She had been pushing her crutch forward into Armour's back. She felt very sexy, but knew that she would have to curb her feeling for at least a little while longer.

It was only a matter of minutes and they hit the A1, and Armour decided to go south for a couple of miles and go into Stamford from the Northampton road… he thought it might not be anticipated.

The fact was that every road into Stamford was being heavily monitored.

Armour and Mac were spotted as soon as they left the A1, and even though heavily disguised by their helmets, they were being followed by the time they reached the T-junction to turn left and head down to The George.

Fortunately for them the bike gave them an edge. They were able to weave in and out of queuing cars at that junction, when all their pursuers could do was radio ahead that they were coming through.

But that was enough. As they passed a turning on the right, a red Cavalier shot out behind them… it was only a matter of 120 yards to The George, and the Home Secretary.

It was plain that a certain amount of desperation had set in when the Cavalier, with no question of intent gunned directly at the tail end of the motorcycle.

Armour, before hearing anything, felt Mac twist in her seat and then felt her body tense. He looked down into his mirrors and saw the danger.

Immediately he dropped a gear and twisted the accelerator grip for what it was worth.

Mac, not expecting the sudden jolt just managed to catch Armour's collar, and pull herself back into a balanced position.

Armour's move was enough to clear them of the Cavalier

for the moment, but they would not be able to stop in the normal way, get off and walk into the hotel. These people were close, and there would be more so very soon.

He was at The George. Braking hard he hung a sharp left, and the Cavalier followed.

He knew the only way to shake them was… a sudden right, along a footbridge, over the river and into a busy park. He carried on along the tarmac path, up the hill, right into the centre of the town.

He had been here before. He powered the machine right and right again, and they found themselves heading back down towards the river.

Narrowly they missed the Cavalier coming the other way, and they could hear a handbrake turn screech behind them.

There was no time for messing, and Armour knew it. He slowed right down, and brought the machine up the steps and bursting through the door of the hotel.

The management were not impressed, and also within seconds security men were there, guns at the ready.

Armour had been ready for this and had been fumbling for his MI5 ID which he still had on him. He revealed it very slowly as the safety catches of the weapons clicked off.

It still took some time for security to accept that they should even speak to the Home Secretary about this, let alone him… but eventually, after Mac's intervention with her special 'letter of introduction' from HRH, they did. Mac had come up trumps every time.

Chapter Nineteen

In a private suite off the Garden Room, the Home Secretary met with Armour and Mac.

He was a tall man with greying dark hair. He looked pretty fit and was well built, with clear skin. He had a jutting jaw with a public school and Sandhurst air of arrogance. His suit was dark, his Italian brogues had an incredible shine, and his tie was regimental.

He was not alone. A grey-haired man with a military bearing emerged from the shadows of the corner of the room, smiled and held out a hand. Armour and Mac each shook it in turn, and there were two security men by the door.

'An aide' was the only explanation the Home Secretary would offer as to the other man's identity.

"I was told you were coming… you have friends in high places, but now you must tell me what this is all about. I really don't have much time, so you had better make it quick, what's all this drama about?" he said, more than asked.

Mac was a little angry.

"This 'drama' as you call it, has cost the lives of at least eight people. People who, if it were not for this document, would still be alive now," was her riposte, and she shook the offending material, still in the duffle bag, firmly in his direction.

"OK, but what is it?" he demanded as if they were tiresome children. At the same time he waved offhandedly at the two security, "Wait outside," he barked at them.

They did as they were ordered, and the Home Secretary turned to them again.

"Now please…"

Armour took the bag from Mac and walked across, pulling open the drawstrings.

"This does not amount to any proof, but it outlines a plan by senior security officers within government agencies and foreign ones, and others, to coordinate covert operations, and make them revenue earning, for the personal gain of the senior operatives involved. The idea is, that knowing what work has been sanctioned, it can be touted to people who might be interested in the same result. And although it is not proof, and so far uncorroborated, it names names. There can be no doubt that this information would be very embarrassing to some important people, if it became public, or known to the proper authorities."

"It is as we feared Bryan," said the Home Secretary to the other man.

"It would seem so," he replied.

Turning to Armour again the politician asked: "When you say it names names. Who, for example?"

"The names are just initials, and the only one that seemed to make sense at the moment, would appear to be Sir Bryan Calder-Maynes, but there is also a M. McM, and a B…F-S…and a C…C," Armour suddenly felt sick to the bottom of his stomach.

Mac noticed him wince, and stared open-mouthed at him as the colour drained away in an instant.

But he carried on: "You", he pointed to the other man,

"are Sir Bryan… and I guess the C.C …probably stands for Ceiran Carmichael, doesn't it Home Secretary?"

A small automatic emerged from inside Sir Bryan's finely woven tweed jacket.

"You have played a very clever game so far, but I have only been half a step behind, all the time. Oh you have been a little lucky at times, and the opposition has been butting in from time to time, which has helped you, and then there was the Prince, but anyway, you have been a very entertaining adversary.

"However as far as the names are concerned, you have been very stupid," said Calder-Maynes, "You should have thought much more about who you should go running to with the information your friend left for you. I'm afraid I am going to have to shoot you for attacking the Home Secretary… I am a very good shot, so no one will be surprised that you die instantly."

But in the second that he finished the sentence Armour saw the faint smile that had been on his lips fade, and the edges of his mouth turned down as his peripheral vision caught a glimpse of a form by the window.

But he was too late to reaction.

The glass shattered and a bullet tore into Calder-Maynes' throat, and out through the back of his neck, splintering bones and ripping through his spinal cord… he was dead before his gurgling body thumped to the ground like a sack of old King Edwards.

As he was halfway down Armour, with Mac in his arms hit the deck as the two security guys outside stormed in and peppered the window where the shot had come from. Running to it, one picked up a heavy upright chair and hurled it through …more glass showered down and the wooden frames cracked and fell away. The two men leapt out and ran off.

Carmichael had backed against a wall as Armour and Mac made for the door. Armour, just within arms' reach of the Home Secretary said to himself: "In for a penny, in for a pound." He snatched the still unopened duffle bag and he smacked him hard across the top of his mouth and nose with his fist, then shook his hand in pain.

Carmichael made only the slightest guttural noise, but shot backwards and then slid sideways along the wall, tripped over the base of a standard lamp and fell to the floor clutching his face, blood from his broken nose trickling through his fingers.

As they left the room two more security men ran up to them, and Armour shouted:

"Quick, they went through the window… that's where the shot came from," and they dashed off after the others.

They were next to a door which said staff only, so he bustled Mac through it. They were in the kitchen.

Armour was just about to move forward toward the back door when he felt cold metal at the back of his ear.

"Please don't move," said a voice, and it continued… "Believe me, I'm here to help you.

"Keep very quiet and turn around very slowly…"

The man was about 36, clean shaven, wiry and fit. Like them all, it seemed, he had closely cropped hair.

"I was told that if for any reason the chopper didn't arrive at Stoke Rochford, within 45 minutes of its ETA, I should head straight into Stamford and help if I could. I have a car across the road, but we have to get to it"

Armour and Mac relaxed. No one else but the Prince's promised driver would have known about the rendezvous at Stoke Rochford.

Out through the door they found themselves in a small courtyard, with a gateway leading out to the road which overlooked the park, and where they had earlier driven the motorbike.

They were surprised to be able to dash across the road and get into the back of the car.

Their good Samaritan gunned the car into action, revved up to speed and executed a screeching handbrake turn. With the car already in second and then third they met the green light that cleared them for the right hand turn which they took virtually on two wheels, and they sped out of the town past the Lady Anne Hotel and out to the A1 and south.

"If you were given alternative instruction to those that Prince Charles first gave, then he must have guessed that something was likely to go wrong," said Armour to the man.

"We don't use full names sir, but yes you are right. My orders are to take you to London. But first of all I have to take you to an airfield where you will have to wait for a short while so I can change the car. Relax, it will be a few more miles first."

In fact it was less than 15 minutes, and they had passed Peterborough, and left the A1 a couple of minutes earlier. They came to an airfield guardhouse, and their man stopped the car by the barrier and got out. He went to the door and opened it. They could see him talking to a guard inside, show him something, wave and then return to the car.

The barrier raised and they drove through.

"Just had to give him some MI5 bullshit," he said and they started to head out across open land, on the airfield perimeter road.

In the hazy distance Armour could see a small air traffic control tower, a few green-painted buildings, a couple of white ones and a few large blue-grey hangers – but they were a good way off on the other side of the airfield, and the airstrip, which was between them and those buildings were a good 400 yards away.

In the opposite direction was the airfield perimeter fence,

at least 300 yards away, through which Armour could see several fields of corn and hedgerows.

They came to a small clump of aging Second World War Nissen huts, some still with corrugated iron roofing which touched the ground on both sides, like a cylinder cut in half lengthwise. Each building was joined by narrow corridors. The old iron-framed windows were large and square.

Their driver stopped and got out. He went over to a door, opened it, disappeared for a moment and then came back and beckoned to them.

He led them in past two doors and he opened the third on the left. Inside, it was clean but spartan and he led them in.

There was some simple furniture, rugs on the floor, two bunks and tea and coffee-making facilities.

"Look I know this is not very special, but I will only be about an hour. This place is sometimes used for operatives working around this area, so it is sort of meant for us rather than civvies.

"When I have found other safe transport I have to clarify where exactly I have to take you… I want to check what they told me on the radio," he said.

"Where did they say to take us?" asked Mac, looking around her.

"Well, my original instructions were to take you to the old Cabinet War rooms in Horse Guards Parade, but then there was a radio message to bring you here, change vehicles and then transport you to barracks off Albany Street, next to Regent's Park. But don't worry, I'll get it sorted out soon and be back in no time. Make yourselves as comfortable as possible. Cheers," he said closing the door. A few minutes later they heard the car drive off.

Suddenly though they felt very lonely, and Mac slid into Armour's arms.

"Do you think we are going to get these documents through to the right people?" she asked, pointing aimlessly at the duffle bag.

"Surely there is only one person left… the Prime Minister… He can't be in on it too… can he?

"He could, but I doubt it, mind you, I have been wrong before… and quite recently."

Armour did not want to think about it for a little while. He walked over the corner of the stark room where the kettle was.

"Want a cup of tea?"

"Mmmm, why not?"

She curled her legs under herself and watched him. She did not mind what happened as long as they were together. She wondered what he would be like in a normal domestic situation. She found it hard to conjure up that image, but did not think that even that would be boring.

They sat, arms around each other and drank their tea from enamel mugs. The sudden silence after the action of the past few days seemed strange and even a little eerie. They both felt it.

"Pete, isn't this a bit of a strange place to keep us… for however short a time?" she said, looking around their 'cell'.

"Why? What do you mean?

"Well, I don't know. We are in the middle of some airfield, God knows where, on our own, with no transport, and no easy way out."

"Well, I know what you mean. But on the other hand, being on an air base means that we are highly unlikely to fall foul of the other side."

"But Calder-Maynes said that the opposition, whether they meant to or not had been a help to us. I think it is our side that we should be most worried about. Being in a government establishment does not exactly give me the greatest confidence in the world."

"OK I share that feeling, but what about if this guy was the rendezvous man at Stoke Rochford, knew what HRH meant him to do, and he got us out of Stamford."

"Yeah… I've been thinking about that… What if he worked for Calder-Maynes and rendezvoused with the rendezvous man… and took his place.

"Considering what has been happening over the last couple of days that certainly can't be ruled out, but why would he then shoot Calder-Maynes, it doesn't make sense."

"But let's say we don't trust this guy… where do we go from here. We are miles from anywhere?"

"I don't know. It is odd."

"My point exactly, I'm worried."

"He said he received instructions by radio, so obviously not from Charles. Someone else has been giving instructions, so this guy could be the right rendezvous man, but now getting the wrong instructions.

"Hey, we'll be alright," and he clasped her in his arms again, and although her mind was racing, she was comforted by his soothing words. The more he thought about their current situation the more he worried. Mac was right. More than ever over the past few days they were alone, but never more exposed or vulnerable.

"I think we should try and keep a look out for anyone approaching. I know he will be in a different vehicle, but it might be worth keeping a look out," said Armour, "You check out the way we came in, and I'll see what more there is around here in the other buildings, and watch that way."

Staveley-Smythe received the call from Blake.

"Yes"

"Blake sir,"

"Yes Blake, what's happening?"

"Well, there's been a right old fracas." He pronounced it

'frack-arse', "at The George at Stamford. Armour and the girl driving into the place on a motorbike, there was shooting, and General Calder-Maynes is dead…"

"What? Armour shot Calder-Maynes?"

"Er, no sir, someone else did. And they then lifted Armour and the girl and got them away. Well, as you know sir we have a chopper in the area. We had a description of the vehicle to them quickly and they were spotted heading south on the A1. It looks as if they have been put into temporary billeting on the field at Alconbury, which is pretty convenient really. Do you want us to move in, there's virtually no one around."

"No Blake. Stay in the area, but keep away, I'll handle this," said Staveley-Smythe and he hung up the phone.

So, Calder-Maynes was dead. That did not bother him, although he was surprised that it had happened, he almost thought the man was invincible. But he, Michael Staveley-Smythe, was now the brains and the power behind the group, and although he was not the most senior person involved, he would be expected to take day-to-day control, and make things happen. It was dangerous, but would be incredibly rewarding. He need only be involved for a couple of years and he could disappear – with a new identity, and a very rich lifestyle. There was nothing stopping him, except that is, for Armour and the girl.

Although dead, Calder-Maynes was still playing in the game, and a short while earlier had been having the same thoughts.

In his car, just before the pre-lunch meeting with Carmichael, he sat and thought for a few minutes and then picked up his mobile. He realised that Armour and the girl getting to Carmichael was likely, but it was unlikely they would reason out who he was or that Carmichael was involved. But if Carmichael let the cat out of the bag – he was apt to run off at the mouth on occasions, there would need to be a contingency plan.

He punched in the numbers, thinking all the time of the area they were in. It could be pretty simple, but he would have to act very quickly.

He checked a few details with West Drayton air traffic control, which handles military flights, rang off and then made another call. He spoke for a few minutes, gave a codeword, spoke again and then hung up.

Chapter Twenty

Flight Lieutenant Jim 'Stack' Halloran was a Harrier pilot and a veteran of various conflicts including covert operations. He had a reputation for great accuracy on bombing raids.

Fact is, that's how he got his nickname… many missiles are designed to smash through concrete roofs and then explode inside a building, but they reckoned Halloran could put a missile down a chimney stack of the target building, without first damaging the roof.

This of course was a mild exaggeration, but, at the same time Halloran did have an extraordinarily precise skill, which had won him honours.

Stack loved to fly. It was his job, but there was more to it than that. When he flew, and particularly the Harrier – most pilots had their favourites – he felt at one with the aircraft, measuring each slight movement it made in response to his manipulation.

Stack Halloran glanced down at his watch. It was 2.27 pm, on this Saturday afternoon.

Paired with a back-up VTOL 'jump jet', Halloran was flying a pretty routine training run, leading in the second pilot… to show how it was done.

With typical secrecy and haste, this 'mission' had little

forewarning, and on this occasion an even briefer pre-flight brief than usual. He knew what the target was, where it was, but not when he was supposed to strike. In fact he was ordered to await final confirmation of the strike before commencing the live bombing run. Halloran's commanding officer did let it slip to him though that there would be top brass eyes on this one, and to make it good.

They had been in the air for about 40 minutes, and from their base in Lincolnshire, they had been out over the North Sea, headed back in towards Newcastle, down the coast to Kings Lynn, and then headed inland, south, south-west.

"Alpha, Tango, One. Alpha Tango One?" Halloran heard over the radio, and he acknowledged immediately.

"Alpha Tango One. Alpha Tango One, strike confirmed, repeat, strike confirmed."

Halloran 'rogered' and altered his course. He noted the second Harrier, Alpha Tango Two, make the same adjustment, and they confirmed with each other their approach to the target, speed and ETA.

Halloran radioed this back to base.

They were now just three minutes away.

This was fun for Halloran. He loved the speed, the accuracy, and the real pleasure in the perfect strike. And although he always liked to do it right, this was just a training flight, even if the big boys were watching and so he relaxed, feeling good.

The weather was clear, but this was not to be a particularly high altitude strike. He and the other pilot had decided to make a run past, make a turn and start the first bomb run... there would be two in all.

On the fly past he could see the old Nissen huts on the airfield, one of which conveniently had a white cross marked on the roof. It was an isolated spot and there was nothing significant nearby.

The missiles which hit on the first run would reduce the place to rubble, but he had been told to make sure of the strike, needed or not, with a second run.

Thirty seconds to go and he made his final turn. Alpha Tango Two was just six seconds behind.

Halloran could see the buildings clearly in his bombsight. This was going to be dead easy. In training flights cameras were usually fitted to the aircraft, so others would be able to see the standard of performance and make comment later, so he decided that precision was again going to be the mark of his calling card.

When satisfied, his thumb squeezed the button, and he felt the familiar jolt as the missile launched and then the slightly weaving trail as it wound its way to the target, and he watched his screen guided the missile in and gave confirmation of the hit.

Terror grabbed Armour in his throat, and it contracted so much that he thought his head was going to burst, and he felt sure he would shit himself.

He heard the aerial scream and recognised it in a flash. In the next moment, as he was flung into a ditch only 40 yards away from the building, everything went white and a horrific heat seared above him, burning his neck.

Mac?… his eyes prickled and he felt sick to his bones and the base of his stomach and all content shifted.

Less than a minute earlier he had watched as Mac wandered off towards the entrance of the building that they had come in through. She had smiled and given a brief wave. He had turned the other way towards a part of the buildings that they did not know.

The further into the building he went, the worse the decor, until he found an area where the walls were a mixture of rotting plaster and peeling paint of bland RAF grey and blue.

He had checked out several other rooms which were empty, or just had a few cardboard boxes and scraps of paper, and a couple of outside doors which were locked.

In the old style curved corrugated roof buildings even the wooden floors had been ripped out and there were a few discarded ammo boxes strewn around.

Armour returned to one of the newer parts and found a room with a desk and blackboard, and a map on the wall of RAF Alconbury, and he made the assumption that that was where they were. He looked at it and it even had the buildings in which they were standing marked on it. At each of the windows he peered out to see if there was anything that might help them.

But at each Armour could see there was as little out this side as there had been on the other.

From the office which he took to be a briefing room, he looked out. A short distance away was a small tank raised from the ground on a metal frame, which Armour took to be for central heating fuel. Around the tank there was a large patch of rough ground.

There were shadows among the clumps of tufted grass.

Suddenly, he noticed one of them move, and raise from the ground to take the form of a soldier huddling an automatic weapon. It was remarkably similar to those one sees on military firing ranges and Armour, though feeling the need to move quickly, stood rooted to the spot, transfixed by the figure in front of him.

His eyes narrowed as he looked, and it was plain that the soldier had seen him. He raised his hand in front of him with his palm towards his own face. He brought his hand quickly towards him in a 'come here… quick' gesture which he repeated three times.

Armour, realising the man appeared to mean him no harm… he would have shot straight away if he had…

Armour tried to open a window, but they were paint-jammed shut. He tried a door but that too would not open.

He fought with the window again, but saw that the soldier was running towards him.

As he got closer, he could see he was wearing a balaclava covering his whole face except his eyes, and the skin around his eyes was darkened by a blackish-green substance.

The soldier waved him back from the window, and mutedly heard him shout: "Get away" and he duly stepped back, strangely bemused by this action. Using the butt of his weapon the soldier smashed his way through, showering glass everywhere.

"Get out," he yelled, and as Armour came closer, the man grabbed him under his arm, and using the window sill as a fulcrum swung Armour out of the building, and then pushing him, half running and stumbling into the open ground.

"What the fuck's going on?" he protested, and he turned, as if to go back to the window.

"What about Mac?"

"Forget it mate, you haven't got time. Come on, this way, move!"

"Why no time?" he said starting to return to the building.

It was then that felt the blow on the back of his head. The soldier had clipped him with the rifle-butt. It was not intended to put him out, but just enough to let the soldier swing him round and continue to run with him.

Then there was the screech from high above them and the soldier launched them both into the ditch, landing on top of Armour, except for his head and shoulders.

Armour fought for breath, and tasted the soil and grass beneath him. As if hitting the crest of a wave, and at the same time being punched in the stomach, his breath suddenly came, but it seemed like an age. He felt a rib crack. Then it was as though a ton of loose earth had rained down on the two of them, along with bricks and splinters of wood. The sky had gone dark. The heat was searing and he heard and smelt burning hair. The breaths that he took were short and foul tasting.

His head pounded.

'God, what about Mac?' was all he could think.

Had he lost her so soon…?

Just as he was about to raise his head, a second chilling scream came, and this time he dropped his face to the ground, knowing what was about to happen.

The little breath he had in him escaped from his body as he tried and only half managed to get her name out.

"Ma-a-a-"

It was like a prisoner's appeal to a hangman, when suddenly there is only air below.

It's too late.

With the horrific burning smell in his nostrils, he buried his head again as the planes returned, unleashed their deadly missiles, and then flew off, eventually disappearing into the distance.

Now the tears flowed freely. Armour raised his head as his body rattled, wracked with shock and grief.

The soldier was already on his feet and walking fast towards the debris. He walked into the smoking wreckage, and he disappeared from Armour's sight.

Apart from the burns on the back of his neck, Armour thought for a split-second that it was a dream, it hadn't happened. But that was silly. He knew it had happened and he knew his life had been saved by the mystery soldier.

Equally he knew that Mac was dead. If he was anything, Armour was a realist. His own rescue was nothing short of miraculous, but that was as big as miracles get…

But now he wished he had died. Faces swirled in front of his face, Burricks, Grogan and Vasilli, even the two hitmen who themselves had been killed in Oxford. He did not care anymore about the secret document still strapped to his back, or what it might mean to the country.

He crumpled to the floor, making no attempt to protect his face except to turn it to the side, and his head hit soft grass.

Watching the smoke rising and other soldiers running past him towards the wrecked building, which was now no more than a hole in the ground, he just lay there motionless with a stink of cordite and sulphur in his nostrils.

He ached completely, he was tired and he had lost the person most precious to him in the world… so what else mattered? Actually he was beyond pain.

Feet were pounding the ground closer and closer to him, and he felt a soldier kneel down beside him.

"I'm a medic, where are you hurt?"

He ignored the inquiry and continued his blank stare through the blades of grass in front of his face.

Without asking his permission the medic was feeling his limbs and then gently, rolled him over. He checked Armour's body for wound and injury, but apart from a few minor burns could see nothing.

"Can you talk?"

Armour was now staring up at the sky without moving from the position to which the medic had rolled him.

"Hello, can you hear me?" the medic yelled, and he waved his hand across in front of Armours eyes which were watering.

He didn't really feel the enthusiasm to come back to reality, he had had just about as much as he could take. But he decided to acknowledge…

"Yeah, yeah. I'm alright," he said, and he allowed the young medic, whose eyes he looked into for the first time, to help him to his feet.

He stood facing the devastation, his face reddened by the

searing heat and tears silently slipping down his face. He couldn't be bothered to wipe them away. He had seen as much as he needed to see.

Taking several steps to do it he staggered and turned away from the scene. As his eyes struggled to focus, he saw four dark green Land Rovers rushing across the open ground towards him…he stumbled a few steps, his head swam, he tottered forwards, and fell to the ground, losing consciousness as he dropped. He lay there with smoke wafting from his charred clothing, the smell of which stuck in his nostrils for just a moment before the lights went out.

"Great shooting," enthused Halloran to the pilot of Alpha Tango Two, as the other pilot, coming up alongside his leader, smiled, looked across an gave a thumbs up.

"Sweet as a nut." he returned.

Stack Halloran radioed base and asked for instructions and got a simple order to return to base. The pilot on his right wing heard the order and Halloran, pleased at a good day's work, the dying sun over the nose of his aircraft, Halloran pulled back on the joystick, lifting the nose, powered up, dipped his right wing and turned towards the north. Alpha Tango Two followed suit.

When he came round it was early morning in the private room of a hospital, he assumed, but did not know where? For a moment he was confused, and then he recalled the nightmare, and then he didn't really care where he was.

All he could think of was Mac.

The only consolation was that there could be little doubt that her death would have been instantaneous. He felt the tears well up again.

"Oh Mac I love you," he whispered finally and drifted back into oblivion… so what?

Peter Aengenheister

During the air strike there must have been more bricks than he first thought, as he lay, this time with his eyes still firmly shut. He felt pummelled and he was having some difficulty breathing. He knew he had at least one broken rib, maybe two. And the sulphurous stench from the missile mercilessly ripped at his lungs every time he breathed. He had been bathed, treated and left to sleep. The earlier bullet graze too had been re-dressed. Unusually he was wearing pyjamas, but it was obvious they were crisply brand new. The room was comfortably furnished and quite plush, and there was a faint light from a dimmed standard lamp a few yards away. He was as comfortable as he could be, he guessed, but the rigours of the last few days and what happened to Mac left him listless. He drifted in and out of sleep for some time, and was only vaguely conscious of the door of the room opening and shutting occasionally.

Finally, he woke, and just lay with his eyes open, calmly but disinterestedly taking in the things around him.

The room was quite large, florally wallpapered in pastel colours, with proper drapes and two deep soft sofas in one corner with a low coffee table in front of them. There was a wash basin with mirror above and a host of gentlemen's toiletries on the adjoining surface, and there was a shower cubicle in the corner. Further along there were coffee-making facilities with an assortment of biscuits. In another corner was a small colour television and video.

He assumed that he was not in further danger, otherwise he would not be alive – and who gives a condemned man assorted biscuits? He looked around to see if there was a button so he could summon attention, but there was none.

Easing his aching body up to a sitting position and he took a sip from a glass of water that stood on his bedside table. Initially it seemed to burn, then soothe his sandpaper-dry throat.

Sunlight was beginning to peep through a crack in the curtains and Armour drew back the duvet cover and swung his legs to the floor. He sat there for a few seconds with a whooshing in his ears. He tilted his head from one side to the other and his neck gave a couple of cracks as the bones found their correct position.

He flashed back to the air strike, and then the moment before that when he had last seen Mac, and the little wave she gave him… something he would never forget. But then there was nothing of the time they had just spent together that he would forget. Whilst they had faced danger almost continuously for the past four days, he had been more alive than he had been in years. It was not just because their lives had been on the line and the adrenalin had been coursing through their veins, but because he had been with her. If she had not been with him, it would have been more simple a job that he had to do, however dangerous. If he had not been thinking about keeping Mac alive he might not have done so much. If she had not been there, they could have been dead the first few hours they hit Oxford. Having Mac there gave it all meaning.

He lifted himself from the bedside, clutching his bandaged ribs, and painfully made his way to the window and gently drew back the curtains.

The light was piercing and he shaded his eyes with his hand for a few moments, his head swam again and he felt slightly sick. He did not recognise the rooftops he saw a little way off, but knew instantly that he was somewhere in the heart of London.

At that moment, there was a soft knock at the door, and he turned as young woman in an informal, but nursing-style outfit entered.

Her eyes moved from the bed to the window and she smiled.

"Ah good, so you're up then. My you had been in the wars haven't you, but nothing too serious…" she had the pleasant lilt of a southern Irish accent.

"Where am I?" he asked, trying not to sound rude, "and what happened to the girl that was with me? What day is it?"

"I'm sorry, you were the only one brought here, and I don't know anything about a girl. It's Saturday morning, and you are in London. Now that you are awake, someone will be along very shortly to talk with you. You of course are perfectly free, but I have been asked to convey the desire of your host that you remain here for just a short while. I will be in the adjoining rooms and can get you anything you want, newspapers for example. That's all I can say at the moment, except, what would you like for breakfast?"

"I couldn't eat anything," he said, and then, "Who is my host?"

"Of course, how could you know, His Royal Highness, the Prince of Wales… Shall I just bring some coffee then?"

So, to the rescue again. He wondered how his Highness had taken the news of Mac's death.

"Yes, that's kind, thank you. How long will I have to wait?"

"Oh the coffee will only be a moment," she giggled girlishly at her own joke, but quickly continued when she noticed that Armour's smile, although pleasant, was a little forced.

"Not long sir, as soon as I tell them you are awake someone will be along I'm sure.

"I'll get you that coffee."

She returned in about three minutes with coffee and also on the tray were a couple of croissants and butter. She set them down on a table in the corner of the room where there were two large easy chairs. She smiled again.

"Won't be long now, would you like a paper?"

"No, I don't think…sorry, yes please, have you got the *Daily Telegraph*?"

She said she could quickly get a copy, and left.

Armour wondered whether there might be anything of the incident in Stamford. He knew there would be nothing about the air strike. Wherever that had happened it would have been a routine occurrence, and with no information, certainly not anything like the truth, nothing worth reporting. An incident involving the Home Secretary was bound to be reported.

Again in a matter of minutes the young woman was back with the newspaper, and then went.

Sure enough it was the lead story on Page Three. The front page was dominated with riots in Berlin involving factions from the far right.

The Page Three headline said: 'SHOOTING SCARE FOR CARMICHAEL', and a rundown headline read: 'Aide dies as ex-mental patient opens up'.

The first few paragraphs said:

'An aide of Home Secretary, Cieran Carmichael was gunned to death yesterday when an ex-mental hospital patient opened fire in a hotel where the Home Secretary was meeting leading Lincolnshire business-men. Mr. Carmichael himself received slight injury in the face during the incident.

'The aide, who has not yet been named died instantly. The Home Secretary was in an adjoining room at the time and was in no danger, although he was slightly injured in the face as security men bundled him to safety.

'The gunman was wrestled to the ground by bodyguards.

'No one else was hurt during the incident at The George at Stamford yesterday lunchtime.

'Although local police have revealed that the attacker was a former mental patient from a nearby home, they have not released his name, where he was in hospital, or why he started the shooting.'

Armour recognised the usual signs of a cover-up. A potential international incident had been reduced to an case of a local with a few stair-rods missing, running amok in a sleepy market town.

Armour sipped the coffee, feeling even more depressed, and the warm coffee burned as it dropped into his stomach.

The door opened and a tall, well-dressed man in his mid to late thirties came in extending his hand.

"Good morning sir, I hope you are feeling all right. My name is James Briars. I am a private secretary to His Royal Highness, who I believe you met a couple of days ago. He has asked me to convey his best wishes, hopes you are comfortable, and he will see you later."

"Thank you," he was slightly surprised, and then he added, "…where am I?"

"This is a part of Clarence House sir. The Prince has asked me to say that you are perfectly safe here, and for the moment, probably for the rest of the day, it would be better that you stay here. He said to say he has the documents you were carrying and that he was meeting with the Prime Minister this morning for private discussions. If there is anything we can do or get for you, you only have to say."

Armour was not in a rush to go anywhere or do anything.

"Do you know what happened to the girl I was with, Claire Willans?"

Briars seemed genuinely hurt that he could not help

"I'm so sorry sir, I don't know. You were brought here on your own."

"Well, that is something you can do for me. Find out will you… I need to know for certain what happened…"

"I will of course do what I can sir. Is there anything else?"

"No, not really. I could do with some more papers to read please… anything will do. I could do with some more coffee."

Armour flopped back down in one of the deep sofas as Briars left the room. He flicked the switch on the television set and the breakfast shows were in progress. He flicked it off again. He did the same with the radio but left some classical music playing as he walked to the window.

The young Irish girl came in and left a few newspapers, which he flicked through. They also carried a very similar account of what happened in Stamford.

He returned to the window, where if he really craned his aching neck he could see Green Park, Constitution Hill, and maybe just the right hand corner of Buckingham Palace. Looking the other way he guessed it was the roofs of St. James, towards Piccadilly Square.

Clarence House, eh, home of the Queen Mum, well certainly no one would be looking for him there. And even if they knew he was there, it would cause a major incident if they tried to do anything. Frankly though he really didn't care. He felt desperately empty without Mac. It was worse not knowing exactly what had happened. He could not quite believe she was dead, but knew that she must be.

Still aching he had a lie down, and woke suddenly when the Irish girl came in and asked if he wanted lunch, and he had a tuna sandwich and some salad. He watched the lunchtime news… more about the right wing rioting in Berlin.

Briars came in about two in the afternoon

"I'm terribly sorry sir, I have not been able to find out anything about the young lady you were talking about. I did raise the question with the Prince when he rang in, but he was in rather a hurry and said he wanted to speak to you personally about what had happened to her."

"He said his discussion with the Prime Minister went very well, and steps are being taken," he said.

Armour was resigned to the fact that Mac was dead. Why would the prince want to speak to him personally if it was not that?

He wished that everyone would just go away.

As Briars left he turned and flopped down in the sofa again and dozed.

He saw himself beside the grave of his parents again. Everything was the same, but when the film running in front of him bought the boy's face into close-up, the tears this time were flowing silently, freely.

The next moment that disappeared and he heard the screech of the Harriers above him and felt the heat and was suddenly bolt upright and awake and shaking. He was gasping for breath and it felt as if he was being stabbed in the chest.

He knew he was never going to be the same again. He knew now that he was going to be as safe as he ever could be and it would appear that what could be done, was being done, but he could not possibly imagine carrying on his life as he had before.

He shuddered at the thought of returning to the *Chron* at any time in the future. The people there may never know the truth about why Burricks was killed, but he did, and he felt responsible.

If it had not been for him, the young man would still be alive – if it had not been for him Mac would be still alive. He could not possibly go back there.

He did not think he would even be able to bring himself to carry on with the refurbishment of his cottage on the edge of Althorp estate. And then he had lost a good friend in Pat Grogan, one of the best…

He would have to move well away, and perhaps to another country. And quite frankly he had lost all interest in journalism for the time being. Well, he had savings and investments, and if he sold the Althorp cottage, he could probably rent someplace in the Ardeche for a year or longer. He wouldn't have to work, but he could imagine doing some local work on the vines. He had once been tempted to stay in a mountain village near Privas a little longer than he meant to by the friendly people and their food and wines.

He could go back there. He thought he might fit in at least, and the rural French have this way of being nosey about people and their habits, but not too bothered about what they did before. They liked you for what you were at that moment and how you treated them. There may be talk, but no one would be as irreverent as to ask.

During the afternoon he slept through an old western film on the television, and when he woke again, roused by the noise of shooting, even though it had not been turned up very high in any case, he switched it off.

This time his mind went back to the nights he and Mac had spent together. He closed his eyes.

He pictured her shape, her form, the eyes he could not tire of looking into, and her smile. He recalled every mannerism. He was torturing himself, but he would not want it any other way.

At 5 pm the girl brought tea and biscuits, and an evening paper. Still no news. At 6 pm Briars entered, bringing some smart casual clothes that were bound to fit.

"Good afternoon sir."

"Hello… eh, Briars. So what's happening?"

"His Royal Highness wonders if you would care to dine with him at 7.30?"

"Sure, where?"

"I will come for you at 7.20 sir."

"Thanks," he said, trying not to sound morose. This guy probably thought: 'This chap is going to dine with the future King of England, and he wanders around with a face like a wet weekend.'

Actually Briars did not think anything of the sort. It was not his job to make judgements and he had long since stopped doing it. He used to, but usually found that he was most awfully wrong about people, and invariably they had good reason for their behaviour.

"Blake sir,"

"Yes Blake?"

"Very dramatic sir, and a mite expensive I would have thought."

Staveley-Smythe was not sure whether Blake was seriously chastising him, or whether he was being tongue in cheek.

"What are you talking about?" Staveley-Smythe felt the blood draining from his face.

"The RAF Harriers sir. They were apparently in the air and on a training mission anyway, but someone arranged for a change of target. Well, I guess it did the job sir.

"There was nothing left of the Nissen hut they were in, but strangely when we arrived on the scene there were a load of SAS boys milling around and it looked as if a couple of them had been slightly injured. I don't know if they had been working in the area. There were also a couple of Royal Protection lads I have seen before."

Staveley-Smythe nearly choked on his coffee.

Who arranged what? He knew Armour and the girl had

been taken to the airfield, but no arrangements had been made since Calder-Maynes' demise.

"You didn't see Armour or the girl?"

"Hardly sir, there was nothing left of that place, it had been hit by four missiles. It's just a big hole in the ground. Personally I would have thought it was a bit of a sledgehammer to crack a nut."

Blake did not normally comment or question.

"Shut up Blake. I didn't arrange this firework display you fool."

"Sorry sir, now that the General is no longer… eh hem, I just thought…"

He told Blake to see if any of the troops on the ground could cast any light, but later would hear that they did not know anything, and if they did, they were definitely not saying anything.

After slamming down the receiver, he made a call to Strategic Air Command and spoke to a Group Captain Dorning about who had given clearance to change the flight plan and target of the Harrier strike. When he learned, he put the phone down and whistled through his teeth – was there no stopping the man – even though he was dead?

However, he certainly seemed to have sorted the problem out. There was no chance that Armour and the Willans girl had survived the missile attack, or the documents,

Blake would have heard. He had no idea why the SAS were at Alconbury, but that was not necessarily unusual.

Royal Protection was a little more unusual, but again not altogether unknown. If it wasn't for the Prince's involvement, he would not have given it a second thought. He pushed it to the back of his mind, it had to be OK. He rang Carmichael.

A lump stuck in Carmichael's throat as his car turned into Trafalgar Square set to go the few hundred yards along Whitehall to Downing Street. This was a trip he had actually made many times, but not usually after being curtly summoned to a meeting with the PM by the Tory Chief Whip.

It had been about 5.30 when he got the phone call. He had been back from Stamford at about 6 pm the night before, and had had an update from Staveley-Smythe about their problem and been reassured that everything was alright. He had decided after his bash on the nose to cancel his engagements, which on that day, Saturday, meant an informal meeting at his club with the member for Rugby and Kenilworth, Jim Pawsey, and a small reception for a group of dignitaries from Botswana.

But he did decide to do some work – he had opened one of his red boxes at about 4 pm and started looking through Cabinet papers.

"Ah, Cieran, Geoffrey here, look, could you possibly come round to No 10 ASAP. We've got a bit of a problem. Listen, can't possibly talk on the blower, but don't bother to bring papers or anything like that with you, we've got it all here. OK… see you shortly," and the phone was hung up.

In between his words Carmichael had managed an 'oh,' an 'ah', a 'yeees' and a 'right', even though Sir Geoffrey Walkworth had not paused for breath.

Carmichael had a feeling of doom. There had been nothing else going on that he should feel guilty about. The elections were a long way off… perhaps a senior Tory had died, or maybe another sex scandal…

The gate at the end of Downing Street was being held open by a police office and his car moved quickly along to the home of his leader.

He alighted, carrying just his briefcase, and moved

quickly up the steps, and the officer outside saluted as the door magically opened before him and he disappeared inside.

He was immediately shown into the Cabinet Room.

Stern-faced Sir Geoffrey, beckoned him to sit opposite Prime Minister, John Major, who was staring down at a document in front of him. When he had done so, Major slowly raised tired and serious eyes towards him.

"What on earth are we going to do with you, you stupid prat?" It was a statement as well as a question.

"Sir?" he was conscious that to have said: 'John, what is this all about?' would have been too informal and very naïve.

"Come on, the document found at this safe house in Warwickshire? Don't tell me you don't know what I am talking about, I've got statements," and he slapped papers down on the famous bowed Cabinet table, and Ceiran saw that Staveley-Smythe's name was on the top one.

It was more than a bluff, but there was no proof. Any evidence would be circumstantial, even inadmissible in a court, and in any case the Prime Minister was not about to let his Party be torn apart by the aftermath of a prosecution of the Home Secretary.

At the same time Carmichael knew that he was finished in politics. Even though there was no proof, the word would be out, people would know. Oh there wouldn't dare say anything, because he would be able to sue for slander or libel, but he was finished alright.

"Yes, Prime Minister I have heard of their existence and have been informed of the allegations that might be made against me. They are wild and spurious and totally unfounded. A complete fabrication, I utterly deny any involvement whatever and vigorously dispute this outrageous slur on my good name.

"However, I recognise the possible difficulty this puts the Party in and for myself as Home Secretary.

"In the circumstances, and to avoid embarrassment to you, the Party, the Government and the country, I hereby tender my resignation."

Carmichael was told that the meeting was over, and when they had decided to say in their statement to the Press, he would be informed. He left for the last time.

It had been at 7 am Saturday morning that there was a knock at the door of Staveley-Smythe's smart home in Nightingales Lane, Little Chalfont, Buckinghamshire. He came to the door in his dressing gown and slippers, and saw a dark blue Ford Scorpio and two black Granadas parked in his gravel drive.

"Good morning sir. Are you Mr. Michael Staveley-Smythe?"

"I am, what is this?"

"My name is Chief Superintendent John Davies and this is Superintendent Mark Marsden. We are from Scotland Yard and I am placing you under arrest on suspicion of breach of the Official Secrets Act. Anything you do say may be taken down and used in evidence against you. You will have to come with us sir, so Superintendent Marsden will accompany you while you get dressed. This is a search warrant," he said holding up a folded piece of paper which he held out to Staveley-Smythe, who stepped back as the two men entered, and others following in from behind.

"This is outrageous," he said to their disappearing backs, with one, Marsden then facing his direction and waiting for him to go upstairs…

On the dot Briars came and escorted Armour through an outer suite and into a wood-panelled corridor, with thick ornamental rugs covering the floor. Briars walked slightly in front as he led the way.

Oil-painted portraits in thick ornate golden frames adorned the coved walls of the drawing room. Uplighting wall lights played on red velvety textured wallpaper, while the room was decorated with Louis XVI bureaux with ormolu mounts, and green covered chairs. There were soft deep cream sofas, foot cushions and ornate coffee tables. William IV and Early Victorian revivalist rococo…

As Armour entered the room with Briars, a golden retriever raised its head and flopped its tail a couple of times, and as his eyes moved around they met the prince who was standing in front of a huge ornate carved Georgian white marble fireplace with Siena Marble slips and in-lay.

The Prince looked serious.

"Good evening, Mr. Armour, it is good to see you again," he said rather stiffly at first. "I hope you are feeling better. Err, I'm sorry I have not been able to speak to you earlier.

"The document you had has, er… certainly put the cat among the pigeons… quite extraordinary."

"Forgive me Your Royal Highness, but can you please tell about Mac… is she…?"

"My dear Mr. Armour, Pete, please forgive me. Forgive me, how remiss. Claire is, sort of, OK, and will be well soon. She suffered some minor burns and a badly sprained ankle."

Armour slumped down in a chair and putting his hand to his head and winced at the pain in his chest, and said: "Thank God… I could do with a drink."

"Forgive me again… a scotch isn't it?" and he poured a healthy portion tumbler, and made himself a gin and tonic.

"I'm so pleased that Claire has someone who is able to put her first. She needs that. I like you Mr Armour," said the Prince.

"Pete, please."

"Of course, and you must call me Charles."

"I'll try. So, where is Mac, I would like to see her."

You should be able to see her tomorrow. She's at the King Edward VII's Hospital for Officers here in town, and they are releasing her mid-morning. I have arranged for her to be brought here. Would you like to telephone her? I hope that you will be able to stay with us for a couple of days."

"Yes, I would very much like to ring her, said Armour and he took a note of the number.

The prince left the room and Armour made the call. He spoke first to a sister on the ward who said Mac was well, but still a little concussed and might be a little confused, but they could talk.

She was relieved to hear his voice and comforted by the fact that he was with Charles.

It was the best possible scenario as far as she was concerned. She felt she could sleep easy.

Armour too was relieved. At that moment there was not a great deal to talk about. It was just good to be in touch and close. Armour was conscious that he was tiring her and for that reason did not try and protract the conversation. She was OK with that and said she couldn't wait for the morning to see him. But she was unable to wait much longer… to sleep.

They whispered, and eventually he hung up, knowing that she would not.

It was about a minute after he had put the phone down, and he was back at the fireplace and making circular motions with his scotch and taking small sips, when the Prince returned.

"Let's go through and eat." he said.

And suddenly Armour had recovered his appetite…

But as they sat down, the Prince said:

"It soon became obvious that you had not made it to Stoke Rochford, but tell me about George. He was a good friend as well as a pilot, I would like to know what happened first hand, as it were, and although they have been notified, I still have to speak with his family."

Armour described events as fully as he could.

Chapter Twenty-One

Mac woke in pain. Her ankle throbbed, her head ached, her throat was sore, and then suddenly she remembered…

She had waved to Armour and turned toward the door they had come in. She peered out and could see nothing significant. Certainly there was no sign of the driver coming back with fresh transport. She could see nothing but a bit of tarmac and a lot of grass stretching for what appeared to be miles. In the distance were some trees.

She tried the door. It was open, and she walked out a few yards.

As she turned to walk back in she heard the repetitive dull thump of someone running behind her, and turned to be grabbed by a man in a balaclava.

Strangely, he was looking up in the air. He turned her 180 degrees from where she was standing and started frog marching her in the opposite direction.

It all happened too fast for her to start protesting.

Just then she heard a faint scream above her head. He obviously heard it too and the pace quickened.

As the scream increased to an ear piercing pitch she suddenly felt herself being projected into the air, and then the wind was compressed out of her by the force of a massive weight on her back.

That weight on her back had saved her life. That weight was a man in a balaclava.

Suddenly the full horror flooded back.

Every breath had gone from her lungs, and when she could force a bit in, it burned as someone literally breathing in fire. She lay with a weight baring down on her, and at the same time the trickle of blood flowed down on to her neck and face. She knew what it was, and as the dust and smoke cleared from around her she saw the redness.

Moments later the weight was lifted and another man in similar attire raised her from the ground and hands engulfed her body, and deposited her in the back of a Land Rover. She passed out.

It was a good few hours later when she woke up in what appeared to be a hospital room. Unlike with Armour… it had been.

As soon as she woke someone was at her side to make sure she was alright, and to explain… but they too did not know anything about Armour, and it was sometime before a senior consultant had come in and explained that the Prince had been in touch to say Armour was alright, and as soon as she was released by the doctors, probably the next day, she could see him, but that he would probably phone that evening.

For her it was a long and lonely day and although totally fatigued she was relieved when at last Armour had rung. His voice was slightly croaky and he only wanted to know about her, how she was. She admitted to being very tired and to having a headache, but not admitting to its severity. They talked for a little while and eventually, after several goodnights, Armour had hung up.

It was strange, but as soon as she came around and realised that the Nissen hut had been bombed, she had also known that Armour had survived and was not hurt. She could not explain why, even when they talked about it later, but she knew. She couldn't wait to see him.

At about 12.30 pm as the two men moved away from the dining table. James Briars came in and waited inside the door. He was beckoned forward by the Prince.

In his hand were a bunch of the Sunday newspapers.

The Prince said: "I thought you, as a newspaper man, would appreciate this. These are the Sundays. This is what the nation will be waking up to."

Armour stared down in total amazement as the Prince spread the various editions out on the floor.

'CARMICHAEL QUITS THROUGH STRESS' said one, and 'HOME SECRETARY OUT' read another. 'CARMICHAEL CALLS IT A DAY' and 'CARMICHAEL CAN'T HACK IT', with a sub-headline saying, 'Home Secretary skips country for rest cure', and so it went on…

There was a lot of speculation in other articles and in the gossip columns, and particularly in relation to the apparent attempt on his life by a madman. None of the pieces by the political watchers was anywhere near the truth.

… And of course, it quickly became clear to Armour there was no way that the government was going to face the real scandal. There was no doubt that Carmichael had to go, but it was far better that it be for a 'normal' reason than, what, treason, deceit, scandal…

"I think, thanks to you and Claire, that we have stemmed a serious problem, and at the same time cleared out some of the rot," said the Prince.

"By the way, I don't know whether you know of his involvement or not, but Michael Staveley-Smythe, whom I know you know, has been arrested. So have various agents and senior members of the security agencies of various European countries."

"I think we owe you a debt of gratitude," said the prince turning to Armour.

"You will have to forgive me Charles, all I want to think about is Mac and our future. Whatever we did, we did because we had to. To a large degree we were pushed into all of it, starting with Vasilli. He set us on this trail."

"Yes, I believe your friend from Russia was a very brave man. I would have liked to have met him."

"I have no doubt he would have liked to have met you", said Armour, "But I have lost him, and Pat Grogan and Mart Burricks, and I have to wonder whether it was really worth it. There is though one thing that makes it worthwhile for me…,"

… And he did not complete the sentence. He did not have to. The Prince was nodding his head in acknowledgement.

They shook hands and parted, and Briars showed Armour back to his room, where he ached… for Mac.

End

Peter Aengenheister

Lightning Source UK Ltd.
Milton Keynes UK
UKHW010625131219
355328UK00001B/170/P